SKINTIGHT

By
Wade E. Beauchamp III

Ink Smith Publishing
www.ink-smith.com

ISBN: 978-1-939156-44-0

Ink Smith Publishing
710 S. Myrtle Ave. Suite 209
Monrovia, CA, 91016

Chapter One
Up In The Sky

I married Deidre because she was a superhero. There were other reasons, of course, like the fact that she was the kindest, funniest, coolest person I'd ever met. But what first caught my eye was the way her ass looked in blue spandex.

The media was still calling her Nova Girl, when I met Deidre, despite the fact that her press kit clearly stated that she wished to be referred to as Supernova ("*the* Supernova" was an acceptable alternate). She was a rookie then, and although she had been instrumental in the Centurions' defeat of the Third Eye, they had yet to offer her membership. She was still a few feats away from her first corporate sponsorship, too. I had seen her on television a few times but never in person until the day I watched her subdue the Atomic Centaur with a Nova Burst. It seemed to cost her little effort, but it nearly blinded me and the two dozen other passengers on the train that the Centaur was dangling over Bostwick Bay.

Afterward, as the freed hostages dispersed, I lingered, staring at Supernova as she gave her report to the police. I gazed at her; that skintight cyan costume, the same color as her eyes, curls so vividly blonde that her officially licensed action figure's hair was painted the same sunny yellow they used for Captain Fantastic's trunks. And that body. My eyes roamed over her arched torso, her hips, down the curves of her legs that

1

disappeared into a pair of magenta riding boots. The suit covered her completely from her neck down, like her body had been dipped and encased in a candy shell. Her symbol—a fuchsia seven-pointed star—stretched across her chest.

I flashed my press pass and crowded in with the reporters. I was betting the word *Photographer* was small enough to go unnoticed.

"Supernova!" I shouted above the others. "Century City Journal. Can you confirm that you've been approached about joining the Centurions?"

She smiled patiently, "No comment."

A couple of correspondents snuck in questions about her powers—"They're perfectly safe to bystanders, I assure you"—and their origin—"Yes, I've had them since birth"—before I got her attention again.

I cleared my throat. "Is there a Mr. Supernova at home?"

She looked at the laminated pass dangling from my neck. She smiled again, the patience replaced by bemusement. "I only date superheroes. Sorry." Supernova began to rise into the air.

"Maybe this is my disguise."

"If it is, it's the best one I've ever seen."

"Maybe I'm really Century Man!" I called up to her but the other reporters, the real ones, drowned me out with their *oh so serious* questions about her thoughts on metahuman registration or security at Casey Asylum. I watched her shrink in the sky until she was a sapphire speck against towering white clouds.

We still had that costume in the closet. It was actually the only one we had the rights to. Technically, Centurions, LLC owned the rights to every other costume (and likeness thereof) she'd worn since. They displayed all of them on mannequins in glass cases in the Centurions Museum, alongside the retired costumes of every person who had ever been a member. But they could keep them, as far as I was concerned. None of them could compare with that first one.

I thought of Deidre in that costume as I made love to her on the floor of our living room, my eyes and hands roaming over the swells of her gloriously naked body. Deidre's attention, however, was split between what I was doing to her and what was on the television. She was on her hands and knees and I was quickly realizing she had chosen that position so she could watch the news. For the third time this morning Eyewitness 8's Lola Oh was interrupting our regularly scheduled viewing, among other things.

"Over the past half hour, the metahuman mercenary group known as Hard Corps has cut a path of destruction from City Hall to Dewey Plaza, apparently en route to the Wertham Building, home of Wertham Biotech," the crouched and cowering reporter told us amidst the occasional hail of debris. "Local law enforcement officials continue to deny that Dr. Estes Wertham himself is being held hostage by the group, despite numerous eyewitness reports to the contrary."

Between groans Deidre said, "Couldn't have happened to a nicer guy."

"A spokesperson for the Metahuman Crime Division told Eyewitness 8 that they currently have no reason to believe this assault is in any way related to Dr. Wertham's grand jury deposition concerning the testing and registration of metahumans," Lola Oh continued, flinching and cringing through the destruction she had strategically selected as her backdrop.

"Careful what you wish for," Deidre said, punctuated with gasps.

As if cued by Deidre, Lola said, "Eyewitness 8 viewers will remember our coverage last year of Wertham's acrimonious testimony before the State Joint Legislative Committee on Metahuman Vigilantism. Many feel this testimony may have led directly to the formation of the Metahuman Code Authority. The MCA has since halted all federal funding of metahumans not officially sanctioned and monitored by the government. This sanction caused a firestorm in the metahuman community, seen by most as being redundant of the Hege Act of '94."

Just then, a car-sized piece of the Wertham Building landed behind Lola, shattering into a cloud of dust and airborne debris that briefly chased the reporter from the field of view. "Conspicuous in their absence are the Centurions, staunch opponents of Wertham and the MCA," continued Lola as the camera found her again.

Deidre said, "I hate how she says '*the* Centurions.'"

"What are you talking about?" I was panting.

"It's not '*the* Centurions.' It's just 'Centurions.'"

I was more concerned with my wife's body than semantics, and I was out of breath. I didn't respond.

Deidre said, "It's like these idiots who call them *the* Grateful Dead. Or *the* Eagles."

I couldn't take it any longer. I said, "Use 'Grateful Dead' in a sentence without the 'the.' Say you went to see them in concert."

"I wouldn't go see them in concert. I hate the fucking Grateful Dead."

"Just say it, smartass."

"I went to see Grateful Dead in concert."

"See how silly that sounds?"

"But it's accurate."

On television, Lola Oh said, "Helix in particular was extremely vocal in his disapproval of the Authority and one has to wonder if he and his fellow Centurions are sending a message to—"

Before Lola could finish her sentence, Deidre reached for the remote control and turned off the television. "Shut up, Lola."

As the screen went black I did my best impersonation of the young woman who had become my wife. "Wherever there's danger, Nova Girl will be there."

"Nova Girl's busy right now," Deidre said. "Now shut up and fuck me, Will."

I did as I was told. Deidre was going to come. She was ready, I could feel it. She was telling me so, but I could barely hear her over my own panting. Almost subliminally I could sense her beginning to struggle against her powers, restraining them, trying to keep them in check as she always had to when she got to this point. I could feel her muscles knot, could feel her frustration as she fought what had to be, I knew, an almost desperate urge to unleash her body on me.

Deidre bucked and I clutched at her hips, seeking purchase there as she beat at me with her body, driving me backwards across the floor. The carpet peeled the flesh from my knees until, finally, we reached the end table next to the sofa and I could reach behind me and brace myself against it. Still she thrust back against me, pushing both me and the table across the floor inches at a time. Her half-empty coffee cup tumbled to the floor by my knees, and its lukewarm contents splashed onto my calves.

Deidre seemed to pause for just an instant, concerned, maybe, about how hot the coffee was on my skin or, more likely, how well my non-super-powered body was holding up.

"Don't stop," I told her and she instantly resumed, driving back against me relentlessly. I grasped at the edges of the table and tried to push back against Deidre but she was too strong and drove me against the table and drove it, in turn, into the wall. The next collision dislodged my photograph of Supernova single-handedly defeating the Quantum Mechanics. The glass shattered as the frame hit the floor.

Deidre's cries grew terse, barely audible over the slapping of her skin against mine and the rhythmic thudding of the table against the wall. The table bit into the contorted muscles in my back and I wanted, for only a moment, to cry uncle and tell Deidre to stop. But I didn't. It hurt, but I could handle it. She drove back against me, her eyes clenched shut in concentration, biting her bottom lip to keep from announcing her imminent orgasm to the whole neighborhood.

I could hear the plaster behind the table begin to crumble, surrendering to Deidre's onslaught. The wall cracked, but it didn't matter. I didn't care if the wall cracked, didn't care if we brought the entire house down around us, I wanted her to come.

Like she used to. Like a tidal wave, a volcano. A force of nature, her powers overflowing and spilling out of her body, engulfing us.

She kept on fucking me. Hard. Harder than anyone could fuck.

Somehow, I heard Deidre's Signet Ring begin to chirp. I told her, but she wasn't listening to me or to her Signet Ring. She was too busy, pinning me helplessly against the table, hips churning in my grasping hands. Just as Psy-Fi had designed it to do, Deidre's Signet Ring grew impatiently louder. The noise was like some pissed-off mechanical cricket. Eventually Deidre could no longer plausibly ignore it.

"Goddamn it." Deidre dismounted me, freed me. I collapsed onto my elbows and watched as she got to her feet and tapped the raised Centurions emblem on the ring with her index finger, silencing it.

"Supernova here," she said into the ring.

"We need you downtown," a voice from her ring responded.

"I know," Deidre said and then tapped the ring again. She stood, her nude body glossy with sweat, and took a moment to catch her breath. "I'm sorry, baby."

I nodded.

Then, with the slightest twist of her hips, she began to spin. Faster she revolved until her body became a blurred five foot, four inch tornado. The curtains in our den rose and fluttered frantically and our home was filled with a blinding burst of light. I had long since grown accustomed to the wind and lightshow that accompanied Deidre's transformations but I would never get used to the sight of her as Supernova. For just a moment she stood poised, resplendent, every inch of her blue costume reflecting light.

Before her secret identity had been exposed, Deidre signed a deal with Clairol to endorse their Nice 'n Easy line of hair coloring products. Although disguise had become moot, Clairol's lawyers considered Supernova's hair color to be an integral part of her image. So, with a toss of her head, and a tweak of her

6

light-based powers, Deidre's shoulder-length chestnut hair became Supernova's sleek blonde waves, modeled, by her own admission, after Marilyn Monroe the day she married Joe DiMaggio.

I smiled proudly at the superhero I married and said, "I love you."

"Me too."

In the moment it took me to tell her "Be careful out there," she stopped being Deidre, my wife of seventeen years and the mother of my children, and became Supernova, Centurion of Truth and Peace.

"I will," Supernova said solemnly and then walked out the front door like anyone leaving for work would do. I watched her lift off and sail effortlessly over our house, gaining altitude in the crisp October sky and banking before aiming her body and shooting like an arrow toward the Century City skyline and whatever menace awaited her there.

I got dressed as quickly as possible for a mere mortal and drove toward the city. I followed, roughly, Deidre's flight path. Century City loomed like some jagged glass and steel mountain range, gleaming towers and spires straining for the sky. From the beltway, not a single building more than a decade old could be seen. The city's near-constant modernization was a by-product of boasting a metahuman population larger than New York and Los Angeles combined. It was a metahuman population that settled its disagreements by hurling one another through skyscrapers.

I drove as far into the city as the police barricades would allow, grabbed my camera bag, and started walking. The Metahuman Activity Alerts broadcast over the radio, television, and internet were intended to minimize innocent bystanders and reduce collateral damage. But, like all the other spectators, I used the alerts to help direct me towards the destruction. The accuracy of the alerts had dropped considerably since news helicopters had been banned after Warhead downed the

Eyewitness 8 Eye in the Sky, but they were still reliable enough to get me close.

The alert had said that the damage was centered on the Dewey Plaza area, but they had sightings as far out as the intersection of Fourth and Mankiewicz. A lone traffic cop tried fruitlessly to divert foot traffic away from the plaza. His fellow officers were presumably choked out by the stampeding crowds. Or, possibly, they were enjoying a doughnut nearby, content—as they had been for years—to turn a blind eye to anything concerning the skintights, as most non-powered folks called them. Even from three blocks away I could hear the deadened noises of crumbling concrete and shattering glass, and the rising and falling cheers of the spectators in response. I began to trot.

Deidre used to laugh at me for not letting her fly me to the scene. She thought I was embarrassed at the idea of having my wife carry me around like a baby in her arms.

"I won't let you get wind burnt," she'd joke. But the truth (and Deidre knew it) was that I had to get my pictures on my own. If my pictures were going to mean anything, I had to get them without the help of powers, especially hers. Before the Knave Incident it didn't matter. It wasn't important how I got the shots, just as long as I got them. And I got them. I had the Pulitzers and *Newsweek* covers and *Century City Journal* front pages to prove it. I was there when the Centurions repelled the Io Invasion. When Psy-Fi returned from the twenty-second century, I was there. When Jinx captured Cybermancer, I was there. No one ever figured out how I managed, for all those years, to be everywhere the action was. No one ever put two and two together. Until the Knave Incident.

The noises had become almost deafening. The crowds were impermeable. I knew I was closing in. I also knew that these people weren't from here. People who had lived here for any amount of time quickly grew weary of the near-daily super-powered fisticuffs that blocked their commutes, disconnected their utilities, and closed their schools. They most certainly didn't park their cars downtown. That was a lesson quickly learned. It only took one instance of your mini-van being used as a giant baseball bat, or one genetically-enhanced ape dropped on your convertible to understand why the subway was much more cost-effective, if not always safer.

The people who lived here weren't awed by the superheroes in their midst anymore than New Yorkers marveled at taxi cabs or San Franciscans pointed out a trolley car. They saw it every morning on the front page and every night on the evening news. It was simply part of their city. Granted, there were occasional especially-large fights, sometimes even with some social or political significance, but citizens of Century City took a far greater interest in the personal lives of their superheroes than their professional lives. It was much more interesting, and the ramifications were most certainly more permanent.

Out-of-towners traveled to Skintight City, as it had become known in other parts of the country, to spend their vacations here in the hopes of catching a glimpse of their favorite spandex-clad hero gliding overhead. There was an entire cottage industry that preyed on these "meta-tourists": bus tours of historic battle sites, maps to alleged secret hideouts, T-shirts and baseball caps emblazoned with your favorite skintight's symbol or logo. I would watch them as they ate Supernova Sundaes at Centurions Café and bought bobble-head dolls of the Skyscraper in the gift shop. But I could only scoff so much because, as Deidre liked to remind me whenever I grew belligerent about it, I helped to create it. It was my photograph of the Centurions in mid-flight on the cover of Time in 1997 that sparked the first real wave of meta-tourism. And it was my portrait of Nova Girl on the cover of *Rolling Stone* that blew it wide open. Basically, I had no one to blame but myself.

Nonetheless, it was exactly that kind of picture I hoped to take today. Not that I really needed to. Despite my arguments against them, Deidre's endorsements had paid for our house, set up college funds for Zack and Luke, and any grandkids they

9

might one day give us. But the pictures gave me a reason to be a part of this, so I came to take them every time Deidre was called into action.

I ducked down an alley and emerged on the very edge of Dewey Plaza, opposite the crowds. At the base of the Wertham Building, much closer than I had estimated, stalked the four members of Hard Corps. I readied my camera and trained it on Dr. Wertham, prone on the fractured concrete of the plaza, curled into a fetal position at the feet of the mind-controlling Headcase. Wertham was the prisoner of the psychosis-inducing powers Headcase had been gifted (or cursed) with at birth. Like most metahumans, Headcase had no idea where her powers came from. She couldn't explain it, didn't know whether it was genetics or magic or simply some accident of evolution. And like most metahumans, she didn't care.

The Hyperborean levitated stoically two stories above Dewey Plaza, his bare, heavily muscled arms folded, directing and overseeing the systematic destruction of Wertham Building, Century City's third tallest. He bellowed commands to the Anvil and Phobos from mid-air, his black cape flapping lazily behind him. I watched through my camera's viewfinder, zooming in and focusing as the two responded to their leader's directions by deepening the gash they had opened in the side of the structure. The two ate away at the structure like some kind of cancer, leaving in their wake a crater of twisted steel and shattered glass almost a third of the way up the ninety-story skyscraper.

"Bring it down!" the Hyperborean commanded in a voice that sent vibrations through the very ground I was standing on. "Bring it all down around him!"

The Anvil extended his arms, his splayed fingers becoming gleaming metal extrusions that stretched out of sight into the bowels of the building. With a heave, he retracted his arms, yanking entire sections of steel column from within the building and casting them out to crash to the earth below. I could feel the ground tremble under the impact of the steel, sinking deep into the asphalt of Mankiewicz Avenue.

10

Phobos, whose powers were still somewhat of a mystery, even to himself, whaled at the building with what appeared to be huge hammers made of nothing more than shadow. With each blow I could see the entire building stagger and, for a moment, I wondered how wise I was to be so close. I watched as a near-constant rain of plaster, wood and glass fell on the plaza below, accompanied by flurries of sheets of paper, computer monitors, filing cabinets, desks and chairs, the contents of an office building vomiting out.

The sudden noises rocked the crowds back half a step, but no more. I would've backed up, too, but I had a job to do. The earth quaked with every blow and still I watched through my camera, taking pictures when I could remember to. I could see the Anvil, his metal tendrils coiled around a steel beam that seemed to stretch across the entire width of the building. I watched as he pressed against it, seemingly unable to move it at first. Suddenly, capillaries of fissures appeared in the concrete façade. There was a deafening crack and then a jagged, vertical fault line formed on the outside of the huge building. With a thunderous boom, the fault extended itself to ground level. There was another boom and the building seemed ready to split in half. Flames now burst from it and glass, stone and steel plummeted to earth. Throngs of gathered spectators realized, for the first time, that they were in danger, and suddenly tried to flee. But they didn't know which way to run.

"Enough!" came a voice came from the sky. It was louder than the sounds of the breaking building, louder than the panicked shrieks of the retreating onlookers. Like avenging angels, the Centurions descended from the sky, more floating than flying, and making sure to give the crowds the eyeful they had came looking for. The sky seemed full of Centurions, their bright costumes reflecting the sun.

They were all human, yet somehow *more*. As they stood in the air, as powerful and glorious as gods, their mere presence calmed the crowd. The onlookers abandoned their evacuation.

Their fear was now replaced by excitement at the arrival of their heroes and protectors.

Suddenly the sky was crisscrossed with streaking colors as the Centurions swooped into action.

"Front page," I whispered to myself. The familiar pewter and orange speed-suit of Trace (known to his friends and family as Andre Marcus) flashed past at unimaginable speed. He was a blur, dragging behind him a sonic boom. Faster than my eyes could follow him, he scooped up Dr. Wertham and deposited him on the far side of the plaza. Before Wertham's hair had settled on his head, Trace disappeared. Going after the people in and around the building, he snatched them up, two and three at a time, by their belts or their collars, and carried them all to safety. I never even saw him move. He was a fading ghost in the place he had been a few seconds earlier. I could only see the after-image of his mirrored visor and that famous Trace smile, like he still couldn't believe how awesome it felt to be that fast.

I watched as the strobe-like image of Trace kept adding to the group of scared but safe Wertham Biotech employees in the plaza. Finally he paused long enough to indicate to a teammate, the Centurion called Skyscraper, that the building had been emptied of innocents.

An accident in the propulsion lab where he worked killed everyone except for German physicist Rudy Fleischer. It spared his life but imbued him with the ability to increase the size of his body. Now known simply as Skyscraper, the only thing limiting his size, Deidre once told me, was acrophobia. Skyscraper had begun his new life by seeking revenge against those he held responsible for what he'd become, but the Centurions had shown him a better way and now he fought alongside them. At Trace's signal, Skyscraper began to grow. His black bodysuit, made from a polymer developed in the year 2172 by the time-traveling Psy-Fi, expanded with him. The symbol on his costume, a yellow upward arrow emblazoned across his torso, stretched until it was the width of a city sidewalk, then a street. He rose into the sky, ten stories, twenty stories, forty stories tall, until he stood astride the plaza like a living colossus. He wrapped his arms, now the diameter of airliner fuselages, around the Wertham Building, and hugged it, keeping it from splitting apart and collapsing onto the population below.

Presto materialized from a belching plume of purple smoke on the ground, black cloak swirling about him. The smell of sulfur from the smokescreen permeated the plaza. He took just a second to adjust his top hat and the bowtie of his stage magician's tuxedo before strolling unnoticed to Headcase and giving her a tap on the shoulder. Before the criminal could react, Presto had produced his wand from his jacket sleeve and snapped it toward Headcase, a smoky fist emanating from it that caught her squarely on the chin with a sweeping right hook. The disoriented Headcase, still reeling from the abruptly severed mental link with Dr. Wertham, staggered. Then, sizing up her opponent in a split second, she righted herself. She knew Presto. They had fought many times before. I could sense Headcase desperately formulating a plan to keep this engagement from being yet another defeat for her.

Presto was the only Centurion without the metagene: sleight of hand, misdirection and illusion were his modus operandi. As a child he had studied the black arts under the tutelage of his great-uncle, the Prestidigitator. For years he prowled the alleys and rooftops of Century City at Presto's side, avenging wrongs as Kid Merlin. As a young man, he had adopted the mantle of the Prestidigitator for himself, immediately (and mercifully) renamed himself Presto and continued the crusade begun by his predecessor. He was well on his way to becoming every bit the crime fighter the original Prestidigitator was.

Headcase knew there would be no outmaneuvering or outguessing her opponent, no way to bring her mind-control powers to bear. Sheer physical force was her only hope and, gauging her timing and speed, she rushed Presto, arms opened wide to tackle him. Headcase tumbled to the ground, grappling with a suddenly vacated cloak. Presto himself stood over

Headcase and watched her scramble frantically to her feet. He removed his top hat and waggled his fingers over it.

"Abracadabra," Presto said. "Or something." He snapped his fingers and a white rabbit sprang from the hat and leapt into the air. The bunny delivered a spinning roundhouse kick to Headcase's temple, rendering her unconscious before seemingly evaporating into nothingness.

Cries of "Supernova!" suddenly rose in a wave from the crowd. I looked up to see my wife soaring in a steep arc over the Wertham Building, a contrail of glowing turquoise behind her. The crowd cheered her entry into the fray. She floated down to the opening carved into the side of the building.

"Anvil! Phobos!" she called.

The two wheeled and launched simultaneous, almost choreographed, attacks. The Anvil's extended fists formed into twin metal clubs, spiked and barbed, and shot at Deidre while Phobos hurled a pair of shadow-axes. At the split second of impact, a glowing violet veil shrouded Deidre's body and shielded her from the assaults. She clenched her brow and twin beams of brilliant light shot forth from her eyes. Even from my spot on the ground I caught the faint whiff of ozone. The bolts of light, purple at their edges and shifting to a blinding blue-white in their core, lanced through the air and struck her opponents with the force of a wrecking ball. The Anvil's metal appendices melted and Phobos' shadow-weapons evaporated to uselessness. Deidre's light rays vanished as quickly as they had appeared. Her adversaries folded onto one another and slumped, unconscious, to the ground.

There was an enraged cry of war and I turned to see the armored Hyperborean launch himself skyward, his massive, clenched fists propelling him through the air toward Supernova. I could see his eyes, flashing white with hatred behind the slatted grille of his helmet, as he raced upward, smoky air swirling in his wake.

"I said, 'Enough!'" The voice that had heralded the arrival of the Centurion's boomed again and I saw, standing in the sky,

14

Helix. His emerald green cape snapped in the breeze like a flag. His hands were on his hips as he defiantly blocked the Hyperborean's path to my wife. "This ends now."

The Hyperborean made no hesitation, no deviation from his course and, with a nod to one another, Helix and Supernova bolted downward, intercepting the Hyperborean in mid-flight, the sound of their bodies colliding like that of a car wreck. They wrestled in the air, somersaulting and diving until, as abruptly as they had entangled, the three super-humans flung themselves free, only to assail one another again, struggling and spinning as I photographed each hold, every dodge and counter.

To the uninitiated spectator, the fights were usually anticlimactic, one-sided, aesthetically-disappointing affairs. They had been conditioned by movies and television to expect to bear witness to epic clashes, magnificent aerial ballets, with the combatants going at one another like tireless pugilists, unstoppable forces of nature. But the reality was much more mundane. It usually resembled a high school wrestling match more than a heavyweight title bout, and ended in an uneasy draw or a choked submission more often than in a knockout punch.

Helix, however, understood—perhaps better than any of them—the value of marketing. Despite his concentration on his opponent, he was keenly aware of the legions of worshippers gathered in the plaza below. There would be no uninspired finish to this brawl, no draw, no truce. Not only would he not let his fans down, he wouldn't let his sponsors down. Pepsi and Chevrolet paid him millions of dollars not only to triumph, but to triumph spectacularly in a newsworthy manner, with their logos stretched proudly across his barrel chest and his bulging arms. The Centurions' Media Guide claimed him to be The World's Mightiest Man, and I didn't doubt it. His body was immense, clad in a gleaming white uniform that clung to every exaggerated, flexing muscle. The midday sun shone on the crown of his shaved head, making the silver stubble there glint.

Around his waist was cinched a jade green sash; his cape swelled majestically behind him.

I watched my wife as she valiantly defended the city alongside this godlike man and couldn't help but swell with pride. Not half an hour ago it was *me* that was fooling around with Supernova. Not Helix. Not someone who could bend steel in his bare hands, or change the course of mighty rivers, but normal, human, me. As they wheeled and soared and crashed in the sky above me, I smiled. I got to make love to a superhero.

The crowd grew frenetic as Supernova, using Helix's body like a fulcrum and hers like a lever, wedged her frame between the contending men and gave Helix the opening he needed to deliver a crushing elbow to the Hyperborean's throat. The Hyperborean recoiled, clutching at his neck, gasping for air. And, in that moment, Helix drew back his mighty fist and swung it at him, connecting with the force of a freight train, shattering the Hyperborean's black helmet and sending him hurtling, head over heels, to the earth. His limp body impacted like a meteorite. The center of Dewey Plaza was suddenly a crater.

The crowd erupted in cheers and, just like that, it was over. The whole thing had lasted maybe three minutes. There was no witty banter or clever repartee, no diabolical villains to reveal their master plans just before being foiled again. In the numerous cartoons and the glut of monthly comic books about the Centurions and their foes, the fights raged on and on, venues changed, the tide turned again and again. But this was real life and the only thing real life had in common with fantasy was that the Centurions always won.

With business-like efficiency, the Centurions went about wrapping up their operation. Psy-Fi, dressed in her usual smart pantsuit, could have passed for one of the dozens of Wertham Biotech executives wandering the plaza. She had been waiting patiently in the wings for the opportunity to apply her technology. She tapped the face of what looked like a simple watch on her wrist and cast a giant net of pure energy around the nearly-bisected Wertham Building, securing it until it could

16

be repaired and rebuilt, or demolished, whichever would be necessary. Skyscraper, relieved of his building-bracing duties, shrunk to half his size and appraised the stabilized building, held snugly by interwoven beams of scintillating light. He reached through a gap in Psy-Fi's energy netting and scooped out the unconscious Anvil and Phobos into his trampoline-sized palm. He knelt to pick up Headcase and the Hyperborean. He then moved down Mankiewicz Avenue in strides the length of football fields, walking down the corridor of high-rise office buildings like he would a hallway in his house, every step registering on a seismograph somewhere. He turned right and disappeared behind the buildings a few block away. He was en route, no doubt, to Bostwick Bay, where he would wade with little effort to Styers Island and deposit the decommissioned Hard Corps members in CCPD's Metahuman Detention Center.

Sprinting in concentric circles at super-speed, Trace caught the wreckage and debris from the building in a controlled whirlwind and swept it into a small mountain in the center of the plaza, where Presto recited an ancient incantation and banished the wreckage to some nether region no mortal would ever see.

Then, like the gods stepping down from Olympus, Helix and Supernova dropped to the ground, arms outstretched like wings, lighting soundlessly before the wildly applauding, unscathed beneficiaries of their amazing powers. They were ready to hold court. The crowd immediately swarmed them, pawing at their heroes, pleading for autographs, taking pictures, proposing marriage, offering to bear their children.

I climbed onto a nearby barricade to see over the crowd into the eye of the storm. I was always surprised at how comfortable Deidre was with this part of it, the hero-worship. The first of many 8x10 glossies was shoved in her face and she signed graciously, over and over again, as she always did. As did Trace and Presto and Psy-Fi, as would Skyscraper, just as soon as he had walked back from Bostwick Bay and returned to his normal size. Whether they genuinely appreciated the adoration

17

Wade Beauchamp

of these people or not was debatable, but each of them knew that preserving their way of life depended in no small part on their popularity with public.

Psy-Fi had to learn the hard way, originally thinking the time and effort it took to interact with the public was better spent developing technology to protect them. She quickly gained a reputation with the media for not caring about the people who looked at her as a role model; the same people Dell paid her to tell which personal computer to buy. Dell dropped Psy-Fi as a spokesperson and, for brief time, she depended solely on the Centurions for the financial support it took to live and work in the twenty-first Century. The Centurions, too, were quick to remind Psy-Fi that they could use all the public goodwill they could muster in a time when the government elected by these people censured their kind at every opportunity. So the Centurions spent as much time as it took to sign every autograph and pose for every picture, even if they respectfully declined the marriage and impregnation offers.

Helix, however, was unparalleled when it came to public relations. Since assuming leadership of the Centurions he had become the most popular metahuman in America and probably the world. More Helix action figures, bed sheets, and Halloween costumes were sold than all other Centurion merchandising combined. Only Supernova came close. Helix pitched everything from fast food to men's underwear. Little boys wanted to grow up to be him, grown men wished they were him, and every woman over sixteen wanted to be with him—Presto had the under-sixteen market cornered. Helix had scores of groupies, women who would do anything to get banged by the World's Mightiest Man. Deidre had heard, and passed along to me, stories about Helix's voracious sexual appetite. The kind of stories that never made it to Madison Avenue. Stories about nights of having over a hundred a women, one after another as they waited in line, without so much as breaking a sweat, leaving not a one unsatisfied. Stories of women wanting to

18

consume his semen in the hopes of gaining super-powers of their own.

As I watched Helix give an exclusive interview to Eyewitness 8's Lola Oh, acknowledging from time to time the chants of his name, I felt suddenly sorry for him. Helix flashed his super-human smile, with his super-perfect teeth, at the Eyewitness 8 camera and, as abruptly as it had appeared, my pity evaporated. I walked to my car and drove away.

Chapter Two
True Believers

Jerry's Place was in the part of the city that was considered "downtown" before World War II, back when it was just Century, not Century City, before downtown migrated up the hill. Metahumans didn't come down here much nowadays. There weren't any genetics labs or high-tech defense contractors here so the supervillainous types left it alone. Plus, the brick low-rises and factories didn't make nearly as glamorous a backdrop as the mirrored and chrome spires of the new downtown. That was perfectly fine with me because the last thing I wanted to see right now was someone in a damn cape.

The bar was always dark inside, regardless of the time of day. Mahogany panels surrounded the horseshoe-shaped bar which itself was surround by well-worn leather stools. I found myself suddenly grateful that no death ray or heat vision had ever been trained on the place. The walls were tiled with autographed black and white 8x10s of the men and women who protected this town before the phrase 'metahuman' had been invented, before the metagene had been discovered. Most of these heroes had no special powers or abilities beyond bravery and the desire to help. I saw Double Decker, the Silk Spider, and the Bouncer. Beside them were American Eagle, Skygirl, Monarch & Page. There were dozens more and I knew everyone. Maybe not personally, but I knew their story. Some died in the

20

war, fighting Hitler or Hirohito; not as a caped crusader but as an American soldier. Some grew old and retired. A few, like Ray Girl, had children who would one day follow in their footsteps. I wondered what they would think of their progeny if they could see them now. I realized I already knew.

Behind the bar, innumerable trophies, some for boxing, some for bowling, lined the shelves where there weren't bottles of liquor. Also behind the bar was the man accountable for about a third of those trophies: Jerry the Third. He stood, patiently polishing a glass in the same spot I imagined his father and his father before him had stood and done exactly the same.

Perched at the bar were Mort and Curt, Jerry's only patrons at this time of day, who both offered me a nod before turning their attention back to their beers and the newspaper spread out in front of them on the bar top. Mort was in his sixties, I figured, and had a frame that seemed to be made entirely of squares: blocks for shoulders, fists, and head. Curt was only slightly younger and Mort's physical opposite, slim and lean, with a white mustache and the quiet demeanor and enduring humor of a lifelong sidekick.

I sat next to Mort and Curt. Jerry put a cold bottle of beer in front of me and went back to buffing his glass.

"What's going on, Will?" he asked. "Heard some rumbling."

"Same old. Bad guys tearing shit up. Good guys trying to stop them."

"Get some good shots?"

"Pardon?" I asked.

"Pictures," Jerry gestured with his glass to the camera still hanging around my neck.

"Yeah. I suppose so."

"How'd your gal do?" Jerry said.

"She held her own," I smiled. "She always does."

"Who they fighting?" Mort joined in with his booming voice.

"Hard Corps."

"Hard Corps," Mort snorted. "Goddamned kids these days." He took a draw off his bottle before beginning in earnest.

"Simple vandals, that's all. Whatever happened to real bad guys? Guys with plans?" He let out a huff. "Hard Corps. Loud-mouthed punks. I swear, if I didn't know better I'd say the fights nowadays were rigged. At least the guys Curt and I fought wanted something." Curt nodded in quiet agreement. And they were right. The pair had patrolled the alleys and docks of Century City as Prizefighter and The Night Watchman, fighting organized crime throughout the 1950's. They'd waged their battle into the Sixties until their opponents took on a decidedly more super-powered nature. "Cash, weapons, gold. Something. My daddy always said a thief is better than a vandal. Because at least the thief gets some use out of what he stole." Again Curt nodded silently.

"Remember that time you two mixed it up with the Mortician?" Jerry asked Mort. "Now that was a fight."

"Yeah," Mort said, chuckling a little.

"I know Curt remembers," Jerry said, laughing a little himself at the look Curt shot him.

"First real meta we faced off against," Mort said. "Boss Marconi had sent him to snuff us out after we busted up his prostitution ring. Big bastard, the Mortician. Meaner than hell. Whole undertaker shtick. Black overcoat and everything. Had this power where if he touched your skin, he could actually suck the life right out of you, right through his fingertips." Curt was shaking his head in remembered disbelief. "Every time he landed a punch we could feel the energy draining out of us."

"How'd you get him?" I asked.

Jerry suddenly burst into laughter and walked around the bar to wipe the tables down. "Tell Willie how you got him, Mort."

"Well," Mort began, laughing a little harder now himself. "While I distracted the Mortician, Curt snuck into Gordon Drugs and bought a tube of lipstick and some control-top nylons." I looked at Curt for verification but his head was hung so low I couldn't see his face. "When Curt came back out, here was the Night Watchm," Mort was laughing so hard now he almost couldn't speak. "Here was the Night Watchman all dolled up like the drag queens down on the docks." Jerry needed the bar to hold himself upright by now. "Curt sauntered right over to the Mortician, who was... he was..."

"Mortified!" Jerry yelped. Curt's head dropped to the bar.

"Yeah, yeah," Mort went on, now in hysterics. "He was scared to death. He thought Curt had turned queer or something. So Curt goes right up to him and plants a wet one right on his cheek. And the Mortician just loses it, and his first reaction is to wipe the kiss off, and when he goes to do it his hand touches his face and the bastard starts sucking his own life out. We weren't even sure if it would work on himself or not, but we had to try." Mort wiped away the tears. "And the Mortician, he pulls his hand away, of course. He wasn't even really hurt. But he was so disgusted by Curt that he just ran away. Heard later that he gave Boss Marconi his money back and told him to get someone else for the job."

"Curt," I coughed, my side hurting I was laughing so hard. "Tell me it's not true." Curt raised himself up and looked me in the eye, but all he could do was shrug his shoulders in resignation.

"Of course, that wouldn't work these days," Mort went on. "Try that now and some crazy bastard will sue you. Or worse, kiss you back."

The rest of the afternoon went like that and before I left for home I'd heard about the time Mort mistook the Crusader for the Jihadist, the time Mort accused Red Raider of being a Communist and the dinner where a drunken Mort addressed General Wrath as 'Genital Rash.' Each tale was related with equal parts longing for the past and resentment of the present. And I realized as I sat and listened to their stories that the frustration Mort and Curt and Jerry felt toward the present had long since taken its toll. And despite their ability to laugh about it, there was a certain despair about their place in the world. At least, I thought, they had found an outlet for it here in this bar. I only wished I could find an outlet for mine.

"Live from Skintight City, this is *Alter Ego*." Eyewitness 8's Lola Oh told me.

I didn't watch *Alter Ego* if Deidre was home. She hated it. She hated Lola Oh and hated the way Eyewitness 8 sensationalized and exploited the Centurions.

"That bitch makes *us* out to be the bad guys," Deidre would bark at Lola. "Jesus, we saved their stupid fucking studio from getting leveled God knows how many times. You think they'd show a little fucking gratitude."

"I admire her integrity," I'd deadpan, fanning the flames.

"Whatever. I'm not watching it and the boys sure as hell aren't watching it. I'll be damned if my children are going to have to listen to their mother called a liar every night. How many times have they had Estes Wertham on? A dozen? And how many times have they had me? Huh? None. That's how many."

But I loved *Alter Ego*. To call it yellow journalism would be a compliment. It was tabloid television at its worst but I loved it. I loved their exposé on teen sidekicks and pedophilia, their in-depth look at steroid abuse among metahumans and their investigation into Pfizer's role in the creation of Skyscraper. It was all bullshit, I knew that (well, maybe not the sidekick/pedophile thing), but I loved it all the same.

Zack and Luke were in bed and Deidre was with still with the team at the Citadel analyzing that afternoon's battle with Hard Corps. So it was just Lola and me. "Tonight we take an in-depth look at the ongoing debate over corporate sponsorships and metahumans," Lola said. I was suddenly glad Deidre wasn't home yet. "Throughout their storied history the Centurions have had a very strict policy regarding product endorsements and advertisements. Century Man made it clear on many occasions that the Centurions were, at least under his stewardship, public servants who would not be entering into corporate partnerships of any kind. This is from a fundraising dinner last year."

An image of Century Man replaced Lola's. "I will not allow this unit or its members to whore out their powers and abilities." I flinched at the choice of words. "We use our powers for the greater good of mankind, not to become overpaid pitchmen."

"One week after giving that speech, the Knave Incident took place," Lola continued, "and in its wake, leadership of the Centurions was ceded to Helix. Helix has wasted no time reversing Century Man's endorsement policy and made it very clear that he does not share his predecessor's opinion on the matter. And neither, obviously, do any of the other Centurions.

"In the eleven months since Helix lifted the sponsorship ban, every single member of the Centurions has received compensation to endorse at least one consumer service or product. Helix counts among his many corporate alliances Pepsi-Cola, General Motors and Hanes. Supernova has appeared in a popular series of television ads promoting Verizon Wireless and is currently in talks to become a spokesmodel for designer Calvin Klein. Trace sprints in FedEx commercials and is a paid endorser for the African-American College Foundation. Skyscraper expounds on the virtues of Cialis. Psy-Fi has a deal with American Express and Presto pitches Reese's Peanut Butter Cups."

Lola took a breath. "With me tonight are Thana Thompkins, formerly known as the metahuman vigilante Jinx, and via satellite in Denver, Michael Shuler, author of the *New York Times* bestseller, *Must There Be a Century Man?* Welcome to you both."

"Thanks, Lola," they both responded. This was going to get ugly.

"Thana Thompkins is no stranger to controversy," Lola said as old footage rolled of Jinx returning Phantom Lord to Casey Asylum. "Her invitation to join the Centurions and that invitation's subsequent withdrawal made headlines nationwide last summer. Her role in the now-infamous Livewire videotape scandal was first reported on this very program. Thanks for coming on, Thana. Let's start with you. How do you feel about metahumans, specifically the Centurions, accepting endorsement money?"

"First off, Lola, I'd like to reiterate for your viewers that all charges in the Livewire case were dropped. I still stand behind the statement I made that all participants understood they were being filmed, and participated willingly."

"Then why did Livewire testify that you had used your so-called powers—" Shuler shot before Lola could interrupt.

"Thana," Lola said, her voice even. "You were there that day and witnessed what has since become known as the Knave Incident, the event that led to the disappearance of Century Man. Please share with our viewers your perspective on the endorsement debate Century Man was at the forefront of."

"I think what Century Man was hoping to accomplish with his in-house ban on corporate relationships was to prevent the kind of conflicts of interest we saw just last month. Four people were hospitalized in the Bostwick Docks fire because the Centurions could not respond fast enough. Trace could've gotten there in less than thirty seconds, but he had been pressured by Reebok to leave the Centurions due to the fact that Nike provided their costumes. People could've died because Trace was unwilling to save them while wearing a Nike swoosh on his uniform. There's a reason you don't see the CCPD shilling for Snickers or the Air Force flying around with giant Budweiser patches on their flight suits."

"Give 'em hell, Jinx," I said aloud.

"Michael," Lola said. "Your turn."

"I think it's safe to say that if Century Man had not gone away, the Centurions would've ceased to be. His outdated moral code kept him from seeing the benefits—no, the *necessity*—of corporate funding and the Centurions would've been run out of business altogether by people like Estes Wertham and Senator Hege. And thugs like Hard Corps and Third Eye would—"

"Why do you watch this shit?" Deidre asked me from the kitchen. I did my best not to appear startled, but it didn't work.

"Scared you," she smiled, carrying a coffee mug of wine into the den with her. She was a brunette again. She was wearing a Century Comets jersey, which came down to her thighs, and big, fuzzy socks. Supernova was nice but it was good to see my wife again.

"Thana's on. She's doing pretty good this time," I said. "So far."

"Give her time."

"Your grandmother called," I said. "She said she'd watch the kids tomorrow night. She made fun of you for going to a Halloween party when you dress up for it all year long."

"You did explain to her that it's not a costume party?"

"She said you could borrow hers."

"Grandma's just jealous she can't fit into it anymore."

"I don't know," I said. "Your grandma's kinda hot."

"Shut up," Deidre laughed.

"I've seen those old pinups, with her flared skirt and bomber jacket. Your grandma was turning heads as Ray Girl before your mom was even born. I bet GIs were beating off to her all over the Pacific theater."

"Shut up!" Deidre squealed and she set her wine on the coffee table and climbed onto my lap, straddling me. I could feel her smile as she kissed me.

"Now, where were we?"

Supernova didn't need sleep but her husband did. I slept halfway through the morning the next day. My body ached when I finally woke. We'd made love until midnight before finally giving up.

My wife hadn't had an orgasm in eleven months. Eleven months, three weeks and two days, to be exact. The last time was the night before the Knave of Diamonds revealed to the entire world in a pre-recorded message aired exclusively on a special two-hour episode of *Alter Ego* that Supernova was, in fact, one Mrs. Deidre Donner, mild-mannered housewife and mother of two. The night before I lost my powers.

I lost my powers in a decidedly lackluster way. I never really thought about how I wanted my career to end until it did. I would've preferred a blaze of glory, saving the planet from an alien invasion, maybe, I don't know. I guess I would've liked to have simply retired after a long, illustrious career. Spent my golden years in the superhero retirement home. I would've preferred almost any scenario to what happened.

The Knave was a second-stringer at best. The Centurions had put him away more times than any of us could remember. Jewel thefts, mainly, hence the awful name. The Knave shouldn't have been able to figure out who Supernova really was. But he did. Somehow. We never did find out how but it really didn't matter. It wasn't the first time a metahuman had been outed and Deidre was thinking about going public anyhow. Had the Knave lain low, stayed out of the public eye for a while, chances are the Centurions would've never gone after him. He hadn't broken any laws after all. But the fact that Supernova's enemies suddenly knew who she really was also meant that they knew who her family was, who her children were. It was too late to keep the Knave from telling but it wasn't too late to make him pay, and it wasn't the Centurions who went after him, it was me. It was Century Man.

I still don't really know what happened. It was just the two of us, the Knave and me. I had made sure of that. There would be no one to save him, no one to pull me off of him. I broke his left arm so badly it hung like a limp noodle from its socket. With the strength of a hundred men I beat at him, punished him. Punished him for what he had done, the danger he had placed my family in. He begged me to stop, swore he had been set up. As he cowered, his head buried in his arms, I went to lift him and throw him to the ground. And couldn't. I could normally hoist a freight train. Could tow a battleship. And suddenly I didn't have the strength to lift a man. My strength was gone, just like that. And suddenly I was just a guy in a goofy costume.

The Knave didn't even realize it at first. Maybe he thought I had granted his pleas for mercy. He was quick to take advantage of my confusion, though, and turned the tables, revisiting upon me the beating I had just given him. And, as abruptly as the fight had shifted, I was pulled free by someone and dragged to safety as Deidre dropped from the sky and finished what I had started. I wouldn't find out until later it had been Thana who had saved me. Deidre had her follow me, afraid I might do something I would regret.

That was the last time anyone saw Century Man. The Centurions went on. Deidre went on. I went on, of course, if only with the strength of just one man. We never told the public who Century Man really was or what, exactly, had happened. Sometimes I didn't even miss it. I didn't miss the fame. I didn't miss the suffocating media or the bickering and backbiting that went on in the Centurions after the bad guys were in jail and our masks came off.

Still, there were certain things I did miss: doing good, obviously. Saving people. Flying. I really missed flying. And I missed having sex with my wife the way we used to. I hadn't made Deidre come since I'd lost my powers. Not for lack of trying, on her part or mine. The problem was simple: Deidre liked it hard. Superhero hard. The strength of a hundred men hard. Hard enough to pull a normal woman apart like a wishbone. But Deidre wasn't a normal woman. She was Supernova. And no matter how hard Century Man fucked her, she wanted it harder. And the harder Century Man fucked her, the harder she'd come. But Century Man was gone and he wasn't coming back.

In 1961 NASA's Project Mercury was in full swing. Alan Shepard had been the first American in space that May and by October it was astronaut Barry Kurtz's turn. But something strange happened when Kurtz's capsule passed through the mesosphere and reached the blackness of space. The spacecraft was bombarded with what Kurtz himself would later categorize as Zeta Waves, which at the time seemed to affect neither the capsule nor Kurtz. Batteries of tests on Kurtz in the days following his flight seemed to confirm that he had experienced nothing outside the known parameters. But in the weeks that followed, Kurtz's body slowly began a terrifying change and by

29

Christmas of '61 Barry's skin had developed a steel-like shell, impregnable and virtually indestructible. Horrified by his transformation, Kurtz, now dubbed Arrowhead by the press, dedicated himself to finding a cure. And although he never found what he was looking for, his work and research gave birth to the world's most respected center for the study of the metahuman condition, known today as the Strategic Metahuman Advanced Research Team, or SMART Labs.

The Centurions had worked closely with SMART Labs since the team's inception. Helix and I had both felt it imperative we understood our powers, and the powers of those we fought against and alongside, as completely as possible. As such I've always had a close relationship with the scientists and doctors at SMART, most notably Dr. Agnetha Gunnarsson. Agnetha's father was the original Captain Sweden, who had been a close friend of Arrowhead and an ally of the United States during the height of the Cold War. Agnetha thought of Kurtz as an uncle and when her father was exposed as a Soviet spy she moved to the States and followed in Kurtz's footsteps, deciding to use her mind instead of her fists to fight for justice.

Since the Knave Incident, I had been making occasional visits to SMART Labs and Agnetha in particular, in the hopes of at least discovering what happened to my powers. Agnetha herself believed she could return my powers to me but I didn't allow myself that optimism.

Deidre didn't know about my trips to SMART. Not since the first few visits anyhow. Despite Agnetha's early progress with me, Deidre felt the best thing I could do for myself was to move on with my life, to learn to live without my powers. She felt the sooner I came to terms with my new, normal life the happier I'd be. And maybe she was right. I did stop coming to SMART for a while but I knew there had to be a reason why I lost my powers, and even if I could never have them back, I owed it not only to myself but to Deidre and the rest of my former teammates to help make sure the same thing never happened to them. So I went back.

Early on, Agnetha seemed excited about our chances of discovering exactly what took my powers. Her initial tests hinted at a larger mystery that she felt just on the brink of deciphering. With each visit to the lab I could sense Agnetha's optimism growing, and mine did, too. But then we simply seemed to hit a wall and the progress stopped. The research that had been so promising suddenly was at a dead end. No more clues. The trail went cold.

To her credit, though, Agnetha didn't give up. She insisted that I continue to make my visits to SMART and I agreed. And despite spinning our wheels for months now Agnetha has never stopped hypothesizing, never stopped testing.

Today's test, I was sure, would prove as useless and futile and all the others. I knew Agnetha felt the same way but she did a much better job of hiding it. I sat in the sterile waiting room, surrounded by white walls, a pristine white floor, and ceiling of white light. I could smell rubbing alcohol. On the counter sat a scaled up model strand of metahuman DNA and on the wall was a chart that read "The Metagene and You." I was naked except for a pair of SMART-issue briefs I was given when I checked in. I looked forlornly at the extra rolls around my middle that had appeared in the year since my body's metabolism had become decidedly un-super.

I heard a soft beep from outside and then the door to my room swung open. Agnetha entered in a whoosh. As always her hair was bound in a flaxen bundle on the crown of her head. A tiny pair of reading glasses dangled around her neck from a slender pearl chain and she was wearing her de rigueur knee-length white lab coat over black stockings and heels. She stalked across the floor, heels clicking sharply, and retrieved a clipboard from the work counter. She snapped on her glasses and glanced over my case file.

"Good afternoon, William," Agnetha said in her thick Scandinavian accent. "Did you remember my photograph this time?"

"As a matter of fact," I said, tapping my fingers against the manila envelope I had brought with me. Agnetha's eyes widened as she slowly took the envelope from my hands and carefully removed a glossy, autographed 8x10 of Supernova. My wife's beaming face filled the photograph, a strand of her blonde curls strategically draped across one eye. Agnetha had been requesting the photograph for months and I had been pretending to forget as to avoid having to explain to Deidre why I was still going to SMART Labs.

I watched Agnetha examine the photo thoroughly, reverently cradling it in her palms, her eyes examining every inch. "Skitsnygg. Var är toaletten? Tjejmiddagen," she whispered to herself, not bothering to translate, even though I could have probably guessed. Then suddenly her expression fell and she cast a scornful gaze my way. "It does not say, 'To Agnetha.'"

"Uh, yeah," I stammered, buying time—worst fears realized. "Deidre didn't really have time to..."

"It was supposed to say, 'To my #1 fan, Agnetha. Love, Supernova.' Why does it not say it?"

"I...I didn't really have..."

"And why is headshot? It was to be from rear. You promised me rear view, William."

"I'm sorry, Dr. Gunnarsson," I surrendered.

She looked back at the portrait and Supernova's bright smile seemed to make Agnetha forget my broken promise. Agnetha smiled back at the portrait. She suddenly slid the picture back in its envelope and turned to appraise me with a scientist's stare. "Have you experienced any changes in your condition?"

"No, not at all. Powers still gone. Nothing."

"Okay, then. Follow me."

"Could I maybe have a gown or..."

"Follow me," Agnetha said and I did as she instructed. She led me out of the waiting room and down a series of similarly white and sterile hallways, her heels echoing throughout. Occasionally we would pass by closed doors and I might hear the muted zap of a bolt of electricity or the faint whir of a circular saw or the unmistakable *rat-a-tat-tat* of a machine gun. Agnetha acknowledged none of it.

Finally we entered a door of our own and on the other side lay a massive room at least half the size of a football field. As we walked in, banks of light fixtures flickered in sequence then slowly glowed to life four stories above us. The room was made entirely of concrete and was empty with three exceptions: a small kiosk tucked in one corner filled with panels bristling with various levers, switches and dials; a cartoonishly oversized barbell that must have weighed a ton or more; and in the center of the space, a giant sphere that extended wall to wall, floor to ceiling. The sphere was a dark grey metallic color and was comprised of adjoining pentagonal and hexagonal panels. It looked every bit like a giant steel soccer ball.

Agnetha handed me a small headset and then slipped into the kiosk and tapped a control. With a hiss of air, one of the lower pentagons near the floor separated from the sphere and swung away on a pair of hefty hinges.

"Please enter the sphere now, Will"

I stepped to the opening and peered inside. It was pitch black.

"Please put on your headset now, Will."

I did as Agnetha said and climbed up a short ladder into the five-sided doorway and into the darkness. The interior of the sphere was smooth and cold, but my bare feet kept me from losing traction. The pentagon sealed silently behind me and for first time since I was child I felt afraid of the dark.

"Please stand on the southern pole," Agnetha's voice came through my headset. In the blackness I slid my feet down the inside of the sphere until I was at the bottom-most point. Like the first hint of dawn, I could see the polygon-shaped panels around me slowly begin to glow with light until I was able to make out the shape of the globe around me. It seemed even larger from the inside.

"I am initiating anti-grav now," Agnetha said. Accompanied by the slightest humming noise, my body began to rise in the air until I was floating unaided in the very center of the sphere, twenty feet above the floor.

And for a moment I was elated. It had been so long since I had felt weightlessness, felt the thrill of flight. But only for a moment.

"Prepare for radiation," Agnetha said.

"What exactly are we doing, Dr. Gunnarsson?"

"You will now be bombarded with solar radiation in the attempt to restart your powers."

"Are you sure this is safe?"

Before I could hear Agnetha's reply, the interior of the globe began to fill with a sound similar to the hum of the anti-gravity, only much louder. Within seconds the entire sphere was glowing golden yellow and getting brighter. I could instantly feel the heat, at first like being in warm sunshine, then soon like being naked on hot asphalt. The light continued to intensify until I had to clench my eyes shut against it and even then I could sense its glare. The heat was now unbearable, I was sure my skin was blistering. I called out to Agnetha to turn the machine off even though I knew she couldn't hear me over the electric thrum. At the instant I felt unable to keep from crying out in pain, the light and heat subsided and then dissipated entirely.

And it was over just like that.

I gently descended through the sphere until I was standing again on the bottom. I checked my skin and not only found no burns or injuries, but not even a suntan. I wasn't even sweating.

The doorway swung open again and I exited the sphere. Agnetha was there, standing by the giant barbell making notes on her clipboard. She took off her glasses and pointed to the gigantic barbell with her pen and said simply, "Now lift this."

With a resigned shrug I went to the weight and wrapped my hands around the bar, and tried to lift it, gently at first and then, when nothing happened, with all my strength.

Nothing. It wasn't budging. I had no idea how much the thing weighed, but it felt like it was anchored to the Earth itself. I couldn't even get it to rock back or forth.

"Enough," Agnetha said. She took me back to my waiting room.

While scribbling a few hasty notes on her clipboard she told me, "As with the hyper-neural steroid mass-injection, the supefluid quantum solvent bath, and the photoelectric vacuum saturation, the solar radiation bombardment has failed to restore your powers."

"My powers aren't coming back, Dr. Gunnarsson. We both know that."

"No," Agnetha said, fixing me with a stern gaze. "Neither one of us know that." She put her notes down and pulled her Supernova picture from its envelope and sighed at it. "You may schedule your next appointment at the front desk."

It was late afternoon when I got home from SMART Labs. The house was empty. On the counter, apparently forgotten, was the top hat from Luke's Presto Halloween costume. This was the third year in a row Luke had gone trick-or-treating as Presto and the second year in a row he had left behind his hat. Zack, despite my suggestions of Trace, or even Captain Fantastic, had insisted on dressing up as Helix. On the refrigerator, under a Supernova magnet, was a note from Deidre reminding me that her mom was coming to pick up the boys after school just above a note from Zack telling me he and Luke had left with Grandma, followed by a note from Deidre telling me to help her pick out something to wear to the party.

I hated the Centurions' Halloween party. Hated it from year one. And it had been my idea. I can't remember now why I ever thought it was a good one. Of course at the time there were only five of us and only three of us were married. Halloween seemed like the perfect time for a bunch of people who had spent their entire adult lives in costume to have a party. The only rule was:

no costumes. At least not your own. It only made sense that on the night when everyone else dressed up like us, we didn't.

It wasn't long before the invitation was extended beyond the Centurions. Within a couple of years the Citadel was hosting dozens of erstwhile costumed crime fighters and their significant others every October 31st. Everyone within the law-abiding metahuman community knew everyone else's secret identities (it only takes one busybody with X-ray vision) so it was the one night we could all take off our costumes and be ourselves around one another, even if we were dressed as pirates or vampires. In recent years attendance had swelled along with the metahuman population and last year there were enough people there that we spilled out of the Trophy Hall into the Simulator Room.

Deidre loved the party, of course. She had spent her entire life with super-powers, had grown up as the daughter of the original Nova Girl and the granddaughter of Ray Girl. She had always felt comfortable around other metahumans in a way she never did around normal humans. Plus, as the wife of Century Man, she felt somewhat like the hostess of the whole affair. And now that she was Helix's second-in-command, that hadn't changed. Whether because of that perceived responsibility, or because of the fact that everyone in America had seen her in a skintight costume from the time she was seventeen years old, Deidre always used the party as an excuse to dress modestly. Muted hues, slacks and blouses. Deidre called it "very Kate Hepburn." I called it boring.

Last year, though, Equinox showed up to the Halloween party in a little black dress that, according to Deidre, had been the talk of the superhero town ever since. She'd never admit it, maybe not even to herself, but I knew Deidre was a little envious. Deidre Donner was okay with not standing out from the crowd, but Supernova was not. Supernova wore an electric blue bodysuit and soared through the sky. Deidre wore sneakers and yoga pants to the grocery store. I decided it was time to remind them both that Deidre could be every bit as glamorous as Supernova.

My first tack was to persuade her to go as Marilyn Monroe. I could even be Joe DiMaggio, I offered. She could wear the famous pleated white dress and I could walk around with a Louisville Slugger slung over my shoulder. "If anyone knows what it's like to be married to the biggest sex symbol of their time," I had argued. "It's me and Joe."

"Whatever," Deidre had said to that, blushing. But it was true.

"Plus, the baseball bat will help me keep Helix away from you."

"Whatever."

Deidre shot down the Marilyn idea quicker than she had Anvil and Phobos. She might not dress up in costume, I conceded, but that didn't mean she couldn't dress up.

I browsed Deidre's closet, looking for the dress they'd all talk about till next year's party and quickly discovered that Deidre didn't own it yet. I turned on Eyewitness 8 to find out where my wife was. A random supermodel informed me that I, too, might be a metahuman and now I could find out in the privacy of my own home with MetaCheck, the home metagene test, available at drug stores everywhere. The model conveniently neglected to mention that MetaCheck was manufactured by Wertham Biotech. After the commercial Lola Oh told me the Centurions were in Ecuador stemming the lava flow after that morning's eruption of Tangurahua. There was some jostling home video footage of the Centurions repairing damage in, what Lola said was, the nearby city of Banos. I figured I had an hour max before Deidre got home, and I had a mission.

I made it to Century Centre mall and back in forty-five minutes, possibly a new record. The mall was full of moms and dads helping their kids pick out last minute costumes. All the good ones were gone. All the Supernovas, Helixes and Traces had been snatched up weeks ago. If they were lucky, they might find a Skyscraper. I knew exactly what I wanted and I found it quickly. I got back home right at dusk, just as the trick-or-treaters were trickling out of their homes onto the sidewalks.

I stopped to light our jack-o'-lantern. which looked suspiciously like the Hyperborean's helmet, on my way inside. Deidre was already home, in the shower washing volcanic ash out of her hair. I was waiting in the bedroom when she emerged. She walked to the foot of the bed, naked and damp, wrapping her wet mass of hair in a thick towel, piling it all on top of her head and tucking it into a snug turban.

"Tough day at the office?" I asked.

"Sorry I'm late. We had to stop on our way back to rescue the crew of a tanker caught in Hurricane Nicole." As Deidre talked she rifled through her underwear drawer. "Then there were the broken levees." She pulled out first one balled-up, smoke-colored wad of nylon and then, after considerable searching, a matching one. "Then there were the tornadoes in Louisiana that Nicole spawned."

Deidre sat on the edge of the bed and began to roll the stockings onto her legs. She stood again, straightening the lace tops around her thighs and then aligning the seams that ran down the back of each leg, and then went back to her dresser.

I watched as she slipped on the underwear she'd chosen.

"Oh, no," I said, shaking my head. "Not the granny panties. Not tonight."

Deidre was shocked. "These aren't granny panties." Deidre was also a liar.

I sprang into action. I went to her dresser and began my own search. "You need a thong, That little black one. The lacy one."

"That's for special occasions."

"Tonight is a special occasion."

"You'd rather take a beating than go to this party."

"True. So ease my pain by wearing nice panties."

"These are nice," Deidre said, looking down at the briefs she had on.

38

"What's the big deal anyhow?" I asked. "You don't wear anything at all under your costume."

"Out of necessity. You know this. And if it wasn't a big deal it wouldn't excite you so much."

"I bought you a dress," I blurted.

"You bought me a dress?"

I nodded and pointed to the closet door.

Deidre gave me an apprehensive glance as she started for the closet. On a padded hanger perched on the doorknob hung the dress I'd found at the mall while Supernova was averting natural disasters and saving sailors. She froze in her tracks, staring at it for a moment before approaching again. It was black, of course, and no larger than a pillowcase. It was dangling from the hanger by its delicate shoulders, so thin it swayed under the ceiling fan, the satin shimmering as it moved. She lifted it and held it against her body as she turned and went back to the mirror, gauging its length against her legs. It was slim and sleek and short. Shorter, certainly, than anything I had ever seen her in.

"Where's the rest of it?" she asked.

"Just try it on. If you don't like it you don't have to wear it."

Deidre slipped the dress off its hanger and then gently bunched the tiny dress into a loose hoop, bowed her head and draped it over her neck. She carefully threaded her arms through and let the dress fall, her shoulders catching it. She looked at the mirror, smoothing the satin to her body with her palms as she examined herself, turning and looking over her shoulder. Her entire back was bare. The hem of the dress floated about her thighs. It was perfect.

"It's kinda short," Deidre said.

"Yep."

For a moment I expected her to peel the dress off in favor of some sensible pants. "I don't know. This just isn't me."

"Exactly."

She checked the mirror again, frowning at her reflection. I could clearly see her panty lines through the wispy material. So

39

could she. "See? I can't wear a thong with this. It's too thin. Everyone will know."

"You're missing the whole point. If you wear those," I pointed contemptuously to the briefs under my wife's dress. "Everyone will know. It's the exact same reason you go commando as Supernova: panty lines. If you wear those, all the women at the party will talk about you behind your back. You know how women are. They'll point and snicker when you walk by and give you a cruel superhero name like Captain Bloomers or something."

Deidre couldn't help but laugh. "Shut up."

"And over time it would evolve to just 'the Captain,' and then to just 'Cap', and they'd talk about it right in front of you, thinking they were being sly, never knowing how hurtful they were being." I mimicked her teammates in the Centurions. "'Hey guys, Mandigore has busted out of prison again. Should we ask Cap to help out?' 'No way. Even Eyewitness 8's Eye in the Sky can see her panty lines.'"

Deidre had disappeared into the closet but was laughing harder now. "Shut up!"

I finally found what I was looking for in Deidre's underwear drawer, disentangling the lacy black slingshot and holding it up for inspection.

"But these," I said. "These will make friends and influence people. These—"

Deidre's granny panties hit me in the face. I turned to look in the direction they'd been thrown from. Gorgeous, my wife stood with hands on her hips, like a boy's dream of what a grown woman should look like. She had put on a gleaming pair of patent leather heels and was pivoting back and forth at the mirror, making sure everything was in place before scooping her damp brunette curls from her neck to let them cascade softly onto her shoulders. I could feel a big dumb grin stretching across my face.

"You like?" she asked.

"I like."

Skintight

"Good answer."

I offered her the lacy thong I'd picked out.

She shook her head. "Commando."

My stupid smile widened. "I like."

Deidre finished getting ready; hair, makeup and the various other arcane and time-consuming preparations a wife makes before going out, all the while quizzing me on the names of the spouses of everyone she could remember inviting. I couldn't think about anything except the dress Deidre was wearing and what she wasn't wearing beneath it.

She finally emerged from the bathroom and asked, "Ready?" as if I was the one holding us up. She picked out a shawl from the closet and draped it across her shoulders, a last ditch effort to cover up. I decided not to argue against it.

"Ready," I said.

"Hold my hand," she said and I did just that. "Here we go."

With her free hand Deidre twisted the Centurions emblem on her Signet Ring a quarter-turn. Even when I had my powers I hated this part. For the briefest of moments the carpeted floor of our bedroom seemed to be falling out from under my feet and even before my body could reflexively struggle for balance I found myself in the cavernous transporter silo of the Citadel. While my stomach righted itself my senses struggled with the conflicting stimuli they were receiving, the warmth of our home instantaneously replaced with the cold sterility of an orbiting space station.

Chapter Three
Secret Identities

In fixed geosynchronous orbit 22,240 miles above Century City, the Citadel kept constant lookout, shining in the night sky like a star. 'A constant reminder and symbol of our vigilance and protection,' we had called it in the press release. With technology and materials from the 22nd Century, Psy-Fi helped Helix and me construct a satellite that continuously adjusted its orbit in ways that gravity alone would not permit, allowing the Citadel to remain perpetually above Century City. We had conceived of a stronghold, a fortress to base our operations, a place to strategize, a place to keep watch over the citizens we had sworn to defend.

And at first that's exactly what it was. Inevitably, though, as the Centurions grew and changed so did the Citadel. We added training facilities and a Surveillance Womb, as Helix dubbed it. A new wing was constructed simply to house the spoils and trophies of our adventures. Lately, however, the Citadel had become no more than an orbiting locker room, a glorified clubhouse for grown-ups who liked to play dress-up and beat people up. A place to have outer space Halloween parties.

Hand in hand Deidre and I made our way through the main concourse of the Citadel, a gently curving passageway of titanium floors and inch-thick aluminosilicate glass walls. By my feet was a puddle of vomit, the sudden change of scenery having been too much, apparently, for an earlier arrival to take. The Earth hung beside us, a giant black ball webbed with strands of golden light; nighttime in Century City. The planet seemed to be just outside the glass, like we could open the window and reach out and touch it.

Deidre and I made our way down the hall, her heels clicking loudly on the metal floor, walking past the cavernous hangar on our way to the repulsor lifts. Walking through the Citadel felt like walking simultaneously into the past and the future. Technology quite literally from the future was juxtaposed with a sense of deliberate nostalgia, as if the whole thing had been designed by little boys from the 1950s, whose world of tomorrow was populated with disintegrator ray guns and silver rocket ships.

Inside the hangar sat Bettie, Psy-Fi's invisible ship, her presence betrayed only by the refueling line seeming to float in midair, the nozzle apparently connected to nothing.

"I wish I had a dollar for every time I bumped my head into that damn thing," I said, looking into the hangar, using it as my reason for falling a step behind Deidre so I could look at my wife's rear end. It looked almost as good in that dress as it did in costume. I missed watching my wife walk. This was the first time I'd seen her take more than three consecutive steps since the Knave told the world who she really was. With no need to conceal her powers any longer Deidre simply flew wherever she went, even if only to the bathroom in the middle of the night or to get the mail.

In the days that followed Deidre's outing I would overhear, maybe in line at the supermarket or on an elevator, people asking one another, "Where were you when you heard who Supernova really was?" like they did with the Kennedy assassination or 9/11. Except the people were disappointed, dejected that Supernova wasn't revealed to be a movie star or a senator or some equally famous person who had been protecting them against countless alien conquerors and power-mad despots. They felt ripped off somehow to realize they had

43

never heard of Deidre Donner before. They felt gypped to find out that she was a soccer mom, a member of the PTA, drove a minivan. Gypped to find out she was just like everyone else. Except, of course, for her amazing powers and abilities. It wasn't long before the name Deidre Donner slipped back into obscurity and she became, at least in the public eye, simply Supernova again. After all, it was no secret that John Wayne was really Marion Morrison or that Bob Dylan was born Robert Zimmerman.

We rode the lift to the Trophy Hall. The doors parted and we emerged into the din of the Centurions' Halloween Party. The hall was full and loud and we stood, Deidre and I, just outside the lift for a moment. We were not really sure where to go at first, overwhelmed by the amount of people.

There were easily a hundred guests, maybe a lot more. I had no idea the metahuman population had grown so large. Even without costumes it was easy to separate them from their spouses. There were bizarrely shaped and colored creatures, barely human, who looked more unusual, I imagined, in ordinary clothes than they did in costume. There were many more, however, whose appearances were quite normal, their true nature revealed only when they used their powers, typically reserved for battle, or to entertain themselves and those around them.

I saw the Toxic Twins tending the bar. I watched Electrolite as she stood on the gridded aluminosilicate ceiling, the Milky Way arching behind her as she made light-puppets with her hands, their obscenity matched only by the hilarity. I could see Starface trying to make her way to the bar, the chrome wings that jutted from her shoulder blades making navigation through the crowd nearly impossible. The "Monster Mash" blasted from Tripwire's head while Solstice and Equinox danced (or at least tried to) in mid-air.

Everyone seemed to be laughing and smiling and I was reminded of how much camaraderie and shared history there was, not just among the Centurions but within the larger metahuman community, especially now that the government seemed bent on sanctioning them all out of business. Thanks to the Metahuman Code Authority and Dr. Wertham, most here were marking their last Halloween amongst us. Those who could qualify for funding would not submit to the registration process and those who complied would be disqualified from attending. It was a safe bet that next year at this time only the Centurions themselves would be here. As Deidre and I made our way to the bar I overheard more than one conversation rehashing year-old arguments and preaching to the converted. "If they outlaw powers, only outlaws will have powers," I heard Black Diamond tell Gun Doll's husband.

But still, whether because, or in spite of, Wertham's Code, these people were determined to enjoy themselves. I made my way through them and fetched a glass of wine for Deidre and a beer for me. When I returned, Deidre reached for her glass.

"Shawl first," I said. Deciding she needed the alcohol more than the modesty, she reluctantly surrendered the shawl, swapping it for the wine and putting her dress on full display.

"Deidre?" the attention came almost immediately. We both turned to see Psy-Fi, who immediately snatched Deidre's free hand and held it out from her body, taking a long look at the short dress.

"Nice gams," said Psy-Fi. Being a time-traveler, she had the unfortunate habit of using slang that was either decades old or decades from being invented. "That dress is the bee's knees. You look great."

"Thanks, Marta," Deidre blushed. "Where's the wife?"

"She's at home," Psy-Fi said, and then clarified, "Home, as in the 22nd Century. She hates this sort of thing."

"So does mine," Deidre said with a pat on my shoulder.

With a knowing laugh, Psy-Fi hugged my neck and said, "We miss you around here."

"Sometimes I miss it myself," I said. "Just sometimes."

With promises to talk more later, Deidre and I parted ways with Psy-Fi and began to mingle in earnest. We talked to Presto and his newest girlfriend, having the requisite laugh at Captain Fantastic's expense for still wearing his underwear on the outside, "Doesn't he know that was over in the Seventies?" We chatted a while with Ultra-Vixen, who asked for Deidre's advice on how to keep certain parts of her considerable anatomy in costume—"Spirit gum." We even ran into Rocket Man and Rocket Queen, who we hadn't seen since we all had agreed to appear at Meta-Con a few years back—"Is body odor a super-power?"

There was one thing, though, that everyone we talked to mentioned: Deidre's dress. Depending on the proximity of their girlfriends or wives, the men either stared at it or futilely pretended not to. The women showered Deidre with praise, most of it genuine, some of it thinly veiling envy. Even passers-by, whether knowingly or not, acknowledged the dress with double takes and whispers. For the better part of our conversation with Trace's wife, Janet, I watched Trace jockey for position around his spouse to get a few stolen glances at mine.

Deidre and I went to the bar for another glass of wine and another beer. We said nothing for several minutes, welcoming the respite. The bar had been set up next to one of the giant glass cases that housed a smattering of the spoils and souvenirs of past Centurion's adventures. Behind the bartender I could see Prince By-Tor's sword and costume.

"Remember that?" I asked, gesturing toward the draped robes with my bottle.

Deidre smiled. "I remember I was so exhausted after that fight I finally gave in and said yes to a date with a very persistent photographer."

"And I remember you stood me up."

"I was waiting on Century Man to ask me out!" Deidre laughed.

I laughed, too. We drank in unison and then I said, "Do you miss him?"

"Who?"

"Century Man."

"While I was waiting on Century Man," Deidre squeezed my hand. "I fell in love with you."

I leaned to Deidre and kissed her on the lips. "Me too," I said. "I've got to pee."

"*Très romantique.*"

As I wove through the crowd it dawned on me that not once did I ever have to piss while in costume, and I almost laughed. Apparently Century Man possessed the bladder strength of one hundred men as well. I left the Trophy Room, walked through the gym and into the showers. I stepped up to one of the stainless steel urinals and began to piss. Suddenly a voice right beside me said, "Hey, baby."

I wasn't sure if it was the fact that it had been a woman's voice or that it was so close that startled me. I'm sure she had seen me flinch.

"It's not like I haven't seen it before," the woman said, peering over the partition that divided the urinals. "And you've certainly got nothing to be ashamed of."

I hurriedly zipped up my pants. "Hey, Jinx," I said. "I had hoped you'd forgotten about that."

I watched her gather the hem of her tiny dress in her fingers, hiking up the red material as she rose on her tiptoes and straddled the urinal. She cursorily surveyed the otherwise empty room and then gave me a wink.

"The line outside the ladies room is a mile long," she smiled at me as she urinated, scarlet lips curling devilishly. "I'll be damned."

"You were good last night," I said.

"Excuse me?"

"On *Alter Ego*," I quickly clarified. "You did good."

"Yeah, that fucking Oh is a real cunt. And Shuler, my god, what a pussy." Thana finished peeing and started looking around for something to wipe with. "Nobody's going to talk shit about you on my watch." With the exception of her shock of jet-black hair, green eyes, and alabaster skin, everything about her was red. Lips, dress, shoes, nails: all red. I followed her to the row of basins along the opposite wall and we both began to wash our hands, our eyes meeting in the mirror as she slipped a wetted hand under her skirt and scrubbed briskly before yanking a bundle of brown paper towels from their dispenser.

"Floating satellite, invisible spaceships, fucking brown paper towels," she said.

I laughed louder than I meant to. "You know Helix."

Thana ran her hands through her cropped hair and tweaked the devil-horns she had sculpted into her hair and dyed red.

"Yes, I do," she said and offered me her unused towels, which I accepted for some reason. Then she turned and walked away. I listened to her heels strike the floor until she was gone.

I studied my expression in the mirror and I watched a resigned smile crease my face. Deidre and I had first met Thana in here, in this room. The Centurions had just returned after defeating the Thirteen, and Deidre, like always after using her powers, was ready to get it on. Our usual place was the showers, the only place in the Citadel that afforded any privacy. As I stepped out of our stall, naked and wet, still semi-erect, I looked up to see Thana standing in the doorway, looking every bit like a lost little girl.

That's the only time I've ever seen her look anything less than supremely confident. Surrounded by some very suspicious Centurions, Thana had carefully explained how she had used her "touch," as she called it then, and convinced Psy-Fi to let her stow away aboard Bettie while the rest of us were fighting the Thirteen. She said that she didn't really have a plan and once successfully in the Citadel she had simply followed Deidre into the bathroom—"You looked like the friendliest one," she told us—to wait for the opportunity to approach her and explain why we should make her the newest Centurion.

She told us about her powers and how she could convince anyone do anything she wanted them to do as long as she could touch them with her bare hands, skin to skin. And how she had run away from home when, in a teenage fit of rage, she had

48

persuaded her mom to commit suicide and how she had nowhere else to go and wanted to do some good in the world to try to begin to atone for her awful sins. It was all bullshit, of course. Except for her powers. Those were all too real. But a few keystrokes on the Centurions' super-computer revealed that Thana's mom was living in Cedar Oaks with her five cats and was doing just fine.

Turns out Thana's only sin was wanting to trade in her barista gig for a life of adventure and excitement. Thana never once told any of the other Centurions what she had seen in the shower. And I realized that, if I was waiting for the right time to thank her for that, it just passed me by.

I finished drying my hands and went back to the party. The room was getting noisier; those whose physiology allowed them to get drunk were doing so, making up for those who could not. Tripwire's head was louder still, music blaring from it, and the floor was full with dancing skintights and their tipsy spouses. It looked like half of Century City was at the bar and I reluctantly joined them, hoping Deidre had kept an eye out for me.

I wrestled my way to the bar and asked for a beer which appeared almost instantly in front of me along with a martini, which I hadn't asked for.

"Mine," Thana said, appearing again. She plucked the martini from the bar and took a sip before taking me by the hand. She effortlessly parted the crowd and she led me to a spot of relatively empty floor away from the bar. Thana took another sip, smacking her lips afterward. "So, where's your better half?"

"She was supposed to be waiting for me at the bar," I said, scanning the room.

"Here she comes," Thana said, pointing with a tip of her martini. Through the crowd I could see my wife making her way toward us, holding her wine glass above the fray. Not ten feet away from me, Deidre's path was blocked by Helix. Despite the party's theme he was in costume, just not his own. He was wearing a spot-on recreation of the original Captain Fantastic costume, complete with the cuffed yellow boots and short cape.

He struck a heroic hands-on-hips pose.

"Halt, Citizen!" he boomed, loud enough for half the party to hear him. "It's not safe to drink alone in this neighborhood after dark."

Deidre laughed. "Hey, Trey."

Helix kept up the act. "Especially not in a dress like that."

I could see that Deidre was embarrassed but she didn't dare show it. She was flattered, too. "And what's that supposed to mean?"

"It means that's a brilliant disguise," Trey said. "If not for my X-ray vision I would have never guessed you were secretly mild-mannered Deidre Donner."

"X-ray vision, huh?"

Trey took a step back and looked my wife up and down. "Strange," he said, rubbing his chin. "Your dress must be made of lead. Either that or you're not wearing any panties."

Now Deidre's embarrassment showed plainly, her cheeks flushing with color. For just a second I was ready to go to her rescue—shoo Trey away and walk her back to the bar with me—but I knew Deidre could take care of herself.

Trey suddenly seemed to realize he'd crossed a line and dropped the Captain Fantastic gimmick long enough to say, "I'm sorry. It's altogether possible I've drunk too much. And to be completely honest, I have no idea whether you're actually wearing panties or not. I've been waiting all night to make that joke to someone."

"Or maybe I'm not so mild-mannered after all."

Trey offered his hand to dance and said, "Prove it."

Deidre took a big swallow of her wine and then set her glass down on the nearest table. She took Trey's hand and let him lead her onto the dance floor.

Thana elbowed me. "You snooze, you lose."

"He's harmless," I said, watching carefully. With Deidre in tow Trey wove his way through the crowd until he found a clearing, spinning as he took her in his massive arms and began to dance with her.

"You don't mind?" Thana asked.

"I don't mind," I said, hoping it sounded more truthful to Thana than it did to me.

Watching Deidre dance, swaying in Trey's arms and laughing with him as they talked, I felt an unfamiliar fluttering in my stomach. For a moment I thought it was jealousy. But it wasn't.

"You sure? Because, for a second there, you looked like maybe you were pissed. You know, like maybe you were ready to go kick his ass *with the strength of a hundred men*," Thana said, that last part a dead-on impersonation of the cheesy voiceover that used to accompany my television PR spots.

"Shut up, Jinx," I said, and we both laughed. I could feel Thana watching me, gauging my reaction as I watched my wife dance.

"You like watching her, don't you?" Thana said, almost making it sound dirty. At first her boldness took me by surprise and then I remembered who I was talking to. I glanced over at her and there was nothing in her expression that would indicate she meant it the way I took it. I said nothing, concentrating instead on Deidre and Trey. I realized suddenly that I had no idea how old Trey was. He had looked exactly the same for as long as I'd known him. I had always assumed it was because of his powers but for all I knew he could've been immortal. Or from another planet. Because of his name there had always been speculation that his powers were DNA-based. But no one really knew.

I watched Trey's hands, wrapping first around Deidre's waist then sliding down onto the swaying curves of her hips, clutching at the smooth satin of her dress, pulling it taut across her buttocks. His hands almost seemed to hold her there before gliding quickly up her naked back, letting her dress fall free.

"Yeah, he's harmless, all right," Thana said.

I could see Deidre eyeing her partner and for a moment she looked uneasy. Then she lifted her arms above her head and dropped them around his shoulders and began to move with him.

Thana said, "That's a nice dress, by the way. Let me guess: you picked it out."

I nodded and drew on my beer.

"She's sexy," Thana said.

"Thanks."

"I'm not talking about her looks," Thana said and then paused to make sure I was listening. "She's beautiful, yeah. There are a lot of beautiful women here tonight. But beautiful and sexy are two different things."

"Yes, they are."

"Sexiness is ninety percent attitude, ten percent looks."

"I like that."

"Feel free to use it," Thana said. She was quiet for a minute or two before starting again. "So, how are things?"

"What things?"

"You know, *things.*"

At first I wanted to tell Thana, to finally tell someone, how things really were. I wanted to tell her how Deidre and I used to fuck like locomotives colliding. For a moment I wanted to tell her how now we did it like arthritic old folks because we were scared to death she might break me.

But only for a moment. Until I remembered who I was talking to. "The only bad thing is having to ask my wife to open the pickle jar for me."

Thana laughed and then took my hand. "You know you can call me anytime, right?"

I told her I did know and we watched my wife dance with Trey for three songs. When Tripwire's head finally fell briefly silent, among the dancers leaving the floor were Deidre and Trey. Thana and I watched unseen as Trey led Deidre to the bar with the same ease and confidence Thana had used to get us out of there. He replaced the wine Deidre had abandoned, and once more wrapped an arm around her waist as he took a beer in his free hand.

"This looks like a job for Century Man," Thana said.

I agreed and excused myself from her and followed in Trey's wake, working my way to the bar next to him. Everything about him seemed to shine; the blinding teeth, bronze skin, the silver stubble on his head. I sat my beer next to his and waited until his eyes caught mine.

"Trey," I greeted him.

His eyes lit up and he shoved his big hand at me. "Will! It's been a while." I could feel him being careful not to grip too hard.

"Too long," I lied. Not long ago I would've called Trey a friend but I'd since found out that Helix didn't spend much time with non-metas.

"So, how's it going?" he said.

"Without my powers, you mean?"

Before Trey could respond Thana appeared at his side, placing herself between him and Deidre. She set her empty martini glass down in front of Trey and let her eyes roam over Deidre. "Goddamn, what a dress," Thana said, as if seeing it for the first time.

"Jinx!" Deidre shrieked and the two snatched each other up in a hug.

Thana took a step back and lifted both of Deidre's arms away from her before saying, simply, "Wow."

"Thanks Jinx," Deidre said. "You look great."

"Shut the fuck up," Thana said, dropping Deidre's arms.

"So," Trey began again. "Deidre tells me you're still taking pictures." He was talking to me, but staring at my wife.

"That's right. That was nice work yesterday with Hard Corps. You might be looking at another Fight of the Year Award," I said. Deidre noticed Trey's gaze now, too, but did her best to pretend otherwise.

"You giving him too much credit," Thana interjected. "The Hyperborean would've handed him his ass if Deidre hadn't been there."

Thana kissed Trey on the cheek as she leaned across him to fetch the fresh martini that had been placed on the bar for her.

53

"Of course, if you guys would've let me join your little club I could've made Hard Corps go away by simply asking them nicely."

"And caught it all on film," Trey added.

"Fuck you," Thana snapped but couldn't help laughing.

"Only if you ask nicely," Trey smiled.

"In your dreams."

"You know you want to."

"You're right, Trey. I'd love to fuck your brains out." Thana picked her martini up. "But I don't think you have any."

And with that, Trey simply smiled and gentlemanly asked Thana for a dance. Thana accepted with ladylike grace as if the prior exchange had never taken place. Deidre and I watched as the two of them disappeared into the crowd. Deidre finished her wine with a gulp and suddenly moved to me and whispered into my ear, "I want you." Her breath was hot and she tugged at my earlobe with her teeth as she pulled away. I wasn't sure if it was Trey or the alcohol that had turned her on but I didn't care. "Now."

We walked to a repulsor lift and I pushed the button. Deidre was toying with the hem of her dress when the lift arrived. We stepped aside to allow the Human Submarine and his wife to step off, and then we entered the elevator.

There were no words. I pushed her forward, into the rear of the lift. I was working her dress up over her hips even as the door was slowly closing behind. I could see the party and knew that we would be seen if anyone glanced our way. Maybe they already had. Deidre opened my pants and hauled out my erection. I hooked her leg in my elbow, lifted it, and slid into her. The hatch finally sealed shut and we began to descend. She coiled her leg around my waist; I slipped a hand into her dress and clasped her breasts.

I watched the display on the lift's control panel. We were halfway down. I hit the stop switch and the lift came to a jolting halt.

"You know there's an alarm," Deidre gasped. She planted her palms against the smooth interior panels, bracing herself as I rose onto the balls of my feet and thrust into her.

Psy-Fi's voice crackled through the small speaker mounted in the lift's control panel. "Repulsor Lift 3, is there a problem?"

Deidre slowed her rhythm, just slightly, asking me with her eyes what we should do.

"Lift 3," Psy-Fi called again. "Stay put. We're sending someone to assist you."

I pushed into her harder. Deidre's eyes fluttered and flashed violet-blue for just an instant, and then closed. She reached up, slipping a hand under my untucked shirt, dragging her fingernails across my stomach.

"Occupants of Lift Number 3, please step away from the door," Marta's voice came from the speaker again, more urgent now. I held onto Deidre, both hands clamped onto her hips hard enough to bruise a normal woman. I began to come. She watched me, eyes narrowing as she smiled, until mercifully my orgasm began to fade, devolving into a series of twitching aftershocks and undulations, like some silent movie death scene.

Deidre sealed a kiss to my lips and then turned to flip the switch. We abruptly resumed our decent.

As the hatch slid open, we were greeted by a concerned Marta, a suspicious Trey, and a knowing Thana, awaiting us in the hangar bay.

"Are you guys all right?" Psy-Fi said, waving her 22nd Century wristwatch over to make sure before peering inside the lift for the cause of the problem.

"Yeah, we stopped the lift," I began, not sure what to say next. "We just..."

"I accidentally bumped the switch," Deidre said, saving me.

Thana laughed once. "Yeah, you bumped the switch, all right," she said, eyeing the blatant lingering erection in my pants.

"The lift appears to be in working order," Psy-Fi said, scratching her head as she emerged.

"The repulsor lift is fine, Marta," Trey assured her, all business.

Thana gestured at Deidre's dress. "Dee, uh, you need to..."

Deidre looked down and saw the hem of her dress tucked into the top of a stocking. She quickly plucked it free and straightened out her dress, smiling sheepishly at everyone. She wished them all a safe Halloween and apologized for our early departure, explaining that we needed to get home to the boys.

"Well, you kids be careful trick-or-treating," Thana winked.

Deidre twisted the emblem on her Signet Ring.

"You looked amazing tonight," I said.

We had transported back to exact spot in the bedroom we had departed from, and I promptly collapsed onto our bed, not sure if it was the alcohol or the teleportation that was making the room spin. Deidre had gotten out of her dress and was climbing into bed.

"Everyone at the party was looking at you," I said.

"No they weren't." I could see her blush and smile.

"Especially Trey."

"Trey looks at anything in a dress," Deidre said, almost embarrassed, trying to downplay the attention he had given her. She was right, but that wasn't just any dress, and Trey did more than look.

"I liked watching you dance with him."

She paused for a heartbeat and then said, "You saw?"

"Of course. Did you like it?"

"Like what?"

"Dancing with him."

"All I could think about was not stepping on his feet," she said.

"Says the woman who can fly."

Deidre laughed at that. "Tonight was nice."

"No it wasn't. I hate that party."

"Not the party, silly," Deidre said. "The elevator."

"Oh. Yeah, that was nice, wasn't it?"

"Yeah."

"Hey, do you remember that time we got it on in the back of the Fantasti-Coupe?"

"You ask me that every time you get drunk," Deidre said.

"I bet you don't remember who we were chasing."

"Fastball."

"Fastball, that's right! And you said—"

"I said, 'The way Captain Fantastic is driving we've probably got time for a fast ball ourselves.'"

"Cap was concentrating so hard on not losing Fastball's van he never once looked in the rearview mirror." I stared at our bedroom ceiling and remembered. "I was kind of hoping he would."

Deidre tried to stifle a smile and then confessed, "Me too."

I looked at my wife. "I want us to be more, I don't know..." I tried to find the right word.

"Adventurous?" Deidre offered.

"Yes," I said. "Adventurous."

"Okay, baby."

"No, I'm being serious. Like that night in the Fantasti-Coupe."

"Okay," Deidre laughed.

"Like tonight."

"You're drunk, Will." Deidre said and kissed me. "Go to sleep."

I smiled at her. "Goodnight, Nova Girl."

"Goodnight, Century Man."

Chapter Four
Excelsior

The dream always began the same.

I was flying in a perfectly clear sky. A thousand feet below me I could see my shadow, a dot crawling across the landscape.

I soared over schoolyard playgrounds and farm ponds, city streets and suburban backyards, catching glimpses of life between the branches below.

And everyone was okay. No one needed help, no one needed saving. No banks were being robbed, no trains derailing, no volcanoes erupting. I had time, free time, to just fly.

I aimed my body toward the skyline of Century City and closed the distance within minutes. The spires and capitals of the buildings stretched skyward and each caught the sunlight and reflected it back, like an army of raised spear points on the horizon. I soared into the city, skimming past the skyscrapers, weaving in and out of them. Beyond the city, across Bostwick Bay out toward open water, on a small man-made island stood Lady Justice, over 300-feet of verdigris-patina copper, blindfolded and perpetually holding forth her sword and scales for all to see. I broke for her and inverted my body, looping in spirals down around the Statue of Justice, the cheers of the tourists below rising to meet my ears.

I was Century Man. The most powerful metahuman of my generation. Perhaps of any generation. The strongest. The fastest. From the beginning, the press dubbed me the Fearless Wonder. And although I hated it, they were right. I was fearless. And why not? What did I have to be afraid of?

As I arched back into the sky I waved at the people and smiled. I allowed myself a lingering glance at them as they waved back. But then, their waves turned into pointing fingers, their smiles changed to dropping jaws. They were pointing past me, into the sky behind me. And I spun in mid-air to see for myself what they saw.

Straight out of the sun, a giant silver airliner was falling from the sky. With my enhanced hearing I could hear the screams of the witnesses on the ground as well as the passengers on the plane. I shot upward, streaking toward the disabled plane. I had time. Time to catch it. Time to save them.

I reached the plane and then reversed course, matching my velocity with that of the aircraft. The plane was in a flat spin, under no control at all. I swooped under its belly, positioned myself and leaned into it, letting the weight of the plane transfer from gravity's grip to my shoulders. I pushed against it in flight, slowing it gradually. I halted the plane's spin, righted it, and slowed it further as I began scanning below for a safe place to set the big jet down. I could hear the exuberant, weeping cheers of the people on board as they came to realization that they had been miraculously rescued.

Then, it felt as if a giant invisible foot had stomped down on the plane from above, with me under it all. It took a moment for me to realize that gravity had simply reclaimed the airplane and it was again falling freely. As was I. I was tumbling out of control beneath the plane. I couldn't fly. My powers were gone.

Below, the water of the bay rushed toward me, the wind buffeting me, deafening as it rushed by my ears. I was going to hit in seconds, the massive airliner seconds behind me. They were all going to die. All of them. Men, women and children. No hope. They were falling too fast. They were going to die. I was going to let them die.

Then I woke up. My heart was a jackhammer in my chest. My body was covered in sweat, my hands trembling.

No matter how many times I had the dream, or a variation of it, there was no getting used to it. At least Deidre wasn't there to see me like that. Her absence usually meant only one thing, and I turned on the television to find out where truth and freedom needed defending today.

There couldn't have been more than a thousand metahumans in Century City. A recent Department of Extra-Human Affairs had estimated the metahuman population in America to stand at 13,272. That's one in 22,000. Less than five thousandths of a percent. Somehow, though, there were always enough metahumans in the same place at the same time to start a fight. Usually in a densely populated urban area. During the morning rush hour.

Today that place was Bostwick Bay Bridge, and what they were fighting about was anyone's guess, including, I was sure, their own. The bridge arced across Bostwick Bay and, from where I stood, its twin steel towers and cables formed a frame for Century's looming skyline. I made my way further onto the pedestrian crosswalk, pointed my camera and zoomed and focused on the figure of a young girl perched atop the bridge's north tower. She called herself Fahrenheit and was clothed only in the constantly dancing, lapping flames that enshrouded her entire body. I took her picture as she pointed at something, a sweeping arc of orange fire spewing forth from her extended index finger. I followed the band of flame and saw Trace, or rather a flickering, zoetrope approximation of Trace, as he raced up one of the bridge's suspension cables towards and past Fahrenheit. His roiling wake extinguished her flames and blew her from the tower. Her naked body plummeted towards Bostwick Bay. Before she had fallen even halfway to the water below, though, Trace was at the street level of the bridge. Smiling that ever-present smile; he cushioned her in a vortex created by his spinning arms, twin silver and orange tornadoes.

He deposited her unconscious, naked form onto the crosswalk not fifty yards from where I stood.

Supernova soared overhead, her eyes flashing beams of pure energy to cleave the morning fog and to evaporate on contact the jagged spears of ice that had been flung at her from the bridge's opposing tower. Another flurry of ice-lances barreled towards her, and she dispatched them with the same ease. Frostbite was this meta-criminal's nom de guerre, and my camera captured the look of bewilderment behind her mask as Deidre knocked her flat on her butt with only the slightest use of her powers. Frostbite scrambled to her feet and examined her silver, fur-trimmed snowsuit for dirt and damage. She seemed more concerned with her appearance than with the imminent arrival of Supernova.

I trained my camera on Frosty's ice-projectile weaponry and wondered for a minute what, exactly, constituted a super-power these days. I imagined this young girl's disappointment when her MetaCheck home test came up negative, almost understood her need to be special as she decided that she didn't have to have powers to be a superhero, or in Frostbite's case, a supervillain. She manufactured an identity for herself, created a stylish costume, and used her daddy's security clearance to steal the technology. I watched her as she looked up just in time to see Supernova dropping the last few inches from the sky. Frantically, Frostbite tried to aim the chrome-plated cannon fed by the tanks, slung, backpack-like, over her shoulders. Before she could bring the weapon to bear, and before Deidre had even touched down, Frostbite watched the nozzle of her cannon turn to slag under the bombardment of those same blue energy bolts that next knocked her out cold.

Helix dove from the sky, a white and green streak, his cape streaming behind him like the tail of a meteor. His fists were aimed at the living rock and lava creature called Magma, who was perilously close to melting away one of the bridge's iron trusses with his smoldering hands. Helix flew directly over me and I staggered in his slipstream. He banked and swooped down

61

on Magma to catch him with a right hook and send him hurtling into a stone pier in a shower of sparks and splattered lava. Helix landed directly over Magma's prone body, straddling him and then lifting him with one hand. Helix's flesh was impervious to the scorching stone and red-hot magma that was Magma's body. With his other hand, Helix delivered a devastating uppercut to his opponent, launching him into the air to tumble helplessly down into the bay below. As Magma hit the choppy water, the hiss of his doused, molten body echoed across the bay. A rising plume of billowing steam marked his point of impact.

Skyscraper, who apparently had been waiting on the shore somewhere, began to wade into the bay, growing as needed to keep the water waist-deep, and scooped the blackened Magma up in his enormous hand. Helix saw me as he took to the sky, and waved as he flew overhead like I was a boy at a parade. He joined Deidre and Trace atop the tower where they were collecting the vanquished members of the Elementals.

Whether he meant to or not—I had little doubt he had meant to—Trey's wave and perfect smile as he rose effortlessly into the sky reminded me of who I used to be. I used to be up there. I used to be him, the one who led the Centurions into battle, the one who waved at the onlookers as I glided over them. The one signing the autographs. The one kids dressed up as for Halloween. I was so big, so grand. But I had been made smaller. There was no escaping it. I used to be the news, now I simply photographed it.

I had suddenly lost my taste for superheroics and decided to forego the customary ass-kissing session that followed a Centurion's victory. As I got on the beltway, a Metahuman Activity Alert gave the all-clear for the Bostwick Bay Bridge area. Right after that, Skyscraper told me I should ask my doctor if Cialis was right for me. He was followed by my wife assuring me that Verizon Wireless has more 4G coverage than AT&T. I turned off the radio and drove home in silence.

There were three messages on our old answering machine. The only people who ever called our landline anymore were

Deidre's grandmother and Deidre's agent, Morris. Deidre's grandmother was convinced cell phones were part of an extraterrestrial mind-control plot, which actually wasn't too farfetched, so I gave her a pass on the landline thing. Morris, not so much. Maybe he was one of the E.T's.

I played the messages as I sifted through yesterday's mail.

"Okay, so look," Morris began his message the way he always did. "Don't forget Meta-Con tomorrow. I know you don't want to do it but it's a Clairol gig and they're handing out free samples of Herbal Essences with every autograph you sign. They wanted you for two hours but I said one or none. I'll meet you there at ten in the a.m. Call me."

The next message was from Deidre's grandmother confirming she would pick both kids up from school this afternoon. The third message was Morris again. "Okay, so look. The Calvin deal hinges on the new costume design. They want to design your Journal Awards gown, too. Call me."

Even before I could get fully incensed at the idea of Deidre changing her costume, the phone rang.

"Hey," said Deidre. "I've got a thing at City Hall this afternoon but I'm free after that. Mom said she would feed the kids. Want to meet me for an early dinner?" She suggested Centurions Café before I could think of an alternative.

"I, uh..."

"Great. I'll be there at five," she said. Then, in a whisper she added, "I'm not wearing any panties."

She hung up. I remembered Deidre's word. *Adventurous.* I forgot all about her agent.

On the roof of Centurions Café was a slowly rotating scale model of the Citadel. It looked like a giant chrome cocktail tray planted top and bottom with all sorts of polished spires and turrets. Inside the restaurant, dangling from the ceiling, was an acrylic version of Bettie, Psy-Fi's starfighter. This one wasn't quite invisible, its position betrayed by the fine layer of dust on its fuselage. The walls were festooned with framed front pages marking the peaks and valleys of a half-century of superheroics. Mannequins in glass cases modeled a autographed bustier worn by Weather Woman and battle-damaged trunks from Excalibur. There was a replica of the Fantasti-Coupe you could sit in and have your picture made.

As usual the dining room was full of tourists. The bar was relatively empty at quarter till five and I climbed onto the end stool and asked for a beer. The bartender said I could get it in a special 22-ounce collectible Helix glass for an additional $1.99.

"No thanks."

A pimply waiter wearing a bunched-up Skycraper costume leaned against the bar a few stools down from mine. My beer arrived and I listened as he provided commentary on the Eyewitness 8 recap of the Bostwick Bay Bridge fight for the bartender, who could hear the TV just fine and seemed on the verge of telling the waiter so.

As Eyewitness 8 returned us to our regularly scheduled viewing, the waiter began telling the bartender, loudly, about some nude pictures of Supernova a friend of his had found on the Internet and how this friend knew they weren't fakes because he could tell a fake. Despite the barkeep's best efforts to ignore him, the waiter told him he had another friend who had downloaded the Livewire video and that Supernova was in it. He was going to watch it and then have the other friend email him the nude pictures so he could compare Supernova's bush, because that was the only real way to tell if the pictures were fake or not. I tried not to laugh. As I was about to ask the bartender for my next beer I saw Deidre in the mirror behind the bar, explaining to the maître d' in the Presto tux and cloak that she was meeting someone.

She was wearing a skirt, not nearly as short as the dress she'd worn to the party, but certainly more daring than her typical weekday mom jeans. She saw me and smiled as she moved down the steps into the bar. I turned and smiled back at her. The young waiter turned, too, and both of us watched my wife walk across the floor.

We kissed when she reached me.

"Skyscraper here is a big fan," I whispered in Deidre's ear, nodding to the waiter. He clearly didn't recognize Supernova out of costume and without her blonde hair.

Deidre gave him a slightly confused smile as I stood, offering her my arm before following the make-believe Presto into the dining room. It was almost as empty as the bar. He showed us to a small, leather booth against the row of tall windows that overlooked the sidewalk and handed us menus as we sat.

"So," Deidre began, unable to resist. "Who was that at the bar?"

"He wants to see your bush."

"Excuse me?"

"He wants to look at your bush in those nude Internet pictures of you and compare it to your bush from your performance in the Livewire video. He just wants to make sure the nudes aren't fake," I said matter-of-factly.

"He told you this?" she asked, hushed and incredulous. "He thinks I'm in the Livewire video?"

"Poor kid," I went on. "He's probably in the bathroom beating off right now."

"What is it with you and beating off?" Deidre laughed. "You've got the Marines on Iwo Jima masturbating to pictures of my grandmother; now you've got a waiter at Centurion's Café jerking off in—"

At that exact moment, the young man in question appeared at our table. "Welcome to Centurions Café," he said. "My name is Todd and I'll be your server today. Can I get you something to drink?"

Deidre did her best to hide her face behind her menu as I told her young admirer that I was fine with my beer but the lady would have a glass of red wine. Todd nodded and walked off.

"So," I said. "Does Supernova's carpet match her drapes?"

"You're a freak."

"I'm being serious," I said.

"So am I. You're a freak."

Todd brought Deidre her wine and took our order. When he was gone I said, "Are you changing your costume?"

"Morris called, huh?"

"Twice."

"Look," Deidre started. "It's just for special occasions. I'm still going to wear my regular costume. The Calvin Klein people wanted me in something they designed. They're designers. That's what they do."

"There's nothing wrong with your old costume."

"I know that. They know that. It's just for special occasions."

"Who decides which occasions are special?"

"They do, but it's not like they're going to have me in it every day. They're thinking ads, charity events, public appearances. Shit like that," Deidre said. "They won't sign on, otherwise."

Todd set our Century Salads in front of us and asked if we wanted any black pepper before leaving us again. We took a few bites each before I said, "What's it look like?"

"You'll like it."

"What's it look like?"

"It's cyan and magenta, just like my old one. A little more skin," Deidre said. "You'll like it. I promise."

I believed her and nodded to tell her so. Our food came and we ate. Deidre had ordered the French Dip with Justice au jus. I tried fruitlessly to find something without a ridiculous name before settling on the Bulletproof Burger. I explained to Deidre the concept of fake celebrity nudes on the Internet, something she claimed to be completely unfamiliar with. She seemed a little embarrassed but still flattered that she might be the subject of such a thing, and we made plans to find some pictures of her later that night. Deidre laughed out loud at the idea of it.

Skyscraper Todd was heading back our way and I said quickly, "I'll ask our waiter if he'll forward those pictures to us when he gets them." Deidre glared at me. "We'll tell him we're starting a collection."

66

Deidre mouthed "Shut" and "up" at me. Todd asked how our food was and we told him everything was delicious. He made a few dessert recommendations—the Psy-Fi Soufflé—"So good you'll want to go back in time and eat it again"—was his favorite. Deidre and I decided to trust him. When it arrived I moved around to Deidre's side of the booth. As we ate it I laid my hand on her leg and let it slowly drift up, pushing the hem of her skirt up with it, exposing her thighs. I fed her a piece of cake with one hand as I slipped the other hand under her snug skirt. She tried not to smile as my fingers grazed her pubic hair. She hadn't lied to me on the phone.

"What are you doing?" she said under her breath, feigning innocence while at the same time spreading her legs apart to give me better access.

"Enjoying my dessert," I replied.

"That's the cheesiest line I've ever heard."

I fed her another forkful as I pressed a finger into her wetness, making her moan around her soufflé.

"How is it?" Todd asked, materializing tableside. I could feel Deidre jump, startled.

"Wonderful," I told him. "A little moist, though." Deidre clamped her thighs around my hand tightly and jabbed an elbow into my side.

"Will there be anything else?" our waiter asked. If he noticed my hand under my wife's skirt, he didn't let on. I shook my head and smiled and he thanked us, left the bill, and walked away.

I looked at Deidre. "Wanna get out of here?"

She gave me a naughty smile. I stood, peeled a few bills from my wallet, and left them on the table. She stood and we started for the door.

"I should probably pee before we leave," I said, changing direction.

"Good idea," she said, walking with me as I knew she would. We walked into the small alcove that led to the restrooms. On one door was the silhouette of a female in a cape above the word *Heroines*, on the other a muscle-bound figure over *Heroes*. Just before Deidre could go left toward the ladies room, I grabbed her shoulders and moved her to the right and into the men's room. I pushed her forward, her heels clicking and clomping, past the sinks and urinals and into the last stall, her hands splaying against the tiled wall as I shoved her in.

"What are you doing?" Deidre gasped, looking at me over her shoulder, almost fearfully.

"Exactly what you want me to," I said, gathering her skirt in one hand.

"What if someone had been in here?

"There wasn't. I was watching."

I latched the stall door behind us and with both hands snapped her skirt up over her hips. I crouched behind her and she bunched her skirt around her waist, making sure it was out of the way. Deidre arched forward; I held her by her ass and sealed my mouth over her pussy and ate greedily. She squirmed above me. My cock stiffened in my pants. Deidre thrust her hips back, pushing against the wall with both hands.

The restroom door creaked open and there were footsteps as someone walked in, whistling to himself. Deidre froze, watching me wide-eyed over her shoulder. I looked up at her, still eating her as we listened to our visitor unzip his pants, humming now as he began to piss, completely unaware he wasn't alone. I could hear the man's stream trickle off to nothing and then heard him zip his pants and walk over to the sink, leisurely washing his hands. He yanked a few paper towels out of the dispenser, whistling again now, and dried his hands thoroughly before I finally heard the open and close again.

"What do you say we go someplace a little more private?" Deidre whispered and I nodded, standing as Deidre straightened her skirt and caught her breath. Almost without me noticing, Deidre dialed her Signet Ring and, in the blink of an eye, the sights, sounds and smells of the men's room of a themed restaurant suddenly were exchanged for of the sterile silence of the Citadel. I had gone completely limp. The disorientation that

68

accompanies a transporter ride had left my hard-on behind at Centurions Café.

"I know a place," Deidre said, stepping out of the elliptical cylinder of the transporter. She took my hand and towed me to the pair of repulsor lifts at the far side of the transporter silo.

"Are you sure we're alone?" I asked as the hatch sealed behind us and the lift began to rise. Deidre was floating an inch or two off the metal floor.

"Just you and me, baby," Deidre said. "Well, you and me and Trey."

"What?"

"Trey has Surveillance Womb duty, but he'll be stuck there for a few more hours."

"Oh."

The repulsor lift slowed and came to a cushioned halt on the uppermost level of the satellite. With a rush of air the hatch slid open and Deidre and I stepped out into the War Room. Dominating the room was a mammoth polished steel table. It was perfectly round, twelve feet in diameter and resting on a single, trunk-like steel pedestal. The Centurions' logo, the original one, was burnished onto the top of it. Around the circumference of the table were the logos of each of the members, with a corresponding chair fashioned of pure black metal. Those chairs hadn't been repositioned since Trey, Deidre and I put them in place. We had hand-formed them from fragments of the neutron remains of the defeated Star Prince. Even when I had my powers it was all I could do to move one. They were meant to symbolize the stability of the Centurions.

On the far side of the table I saw Supernova's seven-pointed star and next to it the stylized shield I used to wear on my chest when I was Century Man.

"I always loved those chairs," I said. "I figured Trey would've gotten rid of mine by now."

"He got voted down," Deidre said.

It was here that Trey and I had envisioned ourselves mapping out strategies and analyzing our enemy's weaknesses like Arthurian knights amid the arrays of the oversized circular screens of infrared sensors and hyperspectral analyzers that lined the walls. More often than not, however, we simply hung out up here, gazing down at the Earth as we shot the shit, usually about which superheroines had the best racks or the Comets' chances of winning the Eastern Conference.

The best view in the Citadel was right here. The Earth filled the viewport that comprised one entire curved wall of the chamber. Deidre dropped my hand and finally touched down on the floor. She walked to the window and turned to lean back against it, silhouetted against the swirled white and blue planet behind her that was big beyond words.

"We've never done it in here," Deidre said, more asking than telling, as the risk we were getting ready to take started to sink in.

"Do you realize how easily Trey could catch us?"

She gave me that little wink of hers that means she's either joking or she's being dead serious, I could never tell which, and said, "Maybe I like the idea of getting caught."

I checked to make sure the lift was still on our level. Even if Trey walked in right now, I thought, Deidre could concoct a believable cover story. Or maybe she'd tell him the truth. Maybe she'd tell him she had transported me to the Centurions' orbiting fortress to fuck me here because we couldn't get any privacy in the men's room of Centurion's Café.

Deidre took the hem of her skirt in her fingers and inched it up and over the swells of her hips. I walked to her, matching her stare, and clamped my hands on her shoulders before spinning her around and bending her over at the waist. She reached out in front of her to catch herself against the glass as I yanked her skirt up over her ass. I unbuckled my belt, the weight of it dropping my pants to my ankles. Deidre's palms squeaked against the cold glass as I entered her.

I looked down at planet Earth and tried to read the geography to get an idea of where Century City was. I focused on the terminator, the line where night was slowly creeping across

70

the globe. I had once read somewhere that at any given time there were hundreds of amateur astronomers training their telescopes on the Citadel, and I wondered how many people were looking up at us right now. With a powerful enough telescope, could someone see us? Was there someone on Earth looking through their telescope and seeing us? Was there a dad in the backyard with his kid struggling to explain what that man was doing to Supernova?

"Look," I said, my hand under Deidre's chin, tilting her head toward Century City's part of the continent. "They can all see what I'm doing to you." I could feel Deidre's chest rising and falling as she panted. I moved my hands around her, opening her blouse and pulling the cups of her bra down, revealing the full curves of her naked breasts to anyone with a large enough lens. I pressed her body against the aluminosilicate viewport with the full weight of mine, her breasts flattening against the glass, on full display for the entire Western Hemisphere to see.

I imagined what our hypothetical voyeur-astronomers were seeing: Deidre's breasts pressed onto the window, two splayed disks, whitened against the glass, morphing and shifting shape as her body rocked.

"They can all see us," I whispered into Deidre's ear. "They're all watching you." Her moans told me how excited that made her. "I want to watch you."

There was a hesitation in Deidre's movements. It was so slight I wasn't sure I hadn't imagined it.

"Show me," she said.

I drove into her as hard as I could, as fast as I could. I rose on my tiptoes to sink into her one last time. I held her to me, my body rigid, every muscle tensed as I issued a final, guttural growl.

I let Deidre slide down the glass until her feet were back on the floor and I slumped into her arms and dropped my face into her shoulder until I realized I couldn't breathe there. I looked out the fogged viewport as I panted. Deidre stroked my damp hair and placed little kisses on my neck. I could see Hurricane Nicole over Louisiana.

When Deidre and I watched Eyewitness 8's *Good Morning Century City* the next day I was a little disappointed to hear not even the slightest mention of strange sightings of the Citadel the evening before. There was no mention of reports flooding in from amateur astronomers across the eastern seaboard, or of a hastily scripted denial from Centurion press agents regarding any indecent exhibitions of affection aboard their satellite. When I quickly scanned the other news outlets as Deidre went to kitchen for another glass of orange juice, I found again not a word about any out-of-the-ordinary occurrences observed on the Centurion's orbiting fortress. Maybe it would be on *Alter Ego*, I thought. It was the sort of story they'd save for Lola Oh.

After returning from a commercial break, Lola used the Bostwick Bay Bridge fight to segue into a brief mention of Deidre's Calvin Klein deal.

"And it looks like Skintight City will be seeing a lot more of Supernova soon," Lola said. "Sources tell us that Supernova has signed a six-figure deal with designer Calvin Klein, which includes a complete redesign of her famous costume. Insiders say the new outfit will be a variation of the old costume, only much more revealing."

"Well, I, for one, can't wait to see it," Brad Bradley, Eyewitness 8's sports anchor, chuckled.

"You'll like it," Deidre said to me, sternly, before I had a chance to open my mouth. "I promise."

"They said 'much more revealing.'"

"It's not *that* much more revealing."

"How much more?"

"I don't know," Deidre stalled.

"You approved the design without seeing it?"

"No, I've seen it."

"How much more revealing?"

"Well, shit, baby, anything would be more revealing than my old one. The only thing that costume doesn't cover is my head."

"How much?"

"My stomach, okay?" Deidre finally confessed.

"What else?"

"My legs."

"Your legs?"

"It's got these... I guess you'd call them shorts. It's got shorts."

"Like how short?"

"Baby," Deidre said, clearly exasperated. "I said you'd like it. I showed more skin at the Halloween party. I show more skin at the beach." She watched me for a minute to make sure she had pacified me for the time being. "It's not like I'm going to be the Nude Avenger or anything. Look, I've got to meet Morris in twenty minutes," Deidre changed the subject unapologetically, "You coming?"

"Yeah."

"You'll need to drive yourself. Morris's set up some kind of fly-in for the fan club members. I'm supposed to make a big entrance and sign a few autographs on my way in to the convention center."

"Nice."

"Yeah. So, I'll just meet you inside." Deidre took a step back and began to spin, lighting up the entire house with a burst of violet-blue energy, and she had become Supernova.

"Have fun," I said to Deidre as she stepped out the front door.

She rolled her eyes. "Sure." She took softly to the air, blowing me a kiss before going supersonic.

With the exception of San Diego's Comic-Con International, Meta-Con was the nation's biggest comic book convention. Last year's attendance was 101,000 and this year was expected to exceed that. Two years ago, organizers had to move the event

73

from the old Century Conference Center to the newer and larger Century Convention Complex uptown.

Originally known as the Century City Comic-Con, the venue change brought a new name ostensibly reflecting the convention's broader appeal, but everyone knew they started calling it Meta-Con to capitalize on the surging celebrity of the skintights. And to be fair, to call it a comic book convention was a little misleading. Sure, there were plenty of comics, dealers and comics creators on hand but in recent years the real draw had been Hollywood. The major studios had long since tapped into the nerd zeitgeist, and every character with a cape was getting optioned for a three-picture deal. The hottest ticket this year was the panel with the cast of the just-released Captain Fantastic movie.

I had been to Meta-Con once before, years ago, on a mission to complete my run of *Justice Guild*. But back then it was no more than a couple dozen folding tables with boxes of back issues in them. Now it took up the entire main hall of the complex as well as all the banquet rooms on the lower level. There was row after row of dealers selling new and old comics, everything from ragged copies jammed into boxes for a quarter each to issues so rare and precious the sellers wouldn't even let them be removed from their Mylar sleeves and handled before purchase. There was an area for the writers, pencilers and inkers to autograph their creations and chat with fans. I saw old-timers who helped usher in the Silver Age of comics and up-and-comers with rock star status. There were toy manufacturers and video game developers. Every publisher, from DC and Marvel all the way down to the smallest upstart independents had come to set up shop. Meta-Con had come a long way. There was a also a booth for Focus Comics, the company that had the publishing license for the Centurions. Every month they put out *Supernova Action*, *Power of Helix*, *Challenge of the Centurions* and so many more. Before I'd lost my powers there was even an *Adventures of Century Man* book, and I thought about going over and talking to the creators, but then I remembered they had no idea who Will Donner was.

The vendors and dealers weren't the real story here, though. Neither were the Hollywood hot shots. What made this all happen were the fans. They were truly the lifeblood of the industry. In fact, most of the creators started out as fans. Many even got their break in the business at this very convention. And there were more fans than ever. Old and young, male and female, black, white and everything in between. No demographic went without representation. And a sizeable portion of those in attendance felt it necessary to attire themselves as their favorite character. By the time I had walked from one end of the hall to the other I had seen seven Helixes, four Supernovas, and a spot-on Trace, beaming just like Andre beneath a mirrored wraparound visor. One smartass had dressed up as a milk carton with a picture of Century Man on the side, "Have You Seen Me?" written above.

I checked my program and found the room for the Supernova autograph session. It was already underway and the line snaked down the hallway and doubled back on itself, and consisted almost exclusively of adolescent girls and grown men. The last guy in line had a piece of paper taped to his back that read, "I am the last in line for Supernova".

I flashed my pass to security and was ushered in. Deidre and Morris were seated in folding chairs behind a long table, a stack of color 8x10s at Deidre's disposal. There was a woman next to Morris handing out free Clairol shampoo packets to every fan, which were greeted unfailingly with a quizzical look and shoulder shrug. There was an empty chair next to Deidre and I took it. Before I could even speak to my wife, Morris was leaning back in his seat and clamping a hand down over my shoulder.

"Can you fucking believe this crowd? No way we're out of here in an hour. I knew I should have held her to two. Should be charging for this shit. Per signature. Should make these bastards buy a headshot to get the autograph."

"How are you holding up?" I asked Deidre.

"Only fifteen more minutes," she said under her breath, then to the forty year old man whose mint-in-box Supernova Ultimate Edition Battle-Ravaged Costume Variant action figure she'd just signed. "Thanks. Have a great con."

For the next two and a half hours I sat by my wife's side as she signed and smiled and posed, all with the patience of a saint. Occasionally Deidre would switch to "Enjoy the convention" for a while and then when she tired of that, return to "Have a great con". The Clairol lady never once wavered from her tried and true, "Would you like a sample of Herbal Essences?" At one point I tried to get up to leave but Deidre held me tight by my wrist and gave me a 'Don't you dare' look. So I sat it out.

Everyone wanted the same three things from her, in varying quantities: something autographed, a picture with her, and answers to their questions. A gloomy middle-schooler all dressed in black wanted to know if Supernova needed a teenaged sidekick. More than one person asked to touch her costume. We met a couple who had named their daughter Nova and I saw more seven-pointed star tattoos than I could count, most in places I would have rather not seen. One young lady even had Deidre sign her left breast, just above the Supernova symbol tattooed there. Another woman told Deidre that her boyfriend likes it when she dresses up like "Slutty Supernova" in the bedroom. A man old enough to be Deidre's dad asked her how she kept her panty lines for showing, and then got his *Nova Girl Secret Origins #1* signed. He had a Supernova tattoo, too.

Finally, Deidre signed a stack of comics for the guy with the sign taped to his back. And when the room was finally empty, Deidre turned to Morris and said, "You owe me big-time."

Morris stuffed the unused 8x10s in his bag. "P.R., baby. P.R."

The Clairol lady asked me if I'd like a free sample of Herbal Essences, to which I politely declined. "We get comped."

"I'm riding with you," Deidre told me. "I feel like I've just gone ten rounds with Pile Driver."

76

Skintight

She tossed her head back, and in the blink of an eye and a burst of light, the real Deidre changed places with the superhero version. We left Morris and the Clairol lady to clean up their wares and Deidre and I drove home.

Chapter Five
Jolting Tales of Tension

Deidre poured herself a coffee mug of wine and collapsed onto the sofa, stretched out. She was wearing her bathrobe, still wet from the shower.

"I almost showered twice. The stench of five hundred nerds is not easily washed off."

I sat on the other end of the sofa and Deidre put her feet in my lap and I began to knead them gently.

Deidre moaned. "That feels good. I'm so sore. I feel like I've been in a fight."

"Are the kids at school?" I asked.

Deidre checked the time and smiled. "They don't get out for another hour."

Then came what sounded like an electronic birdsong.

"Son of a bitch," Deidre spat as she sat up on the sofa. "You've got to be fucking kidding me." I could hear her Signet Ring chirping clearly now. She tapped the ring's face and sighed, "What is it?"

"Hellkat," came the terse response from the ring. It was Presto calling from the Surveillance Womb.

"Where?"

"First National Bank, downtown."

"I'm on it." Deidre tapped her ring again. "Why does it always have to be downtown?"

She stood from the couch, pivoted once on the ball of her foot, then launched into a spin. The room filled with a violet flash of light and Supernova stood before me. "Why can't they rob a bank out in the country? You'd think they'd want to minimize things like property damage and risk of death or dismemberment." She walked to the front door. "I mean, just because they're going to jail for robbery doesn't mean they want a murder rap. Or a multi-million dollar lawsuit." I watched through the open door as she lifted into the air and out of frame. And then dropped back down until she was just a few inches above the sidewalk. "Bye. Love you." Then she was gone again.

The First National Bank of Century City was in the very heart of downtown. It had actually become one the cities most recognizable edifices, not because of the building itself, but because it was adjacent to Century's famous Champions Fountain. Champions Fountain (or more accurately, *Fontana dei Campioni*, as its Italian sculptor named it) had been a popular target of tourists since its dedication. Its polished marble depicted a pair of nameless metahumans, one female, one male, ascending skyward with arms raised overhead, chests bowed and muscles flexed, burbling streams of water spouting all around them. It was ridiculous. And the best angle to have your picture taken in front of Champions Fountain just happened to put the First National Bank in the background. I felt like the only person in town who saw the irony.

On an afternoon like this, with the sun shining down from a clear blue sky, not even the police surrounding the bank could scare off visitors to the fountain. Even as the CCPD called into the bank through bullhorns, rifles trained, children splashed in the fountain's pool and climbed on the stone heroes.

I snapped a few shots of the barefoot kids playing, making sure to get the armed task force in the background, before moving closer the bank. Given the time it took me to drive here, I was sure Deidre had subdued Hellkat by now and would be dragging the criminal's unconscious body out the front door any minute.

I hadn't even finished that thought when the big glass and brass doors blew outward with a crash. Hellkat was shot through them, tumbling head over heels through the air, her body propelled on the leading edge of iridescent bolts of blue energy launched from Deidre's eyes. A blizzard of hundred dollar bills flipping and fluttering to Earth all around her. Hellkat spiraled head-high across the square and landed with a splash and a thud in the pool at the feet of the marble marvels. The children screamed, like only children can, and scattered, dashing dripping wet into the outstretched arms of waiting mommies and daddies.

It took a few seconds but Hellkat got to her feet before the hushed crowd. The police all did about-faces and re-aimed their weapons at her while their commanding officer continued to bark useless orders for her to surrender. The observers that weren't too stunned to look away were scrambling on their hands and knees to collect as many hundreds as they could.

Hellkat was panting, bruised and battered. Her bottom lip was split and a trickle of deep red blood ran from the corner of her mouth. Her black cowl was torn away near her temple and an errant tuft of her red hair spilled from the gash. Even in this disheveled state it was easy to see why Hellkat, despite (or some would argue, because of) her criminal behavior, had always been regarded as one of Century City's sexiest super-types. She was still the only villain to ever make *Meta People*'s list of 50 Most Beautiful Metas, no matter that no one really knew what she looked like behind her mask.

Hellkat stood and waited for her unseen assailant to give chase, focused intently on the entrance to the bank building. She seemed oblivious to the police and to the crowd of watchers. I photographed her as she stood in the fountain pool, soaking wet and seething. She wore very little, and what she did wear was black and made of gleaming PVC, her powder-white skin in sharp contrast where it was frequently exposed. She dressed in
80

boots that laced to mid-thigh and opera gloves with the fingers cut out to expose her nails, which had been filed into razor-sharp claws. A ribbed corset cinched her waist into an hourglass, and her bottoms were no more than a series of straps, an ankle-length braid of leather dangling behind to mimic a cat's tail. She wore a black cowl that covered her entire head with the exception of two slits for her eyes and an opening for her nose and mouth. In the back of the hood there was a circular opening through which a waist-length ponytail of vermillion hair was threaded.

Hellkat grew impatient and cracked her trademark cat o'nine tails with a loud pop, hoping to draw out her opponent. The crowd was growing restless as well, craning their necks to watch their hero emerge from the bank and resume the fight.

"Looking for me?" Deidre's voice came from above. Every head in the square turned and saw Supernova perched casually atop the upward thrust fists of the figures of Champions Fountain, waving at Hellkat with a flick of her wrist.

"There you are, bitch," Hellkat snarled and drew back her whip and leapt upward through the air at Deidre. Hellkat swung the cat o'nine tails overhead and Deidre easily deflected it with a flash of her eyes and a quick burst of energy. Hellkat scaled the fountain with feline dexterity and drew her whip back once more. But Deidre had taken to the air, floating just out of reach of the leather lashes.

"No fair," Hellkat chided. Deidre answered with a series of blasts, a line of energy bursts that forced Hellkat back to the ground. Hellkat landed on her feet and spun to face Supernova again. But then she realized that Supernova's latest shot wasn't meant to simply brush her back, and instantly she was diving, a cat-like leap that landed her just outside the fountain pool.

Hellkat was a metahuman, but one of a lower level. Her only real powers were her reflexes and agility. And despite the fact that she had always been a simple smash-and-grab thief, she had somehow managed to become one of Supernova's signature enemies. She never seemed to fight Helix or Trace. Just Deidre.

Even the press typically prefaced her name as, "Supernova villain, Hellkat." That was always one of the aspects of super-powered crimefighting that amused me. Each of us had our own little rogue's gallery, villains that seemed to run afoul only of a certain hero. I had the Knave, of course, Mongoose and Diehard the Hunter. Deidre had Hellkat, Bounty Huntress and Carmen Monoxide. Helix was partial to Clockbuster, Master Assassin and Mandroid.

The ground trembled from the force of Deidre's next blast, huge chunks of concrete flying in all directions, sending Hellkat sprawling. Deidre landed nearby and moved in closer. Hellkat wasted no time in springing to her feet and charging at Deidre. Deidre loosed another blast from her eyes, but Hellkat leapt above the streaking blue line of energy, leaping forward and spinning in mid-air to catch Deidre in the temple with a roundhouse snap-kick.

Deidre staggered backwards, but didn't fall. Hellkat planted her feet and slung her whip once around her head for momentum then brought it across Deidre's shoulder with an ear-splitting crack. The strike opened a gash in Deidre's blue costume, but couldn't break her skin. Hellkat lunged forward again, an open-handed left slashing across Deidre's face, but her claws left no mark in Deidre's impenetrable flesh. It did piss her off, though.

Anger clouding her judgment, Deidre lurched at Hellkat, launching a heavy punch that was easily ducked, throwing Deidre off-balance. Hellkat sprang from her squatting position and sprang into the air, side-kicking as she did, slamming a boot into Deidre's chest and sending her flying backwards into the pool.

The crowd had surrounded me, all of us trying to keep our vantage points open. From behind me I heard a young man say, "A chick in spandex and a chick in black leather fighting each other with super-powers in a water fountain. God, I love this city."

Hellkat smiled wickedly and stalked to her fallen prey. Even as Deidre moved to her hands and knees to get up, Hellkat slashed the cat o'nine tails across Deidre's bowed back in a rapid, looping series of blows, slicing and shredding her shining costume. Deidre somersaulted away from the attack and scrambled to her feet in the calf-deep water. Hellkat joined her in the pool, confident now, closing in. She leapt forward, diving toward Deidre, going for the victory.

But Deidre caught her mid-air with a sizzling burst to the midsection, and Hellkat fell to the ground in a useless heap, face down in the babbling water. The crowd burst into cheers. Deidre knelt next to her felled enemy and verified her state of unconsciousness before hoisting her limp body with one arm. She rose into the air, to the tip of the fountain's statues, where she looped Hellkat's leather tail around the upward-pointing hands of the stone figures and left her dangling there.

Below, the police were cautiously wading into the pool, pistols drawn.

"She's all yours," Deidre said to them, and with a wave to the applauding onlookers, she stretched her arms above her and shot into the sky.

I knew Deidre was on her way to Citadel to file a case report, so I made sure Jerry's was on my way home. The place was actually half-full but I still managed to find a seat at the bar next to Mort and Curt.

Jerry put a beer down in front of me and pointed to the television hanging behind him, already showing replays of the fight. "Quite the knock-down drag-out, huh?"

"Yeah. I almost started to get a little worried."

"Nah, nobody can take your old lady, Willie. She's a tough one."

I nodded. So did Curt.

"I still say it's a sad state of affairs when a man can't beat his wife in an arm wrestling contest," Mort said, giving me a wink.

"You'd know, wouldn't you, old man?" Jerry came to my defense. "Why, just last week Miss Louise gave Mortie here a shiner when he forgot to take out the trash." I could see Curt holding back a laugh.

"Goddammit! I told you how I got that black eye, Jerry," Mort said.

"Oh, yeah, that's right. Why don't you share that little incident with Willie."

Mort took a draw off his beer and sat in silent defiance, refusing to talk.

"Okay, I'll tell him for you," Jerry said. "Because the truth is better than fiction in this case. Old Mortie here fell asleep in his easy chair watching *Cops*. Well, when he came to, he staggered into bed, where Miss Louise reminded him that he still needed to take his stool softener."

"Blood thinner," Mort corrected.

"Okay, blood thinner. Well, since Mortie had fallen asleep in the chair, his hemorrhoids were acting up something fierce."

"I hate you."

"So, after applying a little butthole salve, he went to take his stool softener."

"Blood thinner."

"Blood thinner. So his fingers were all greasy from playing with his asshole, so his hand slipped off that child-resistant cap, and Mortie cold cocked himself right in the eye." Curt was looking the other way, but I could see his shoulders bouncing as he laughed silently to himself.

In a blatant attempt to change the subject, Mort pointed his beer bottle at the television. "Look at this shit." It was footage of Hellkat from the fountain fight. "Since when is it okay for these kids to run around in their bedroom clothes, for Christ's sake? I mean, look at her. She ain't got nothing on but a pair of panties and some sort of brassiere." Curt nodded in agreement as he gazed at the scantily clad woman on TV.

"And boots," Jerry observed.

"And gloves," I added.

Skintight

"Goddammit, you know what I mean," Mort spat. "Girl's practically naked. Ass cheeks all hanging out." Curt nodded again, still gazing. "Back in my day, you wore something like that in public, you got hauled off for indecent exposure. Goddamn kids these days, ain't got enough sense to put their damn clothes on. Dressing like strippers to fight crime. She's looks like a goddamn... what do you call it? Dominator?"

"Dominatrix," Jerry helped out.

"Yeah. Dominatrips." I knew not to make eye contact with Jerry after that one. "And where are all the capes? Why doesn't anyone wear a cape anymore? And don't get me started on all these kids getting tattoos and body parts pierced..."

Jerry shot me a quick glance that I knew was a plea for me to do exactly as Mort had said and not get him started, so when Mort took a breath I seized the opportunity to redirect him. "What was the best costume you ever saw, Mort?"

He fell silent for a long moment, thinking, staring through the back of the bar as if looking back in time. "Best costume ever," he then said quietly. He rubbed his square chin.

"What about Gypsy Moth?" Jerry chimed in.

"Nah," Mort said, shaking his head. "Too much taffeta." Curt's frown seemed to validate Mort's opinion.

"Speedstress," I offered confidently. "The little wings on her boots? Yeah."

"That was nice," Mort conceded. "Nice outfit. But not the best ever."

"Who, then?"

Mort made us wait for it, then finally said, "Skygirl. Now that was a costume." He went quiet again, no doubt picturing in his head Skygirl soaring across an appropriately sepia-toned sunset. "The goggles are what did it. The goggles and that skirt. Classy. Left just enough to the imagination. Not like these girls nowadays." Mort seemed genuinely sad for a moment.

"Not all of them," Jerry said. "Take Willie's old lady."

85

Mort built up to a nod, then said, "Yeah, that's a pretty suit Deidre's got. A little too tight, if you ask me. But nice colors. And at least she's covered up."

Curt nodded his approval.

Then Mort added, "Just needs a cape."

I spent the next hour talking about the good old days with Prizefighter and The Night Watchman until I missed them myself, despite the fact that the good old days, if there ever were such a thing, were long gone before I was born. I finished my last beer and went home.

Before Deidre could leave the Citadel she got the call to help Trace with the wildfires in Colorado. As soon as we sat down for dinner with the kids, she got a call to rescue the crew of a sunken Russian nuclear submarine in the Barents Sea. When she got home the second time, she sat down to finish her cold spaghetti while we watched the Eyewitness 8 coverage of the Hellkat fight.

I said to Deidre, "The Department of Public Works has already called about the damage to the fountain."

"I love it. No, 'Wow, Supernova, thanks for saving millions of dollars and countless lives'. Just hands me the fucking bill. Oh well. It was an ugly fountain anyhow."

"I kind of liked it."

"Remind me to call Morris. He can probably get Verizon to cover the damages and get it renamed the Verizon Champions Fountain or something." Deidre took her dirty dish to the kitchen sink. "Where are the kids?"

"They're spending the night at your moms. She's taking them to see the Captain Fantastic movie. They flipped out over the twenty foot tall inflatable version of Cap in the parking lot of the Cineplex."

"Sounds like our kids. They've got a friend of the family who can grow his body to the size of the Holloway Building and they go nuts for a fake blow-up guy." Deidre shook her head and chuckled. "Anyhow, I told Mom I wanted to see the movie first, to make sure it was okay for them."

"It's PG," I said.

"I was thinking more about historical accuracy."

"They've taken some creative license, sure," I said. "I caught some footage at Meta-Con and they have Cap saving the President from Doctor Demon instead of Astro-Squid."

"I guess the notion of a giant conqueror squid from outer space was a little too much for even Hollywood."

"All the fanboys on the internet are complaining about it."

A little grin crossed Deidre's mouth. "Speaking of the internet, when are we were going to check out the nude Supernova pics my friend at Centurion's Café told you about?"

"You serious?"

She nodded. "But you better hurry before I change my mind."

We took the laptop to our bedroom. Deidre climbed onto the bed next to me and watched as I typed "nude supernova pictures" into the search engine. Instantly the results began to stream in, faster than I could count.

"Wow," I said, watching as the list grew pages at a time.

"What?" Deidre asked. "Are all those pictures?"

"Those are all websites with nude pictures of Supernova."

"Holy shit," Deidre said, her eyes flying open.

"Well, claiming to have nude pictures of Supernova," I corrected myself. "Obviously they're not real." Then, with mock suspicion, "Or are they?"

Deidre punched me in the arm, hard. "Show me," she said.

Among my choices were *www.supernova-nude.com*, *www.xxx-metas.com* and *www.metanudes.com/supernova*. XXX-Metas boasted 843 free nude metahuman galleries, movies and new daily nudes, in categories like "Super MILFs", "Bad Guys", and "Teen Tight'uns".

"Eww," Deidre groaned, and then laughed. "That's so bad."

"It really is."

"Click it," she said.

I double-clicked the link and watched Deidre as she watched the page load. I was kept busy by closing the swarm of pop-ups for things like Secret Identity, the strip club on the outskirts of town where all the dancers dressed like skintights, and the Hyperborean dildo, which featured an image of the leader of Hard Corps himself and claimed that the officially licensed 8-inch silicone phallus was an exact replica taken directly from a mold of his erect penis. "More lifelike than ever!" it promised.

"The son of a bitch has licensed his pecker," I laughed.

Deidre said, "Can't believe Trey didn't think of it first."

XXX-Meta's homepage was a cycling, flashing collage of images and ads. Near the top was a row of publicity headshots of Starface, Rocket Queen, Electrolite, and Supernova, all under the heading "Updated FREE Galleries!"

I glanced at Deidre. Her expression asked me what I was waiting for. I clicked on the manipulated photo of her on the screen. Her Rolling Stone cover portrait from '97 dominated the page. There were links to twenty-three different galleries superimposed on this background. By the time we got to Gallery Two, the novelty of seeing Deidre's head Photoshopped onto Playboy centerfolds had worn off. Above one shot of a blatantly brunette Playmate wearing Deidre's head was a flashing, animated banner for XXX-Metas that proclaimed them to be the only site on the internet where we could watch the real Livewire video.

Deidre pointed at Livewire's orgasmic expression and said, "Click it."

"They'll want a credit card number," I said. "And the movie's probably about as authentic as these pictures of you."

"Just click it," Deidre said, and I did. Immediately a prompt for my user name and password popped up.

"See?"

"How do we get a password?" Deidre asked.

"We give them our credit card number."

"So give it to them."

Skintight

I eyed my wife to be certain she was serious before fetching my wallet from the kitchen. We signed up and, as soon as we had logged in, the movie began to load. Deidre and I sat and waited in silence until a jostling image of Livewire's face suddenly appeared on our monitor. Held in her mouth was one of the largest erections I had ever seen.

"Damn," I said, barely aloud. Livewire held the shaft in her hands, her fingers unable to completely encircle its diameter.

I watched Deidre as she watched the computer monitor. The owner of the erection was not new at having it fellated, or having it filmed, and made sure to guide Livewire's movements to allow the camera the best view of what her mouth was doing. A faint flicker of electricity flashed through Livewire's tangled hair as the man brushed it away from her face.

"So, where's Thana?" Deidre said in a whisper, as if she was worried Livewire might hear us.

"She's got the camera," I said. "If you watched *Alter Ego* you'd know this."

"Do you really think Thana used her powers on Livewire?"

"I don't know. She looks pretty willing to me."

"Yeah," Deidre agreed. "But that's how Thana's powers work. She could have made Livewire want this by just laying a hand on her shoulder and telling her she wanted it."

Livewire was in full costume, her tight black vinyl corset made her waist unnaturally narrow, and her trademark fishnets disappeared into her shiny thigh-high vinyl boots.

"Nobody wears spandex anymore," I lamented.

"Captain Fantastic," Deidre corrected me.

"And you," I said. The man in the movie squeezed his hand around the base of his shaft and helped Livewire fit a few more inches into her mouth.

"I wear a nylon/Lycra blend, thank-you-very-much. I haven't worn —" Deidre hushed as she saw, at the exact same moment I did, a Signet Ring on the man's middle finger. "Did you see that?"

I nodded, watching as the camera pulled back to reveal a naked man over six feet tall, his exaggerated musculature almost disproportionate to even his considerable height, dwarfing Livewire. The angle widened still until the man's face became visible. He was smiling, eyes flashing with anticipation behind a nondescript pair of eyeglasses.

"Trey," I said.

"It does look like him," Deidre nodded with a chuckle.

"It *is* him."

"That's not Trey," Deidre shot back. "That guy's wearing glasses."

"That's his disguise."

"His disguise?"

"When he's not being Helix," I said.

"A pair of glasses?" Deidre asked, incredulous. "That's a disguise?"

"You didn't recognize him," I justified. "And you work with him."

The camera panned to show that another naked man stood nearby watching. He had the lean build of a sprinter: his torso was ridged and angular, and his buttocks and thighs bulged with muscle. On his face was the most famous smile in Century City.

"Andre," I said, even before he suddenly flitted away from the camera at super-speed.

"Oh my God," Deidre said, half gasping, half laughing. "Poor Janet. Do you think she knows?"

"I don't think Janet cares. She knew what she was getting into when she married him."

"Yeah, she gets into a new BMW about every twelve months," Deidre added.

"They don't call him the Fastest Man on Earth for nothing."

I looked past Andre and saw behind him the bank of processors that kept the air in the Citadel an earthly mixture of seventy-nine percent nitrogen, twenty-one percent oxygen.

"They're on the Citadel," I said. With a glance at the camera, Andre closed in on Livewire and began to peel her costume from

90

her body, unlacing and casting aside her corset faster than the camera could record. He reached around from behind to squeeze her breasts. Now Trey was kneeling and Livewire moved lower with him, going onto her hands and knees, making sure he didn't escape her mouth. Andre dropped to his knees behind Livewire, his big hands roaming over her bare back before gathering the waist of her vinyl trunks and snatching them back and down, leaving them stretched tightly across her thighs momentarily before giving them swift yank. The vinyl tore apart at the crotch. Livewire wriggled to allow Andre to pull the torn trunks completely off her. He tossed them on top of her discarded corset. She was now completely nude except for her boots and fishnets. On each of her ass cheeks were identical, mirrored tattoos of pointy, cartoonish lightning bolts.

"Nice tattoos," Deidre said. I couldn't tell if the compliment was genuine or sarcastic.

Andre began to knead Livewire's naked ass and then slapped at it, a little too hard to be playful. He positioned himself between Livewire's legs, taking his erection in his fist and aiming it at Livewire's ass. I could see Deidre breathing a little heavier, crossing and uncrossing her legs. Oblivious to Andre's intentions, Livewire worked on Trey until Andre pushed hard enough to slip inside of her. She tried to yelp, but Trey was in her mouth so completely that the sound was merely a muffled whimper.

"Ouch," Deidre said, watching as the camera zoomed in on the point of penetration. Our computer screen was filled with the image of Andre's muscled stomach pressing onto Livewire's ass, his hands clamping onto her hips as he made his cock disappear inside of her, her twin lightning bolts striking at it.

"Jesus," Deidre said, lowering her head and cupping a hand over her mouth as if that would keep any more curses from slipping out. "Is she invulnerable?"

"I hope so."

Livewire gazed up at Trey, jagged veins of blue electricity streaking from the corners of her eyes. A tiny electrical storm

91

was raging now in and around Livewire's hair. The camera closed in on her face. Forked streaks of lightning, humming and sizzling, escaped her clenched eyes. Thana was moving with the camera, concentrating on Andre now, the frequency of his penetrations increasing until his entire body seemed to resonate. His shape became a blur, moving so fast that he seemed to be simultaneously in and out and all points in between.

Thana panned to Trey just as his body clenched, his movements abruptly halting like a wrench had been thrown into some rapidly spinning gear inside of him. He pulled free of Livewire's mouth and she threw her head back, gasping for breath. Trey groaned and announced to all present that he was going to come. His immense body suddenly convulsed and I could see the excitement in Livewire's eyes, and Deidre's, too, as they flashed up at Trey. Livewire dove and caught him with her mouth once more, sucking purposefully. Again Trey frantically snatched his erection from Livewire's mouth and aimed it away from her. Livewire lunged for it once more but Trey swatted her away with his free hand just as he began to discharge. He issued some guttural, inarticulate plea as the first stream shot from the tip of his cock like a laser beam. There was a sound like the report of a rifle and the camera panned quickly to the far wall and zoomed in on a small indentation about the size of a marble where his semen had impacted.

Andre dashed to the dent and rapped on the metal wall panel with his knuckles, careful to avoid the splatter.

"Titanium," he assured the camera. To Livewire he said, "That would've blown your head clean off."

Thana zoomed in on Trey, kneeling on his haunches, panting as his erection pulsed in his hand. As abruptly as it had started, the movie ended and our screen went blank.

We were quiet at first until Deidre finally exhaled and said, "Wow."

"Yeah."

Deidre watched the empty screen for a moment before starting again. "I had no idea."

"Yeah."

Suddenly Deidre looked at me and said, "Let's make a video."

Before I could answer, she was shoving her phone into my hands. I took it, not quite sure what to do.

"Start videoing," Deidre said.

She reached into my pants, wrapped a hand around me and pulled me to my feet by my hard-on. I trained the phone on Deidre and started recording.

"Lie down," she said. I sat on the floor, videoing the whole time as Deidre stripped naked. She put a bare foot on my chest and pushed me onto my back and stood astride me. "I said, *lie down.*"

She reached between her legs with one hand, cupping her breasts with the other. She bent her knees a little as she began to finger herself. She bent deeper and reached down to take the phone from me, turning it around to video me as she slowly lowered herself onto my face, her knees sinking into the carpet on either side of my head. Deidre moaned, bucking her hips, grinding over my open mouth. I could feel her body begin to shake. It was taking a concerted effort from her to keep the phone pointed in my direction.

I pulled away with a gasp. "Did it turn you on?"

She wrapped her free hand around the back of my head and pulled me hard against her. "I didn't tell you to stop." She was barely holding the phone now. "Just don't make me come."

I pulled back again. "Why not?"

"I'll break your neck."

"What?"

"If I come, I'll hurt you. Bad. You know this."

I went down again. And then her goddamned ring began to chirp.

"Don't stop." She clenched a fist in my hair, her chest heaving, her thighs clamping around my head. And her ring got louder.

I tried to remind her of her duty, but my words came out all muffled. Then she slumped to the floor and let her phone tumble out of her hand and onto the floor with a bump. "Every fucking time." After a moment, and with a sigh of resignation, she tapped her ring. "What?"

"We've got a hostage situation on Styers Island." The response came. It sounded like Psy-Fi.

"The prison?"

"Yeah."

"Where are the police?"

"They're there. The girl says she'll only talk to you."

"The girl?"

"Yeah. You'll see when you get here."

"I'll be there in five minutes."

Deidre scrambled to her feet and immediately went into her dervish-like transformation. I wanted more than anything to pull her back to the floor and tear that skintight blue costume off her. And I could see in her eyes that she just might let me. But we both knew better.

"Go get 'em, baby," I said.

"Don't wait up." Deidre opened the bedroom window and disappeared into the night.

I climbed into bed and turned on Eyewitness 8. They were live on the scene with their Mobile News Room, but they didn't know any more about what was going on than I did. It didn't take me long to fall asleep.

Chapter Six

Tick. Tick. Boom.

I was flying, this time through the city, as fast as my body would go. It was night. Less than a minute until midnight. Somehow I knew that. There was a bomb, a hydrogen bomb, at Central Terminal. The bomb was big enough to destroy the entire city. I'm not sure how I knew that, either, I just knew. I also knew that I had less than sixty seconds to get to that bomb.

With single-minded determination I rocketed through the city, the buildings on either side of me fading into a wash of reflection and light. I pushed my body to its uppermost limits, moving at such velocity that everything around me tunneled into a blur, only the pinpoint in the distance still in focus. Forty-five seconds now.

Then a dead-end. I banked hard left, my body rolling, threading the needle of space between two buildings. Then shooting back out into the open. The wind whipped by me with a howling scream. The sweeping arches of the terminal building loomed ahead. Not far now. I could feel each second tick away. Less than thirty seconds.

I lost altitude. Five stories. Then twenty. Not again. *No.* My body careened out of control, headlong, diving and spinning. Only ten stories to the pavement. Impact. My body bounced and then tumbled along the street before slamming to a halt. I wasn't hurt, not badly anyhow. I had enough of my powers left to keep that from happening. I got to my feet and began to run. I could see the terminal, lit up in the night, not a hundred yards away. Almost there. There was still time. I sprinted down the empty street. Night became day. The city flared into blinding oblivion.

I awoke to the rhythmic vibration of our entire house shaking and the *clang-chunk, clang-chunk* of Deidre exercising in the basement.

I went downstairs and poured myself a glass of juice, then went down to the basement steps and plopped on the bottom tread to watch. Deidre was wearing a tiny pair of workout shorts and a tight tank-top with *Centurions* printed in block letters across the chest. Her entire body was covered with a glowing sheen of sweat. She was deadlifting the rear axle, wheels and all, from the monster truck Kap'n Krush tried to flatten city hall with a few years ago.

"What happened last night?" I asked.

Between grunts and breathless heaves Deidre said, "We got hot and bothered watching that video, you were eating me, I was getting ready to fuck your brains out, and then we got interrupted."

"I meant at the prison."

"Oh. Remember the Goth girl from Meta-Con?"

"Which one?"

"The one that wanted to be my sidekick."

"Yeah." I could feel the foundations quake every time Deidre set down the giant axle onto the high-carbon steel floor plating we installed over the concrete when we bought the place.

"She's a meta."

"And?"

"She can make your brain activity stop just by looking at you."

"Holy shit."

"Yeah, seriously." Deidre dropped the axle, sparking against the steel floor, and left it there. Her body was lined and curved with the contours of her energized muscles. She drifted, a few inches off the floor, to her weight bench and grabbed a towel and a bottle of water. "Wanted to call herself Braindead."

"Nice."

"Yeah. Well, she *really* wanted to be my sidekick. So much so that she shut down all the inmates' brains as an audition."

"Sweet kid."

"Actually she is," Deidre said between swigs of water. "And she's the most powerful meta I've seen in a long time. She just doesn't know what to do with it yet. She's got trouble at home, trouble at school. No friends because everyone's either scared shitless of her or thinks she's a freak."

"What'd you do?"

"I called Psy-Fi and she came down to the prison. Psy-Fi's going to start working with her, giving her some training on the Citadel."

"You're going to make her a Centurion, after she took people hostage?"

"I didn't say that. Not to her anyhow. Besides, would you rather we left her to her own devices? Or put her in some kind of juvenile corrections facility, where she could learn how to really misdirect her feelings? Maybe she could hook up with D.E.S.T.R.O.Y. when she graduates?"

"Of course not. That's not what I meant."

"We've given her some direction, a purpose in life now. And you know what? She smiled. She seemed happy. Maybe for the first time. And she didn't hurt anyone. She can jumpstart the prisoner's brains as easily as she stopped them. They didn't even know what happened."

"I don't know, I don't think she's the kind of—"

"You're not a Centurion anymore, Will." I could see that Deidre regretted the words as soon as they came out. But she had said it all the same. Not that I needed to be reminded. "I'm sorry, baby. I didn't mean..."

"It's okay," I said. And it really was okay. She was right. "It's not my place to—"

97

"Of course it is. You're my husband." Deidre came to me and kissed me. I watched her float back to the truck axle and then I went back upstairs.

"Where is Century Man? That has been the enduring question on the minds of all Century Citizens since the leader of the Centurions vanished after a minor skirmish with the Knave of Diamonds one year ago this week. And it's the question we intend to answer tonight. I'm Eyewitness 8's Lola Oh, and welcome to a special two-hour *Alter Ego*.

"On the eve of the anniversary of his mysterious disappearance, we talk to eyewitnesses and metahuman experts who claim, amongst other things, that Century Man is still operating under a different identity, that he somehow lost his powers in that fight, or that he was actually killed in the Knave Incident. We'll look at each of these theories, and others, as we try to uncover the truth behind Century Man's fate.

"We'll talk not only about the strange circumstances surrounding his disappearance but the spectacular career that preceded it. Why was he so loved? What was he like under the mask? What were the feats that won his place in history?

"Leader of the Centurions. We'll hear from Century Man's successor, a man who also happened to be his best friend. What was all that charisma like close up? What was it like to serve at his side?

"Becoming a legend. From the near-tragic mistake in Corto Maltese to his exquisite shot-calling in the Hyper-Time Crisis, Century Man rose to prominence swiftly and powerfully. That day last November. A skirmish with a small-time hood seemingly robbed Century City and America of its greatest champion. With me tonight is Hal Larsen, former executive editor of the *Century City Journal* and author of *Super Guys*. Hal, thanks for doing the show."

Luke and Zack dashed into the living room in a breathless whoosh. "We want to watch Super Squid Squad," they said in unison.

"Ten minutes, okay?"

With practiced precision, they slumped their shoulders and shuffled out of the room.

Lola went on. "What made Century Man who he was? He hinted at a family, there were rumors of a family, and we'll probably never know for sure now, but how does someone do what he did?"

"Well, he was a man who perfectly understood the power of public opinion," Hal Larsen said. I'd never met this person in my entire life. "He showed people what he wanted them to see. He hinted at having a family because, just like the President of the United States, people want their leaders to have the same values they have. In America that includes getting married and having children. The truth is that Century Man simply would not have had time for a family."

"So you're saying it was all a carefully cultivated image?" Lola Oh asked. "There was no family?"

"I think it's highly unlikely. I'm not saying Century Man lied, because, technically, he never said he was married, but I think he knew what the people expected of him." While Hal talked, images of me accepting my second and third Hero of the Year Awards flashed on the screen before going back to Lola.

"Let's show a very serious moment here. We've got a clip I want to show," Lola said, waiting for the clip to begin. An image of me replaced Lola. I was standing behind a podium crowned with microphones. Behind me stood Deidre and Trey.

"I call upon Lord Dethlok to halt and eliminate this clandestine, reckless and provocative threat to galactic peace, and to establish stable relations between our two worlds," I said in the video. I had forgotten how big my original mask was. It looked like it was swallowing my head.

"That was Century Man during the thirteen-day standoff that led to the Navies of Io invading Earth," Lola said. "The question: Is that his greatest accomplishment? Saving us during, arguably, our darkest hour?"

"I think the thing that can be said after Century Man," Larsen said. "Is that we live in a less dangerous city, a less dangerous world, than we did before there was a Century Man."

"Well said," Lola nodded. "We'll be right back to talk about the Knave of Diamonds and how the Centurions have changed in the past year. And we'll hear from Helix, the man who replaced Century Man as leader of the Centurions."

I heard the bathtub upstairs draining. I knew Deidre would be down as soon as she dried off, and I would have the choice of watching *Alter Ego* with her running criticism or not watching it all. I was watching a black & white rerun of *The Adventures of Captain Fantastic* when she came into the den in her customary socks, Comets jersey, and coffee mug of wine.

"Turn it to Century Sports," she said as she sunk into the sofa and curled up next to me. Her body was warm; her hair was still damp and smelled of that fruity herbal shampoo she pitched.

"They're getting ready to talk about the AirCare rescue the guys you pulled off today."

"Turn it to Century Sports; I want to see the Comets score."

I changed channels and we sat through the over-dramatized highlights of at least half a dozen other games before learning that the Comets had won their fifth straight game with a 23-yard touchdown run by DeShawn Greene.

"Yes!" Deidre said, pumping her fists.

"You know he's a meta."

"Who? DeShawn?"

"Yep."

"Bullshit."

"He is."

"That's against the rules," Deidre argued. "The league tests for it."

"It doesn't show up. He's just barely got it. Just enough to make him a little faster than everyone else."

"Bullshit."

"Ask Andre," I said. "He's his cousin."

Deidre laughed. "I don't think I'll ever be able to talk to him again without thinking about that video."

"You mean, you'll never be able to talk to him again and not think about his big dick."

"Shut up," she laughed harder. Then she said, "Want to go upstairs and watch a video?"

Deidre and I had watched the Livewire video at least half a dozen times over the past couple of weeks. We videoed ourselves having sex every time after we watched it, and then we'd watch *that* video. Which led, of course, to more sex.

Not every time, but usually, Deidre would wonder aloud what it must have been like for Livewire. What was it like to get taken like that, with varying degrees of reciprocity and complicity on her part, at super-speed, or by the strongest man on the planet. Every time, inescapably and with maddening clarity, I would imagine Deidre in Livewire's place. And just as quickly I'd shake the image from my mind, only to have it instantly return.

Downstairs I could hear the channel change to a constant chorus of cartoon boinks and splats, accompanied by bursts of laughter from Zack and Luke. We climbed onto the bed with the laptop and I logged onto XXX-Metas. I searched for something Deidre and I hadn't already watched a couple of times. We found a new video purporting to be of Macro-Man and Devil Doll but we quickly realized it was another fake. There seemed to be more of those on XXX-Metas than the real thing.

"So, when Skyscraper gets big, his dick gets proportionately bigger, too, right?" Deidre said.

"I would assume so, yes. And exactly how much time have you spent thinking about Skyscraper's dick?"

"Like you haven't wondered about it, too." Deidre finished off her wine. "Think there are any videos of him on here?"

"Even if there are, he'd have to be normal size. Who could he screw when he's big? Think about it: he sizes up to, say, twenty stories, that means he's roughly forty times his normal height. Which means his dick would be roughly forty times its normal length and girth."

"Sheesh. 'Girth.'"

"Width, girth, whatever. So let's say his dick is normally six inches erect, that means at twenty stories high he'd have a hard-on twenty feet long."

"Wow."

"As impressive as that is, it's a little impractical."

"You can't tell me you wouldn't want to see a dick the size of a tanker truck."

"Even if I did want to see it, it's not like he could actually use the thing on anyone."

"What about Giantess? Her pussy's got to be huge." Deidre offered.

"How much wine have you had?"

"Skyscraper could fuck Giantess."

"She's fifteen feet, max."

"So Skyscraper only goes up to twenty feet. I'd pay to see that."

"You're sick."

"Oh, okay. I'm the sick one." Deidre rolled her eyes at me. "Who would you want to see?"

"Hell, I don't know," I answered, pretending like I hadn't thought about it.

"What about Fahrenheit and Flamethrower?" Deidre said. "Could be kind of a fire-fuck." She laughed out loud, as if she didn't realize how funny that would sound until she said it.

"Yeah, if you could see through the smoke. What about the Jackal and Tigress?"

"Ooh, feral. I like it."

"Mom!" The call came from the den downstairs. "When's dinner going to be ready?"

"When the pizza guy rings the doorbell," Deidre hollered and then instantly slipped back into character. "What about Hard Corps and Mistress Kali? There's four of them and she has four arms."

102

"The Contortionist and Miss Malleable," I offered.

"In a sixty-nine."

"Yeah. What about Helldiver and Hellkat."

Deidre laughed. "That doesn't even make any sense. Just because they've both got 'Hell' in their names? You just want to see Hellkat *nekkid*." She punched me in the shoulder.

"Maybe. Who would you want to see naked?"

"Hmm..." She pretended to think about it but I could tell she already had someone in mind. She said, "You'll laugh."

"I won't. Scout's honor. Who?"

"Cap."

"Captain Fantastic?"

She nodded and then hid her blushing face behind her hands.

"You want to fuck Captain Fantastic?" I broke my promise and started laughing.

"Asshole," she said, punching me again, harder. Now she was laughing, too. "Not now, smartass. Back in the day. And I never said I wanted to fuck him."

"Wow. Okay."

"He was hot!" Deidre protested. "Those arms? Every girl my age had his poster on their bedroom wall."

"Okay, okay," I conceded. "What about now?"

"Eww. He's like 70."

"No," I chuckled. "Who would you want to see *nekkid* now?"

She hung her arms around my neck and kissed me. "I see him naked whenever I want to."

"You know what I mean."

"Nobody else."

"Bullshit. If you had a free pass and could fuck anyone, who would it be?"

"Fine, I'll play along," she said. "Anybody?"

"Anybody."

"Free pass?"

"Free pass."

Again Deidre pretended to not already have someone in

mind, looking at the ceiling long enough to plausibly have given it some thought. "The Hyperborean."

"Really? The Hyperborean?"

"You said free pass!" She knocked me over and pounced on me, bouncing on the mattress.

"The Hyperborean?!" I said, struggling for breath as Deidre jabbed her index fingers into my ribs. "You hate the Hyperborean."

"But his arms." She rolled onto the bed beside me with a mock swoon. "I'm powerless to resist." She fanned herself.

"Don't get me wrong," I said, still gasping. "I would watch that video."

Deidre eyed me for a second. She said, "Know who I want to see a video of?"

"Who?"

"Supernova and that stud she's married to."

"Yeah?"

"Oh yeah."

"Put the suit on."

"What?"

"The Nova Girl suit. The old one."

A smile slowly curled the corners of my wife's mouth. I watched her pad to the closet. She filed through the rows of sweaters, slacks, and blouses until she reached the end and carefully withdrew the garment that hung furthest in the back. She held it out before her as she returned, and laid it on the bed with reverence. She gently arranged the arms and legs, smoothed the whole thing, and we stood together and looked at it. The suit glittered like an aqua pool on the bedspread. Deidre crept to the bedroom door to listen and make sure the boys were still securely in the thrall of Super Squid Squad.

She was unable to turn the lock before Zack called her again. "Mom!"

"In a minute, Zack!" Deidre began peeling off her Comets jersey.

"Mom! Come here!"

104

"I said in a minute!"

"I think you need to see this," Zack said. Something in his voice made Deidre pull her jersey into place and trot downstairs.

Super Squid Squad had been preempted by Eyewitness 8's Lola Oh, informing us that Century City was under attack.

In the skies over Century State University's Hoffman Planetarium hovered three giant machines, vaguely humanoid in shape and several stories tall. They had materialized, seemingly, out of thin air, announcing to everyone within range of their metallic, distorted voices, "Attention inhabitants of Earth: we are the Priests of Syzygy, and we are now in control." Within minutes, Helix had arrived. Supernova was only minutes behind.

As I photographed them, Helix and Supernova attempted to communicate with the massive, floating robots, but apparently to no avail. Servos whined and massive, ancient gears crept into motion, groaning and grinding, shuddering. Flakes of ferrous rust showered the students gathered below. The machines discharged bursts of steam from various valves as they lumbered in mid-air toward the darting Helix and Supernova, arms slowly extending outward like decrepit old men trying to catch dragonflies.

Helix shot toward the closest one and struck his fist against its chest casing, causing its pitted and rusted metal epidermis to cave in and crumple like foil. Deidre floated high above, and from her eyes came beams of energy that sliced silently and effortlessly through the second and then the third Priest. The smell of burnt insulation and fried circuitry spilled out into the crisp fall air. Out of the sky the three would-be world conquerors tumbled, and immediately Helix swept beneath the one he had disabled and caught the huge thing with one hand. He glided under a second falling machine and snagged that one with his other hand. Supernova used both hands to catch the remaining robot and with Helix leading the way, the two towed the Priests of Syzygy into the sky.

Suddenly that gray sky seemed to split, and from the blinding fissure poured dozens of giant machines similar to the three decommissioned ones, but infinitely faster and considerably less aged. Their skins shone brightly, their polished metal was without flaw, armatures studded with weaponry and deadly looking appendages. Helix and Supernova dropped their defeated cargo onto empty Keith Field below them, the home of the Century State Mustangs, and prepared to face their new treat.

The machines swarmed around them, enclosed them, and blocked them from my sight. As the last of the robots swirled into position, a broad, flat band of bluish light cut a swath through them, vaporizing a quarter of the invaders on contact. Helix bolted to Deidre's side, back to back with her to guard her blindside from the circling machines. A hundred machines, two hundred now, emerged from the portal in the sky and collected into a ring around the pair of Centurions. With a hastily signaled strategy, Helix and Supernova launched themselves at their assailants. Helix swatted them by the tens to the ground and into the clouds while Supernova disintegrated twice that many with scything bursts of energy from her eyes. Helix used his speed and incredible strength to slice through them, opening gaping holes in their ranks, the dented and disjointed machines plummeting to Earth in droves. Supernova released energy beams at point blank range, picking off the machines in batches.

They worked as one, back to back, defending each other. Helix batted away each approaching robot until the balance of the invaders was formed into a tightening circle and, when they advanced, Supernova released a Nova Burst, the rapidly expanding sphere of energy frying and dropping the surrounding machines en masse. The sky was as suddenly empty of them as it had been filled.

On Eyewitness 8's Evening News that night, Lola Oh was talking over footage of Supernova and Helix as they fought against the Priests of Syzygy. Lola called it "the weakest alien invasion Century City has seen since the Nanonauts," which is saying something considering the fact that in 1993 the Nanonauts had "successfully occupied" every living creature on Earth before people began to notice their piss smelling strange.

I found Deidre in her bathroom. She had just finished her bath and was in her robe, standing with her back to me. The vapor still hung in the air from her bath water, always hot enough to scald a normal person. I went to her and saw over her shoulder that she was looking at my camera. She was scrolling through the shots I'd taken of her and Trey earlier in the day.

"Nice shots, huh?" I said.

Deidre nearly jumped out of her skin. She glanced at me and then looked back down at the camera. "Yeah."

Together we looked at the images of the dense, flying hardware that was the Priests, Deidre and Trey in the middle of it all, their bodies harder still. I looked at Deidre fighting those machines, using her powers, all her strength, unbridled. Even in the still photographs their bodies looked fluid, the movements of their muscles like a dance, their brightly-colored costumes clinging tightly to every raised curve, every flexed angle as they struggled in unison.

I clamped my hands onto Deidre's shoulders and pushed her to the bathroom counter, stumbling as we went, knowing full well she was allowing this, knowing I couldn't have moved her an inch if she didn't want me to. I bent her over the counter, bunched her robe around her waist, and pressed into her. With her forearms, she cleared the counter, lotions and perfume bottles crashing to the tile floor at our feet. She arched her back like a hunter's bow being drawn tight.

I lowered myself onto her, searching with my mouth in her damp hair for her ear. "What if this was him?"

She clasped the edge of the counter and pushed back against me. "Who?"

"Don't. You know who." I drove into my wife with all my strength. "Would you like that?"

I was scared she would say yes and I was scared she would say no. She said nothing, only groaned.

"Show me," I said. "Show me what you would do."

Deidre thrust back against me, bucking off the counter and slamming against me until she knocked the breath from my lungs. Her body was trembling. I was becoming aware of the orgasm building deep within her. *Maybe*, I let myself think. *Maybe this time.* Every individual hair on her body seemed to bristle. Eyes clamped shut. Her jaw clenched. *This time.* A low, guttural growl slipped from her throat.

Then nothing. She quit. She dropped her head onto the counter. "I'm sorry, baby."

"Don't be."

We slumped to the bathroom floor, exhausted, silent except for our breathing. Finally Deidre said, "What if I said I wanted to."

"I know you want to. I know you're trying. And I know you don't want to hurt me."

"That's not what I meant." She watched me for a minute, making sure what she'd said was sinking in.

"Okay," I finally said.

"I'm serious. What if I said I wanted to?"

"Okay."

"I'm *not* saying that, but what if I were?"

"Then I'd say yes."

"Really?"

"I don't know. Maybe. Yes."

She thought for a while and then said, "It would have to be my way. All the way. My rules."

"Absolutely."

"My decision, my choice. One hundred percent, or not at all."

"Agreed."

"I'd decide when, where and how. And if I changed my mind about it, we'd never mention it again. Not one word."

Deidre seemed even more surprised at what she was saying than I did.

"And not Trey," she said. "It couldn't be him. It couldn't be anyone we know."

"We know every meta in Century City, and obviously it would have to be a meta."

"It just couldn't be a teammate. Or a friend. Or a friend of a friend. It would have to be someone I'd have zero chance of ever running into again. And if I ever did, someone I could plausibly pretend to have no idea who they were."

I nodded. "Okay."

"Completely anonymous," she said. "No strings attached. Our little secret, never tell a soul, swear to god. That sort of thing. I wouldn't want to get to know him. I wouldn't want to know what his secret identity was or what his hobbies were or any of that shit. I wouldn't want to care."

"Okay."

Deidre stared at me for a minute. "Okay."

The next day I met with Dr. Gunnarsson again. I was examining the oversized cutaway model of the heat-vision-capable eyeball when Agnetha burst through the door.

"Good morning, Will."

"Dr. Gunnarsson."

"Have you experienced any change on your condition since our last session?"

"No, ma'am."

Agnetha looked over my chart.

"Will, I have made the discovery via the internet that Supernova will very soon be attired in a different costume. Can you confirm this?"

"I... yeah. Yeah, that's true, Dr. Gunnarsson."

"Have you seen this new costume, Will?"

"No, not yet."

"Has Supernova described this new costume to you?"

"Yeah. I mean, kind of." I knew what Agnetha wanted to hear. "She says it will be a little more revealing."

"Will it show Supernova's legs?"

"I believe so, yes."

"Will it show Supernova's stomach?"

"Yes."

"Smultronställe." Agnetha said under her breath. She seemed lost in her thoughts for a minute or two. "Jobbar du naken?" I would have given anything at that moment to have had Mindswipe's power and been able to see exactly what Agnetha was thinking.

Then she snapped out of it. "We will try something different today. You will follow me."

Agnetha led me to a room not much larger than the one I was waiting in. Inside was a chiropractic table with black leather cushions. There was a small metal tray attached to the table's base, and on it sat a headset and what appeared to be a gun of some sort.

"Facedown, please," Agnetha said, gesturing toward the table and, despite my reluctance, I climbed on. I watched over my shoulder as Agnetha snapped on a pair of latex gloves then lifted the gun from the tray. It looked like a futuristic version of a Nazi Luger pistol, with a hypodermic needle for the barrel and a small glass vial attached on top and filled with a silvery liquid that looked like mercury.

"What's that for?"

"This is the nanobot injector."

"What are you going to do with it?"

"Inject nanobots."

"Of course you are."

"More specifically, I am going to inject you with a fluid carrier containing billions of nano-robots, who will infiltrate your body at a molecular level and attempt to deduce the cause of your power loss by analyzing your cell structure. Please pull down your shorts. The injection will be in the buttocks."

With even more reluctance than I mounted the table with, I pushed my shorts down enough to expose some vulnerable butt cheek to Agnetha. She swabbed a spot with an alcohol wipe and then aimed the needle-pistol right at my ass.

"You may feel a slight pinch."

I had to bite my lip to keep from calling out my pain as Agnetha drove the needle in with the delicacy of a carpenter pounding home a nail. Then came the injection itself, which felt as if ignited napalm was being introduced into my body.

"You may feel a sensation similar to that of urination, which is normal."

Instantly I could feel the heat of the injection spreading throughout my body, running down my legs and up my torso. And immediately my bladder began to involuntarily empty itself. Or at least I thought it was. A quick glance below confirmed Agnetha's warning that despite my body telling me differently I was not, in fact, pissing all over the place.

I watched the metallic liquid drain from the vial, then Agnetha held the tip of the gun between her fingers and detached it from the needle section, which she left hanging in my flesh. She fished the cord of her headset into her hands, then inserted the small jack on the end of the cord into the open end of the needle assembly.

Agnetha put on the headset and adjusted the microphone. "Ready?"

"I suppose so."

"I was talking to the nanobots."

I slowly came to terms with the fact that my doctor had headphones jacked into my backside and was having a conversation with microscopic robots swimming in my body. Agnetha seemed to be speaking in some type of code. She used words like 'ribosomes' and 'cytoplasm', terms I knew I should remember form high school biology. Then I heard phrases such as 'decreased mitochondrial transmembrane potential', 'mitotic fraction' and 'aberrant metaphases'. It might as well have been

Swedish. After about half an hour of this, Agnetha unplugged her headphones from my cheek and then removed the needle.

"The nanobots will reside in your body for the next few days, monitoring it, accumulating data which they will communicate to me on your next visit. Then I will compare that information to similar data we compiled on you when you were super-powered. Theoretically this will give us some insight into the changes your body has undergone and hopefully illuminate a path to reverse those changes."

Agnetha carefully affixed a band-aid on my puncture wound then told me I could pull my shorts up. "You will experience some soreness in your buttock tomorrow."

It was midnight and Deidre was with the rest of the Centurions in Honolulu, attending the ribbon-cutting of the newest Centurion's Café. It was only 7:00pm there. Or maybe 8:00, I could never remember. Either way, it was late where I was and the channels were filling up with reruns and infomercials. I started to turn off the television and head upstairs when I heard a couple of names that caught my attention.

"Helix and Supernova! From the earliest days of the Centurions, their names have been synonymous with strength and power. Their skill and courage have made them the most beloved superheroes in the world." Throughout the voiceover ran footage of Supernova and Helix, side by side, as they apparently fended off super-powered world-conquerors, averted natural disasters and otherwise championed the oppressed in general. It was all terribly staged. "People across the globe have marveled at their exploits and wished..." The image switched to a overweight man anchored to his couch by a bowl of potato chips, who said on cue, "If only I could be like that!"

Then Helix himself took up my screen. He was in full costume. "Well, now you can be!"

Standing next to him, also in costume, was my wife. She looked at Helix's spandexed physique with exaggerated admiration. "They don't call it Skintight City for nothing!" Then she turned to the camera. "Do you want to tone up your body? Gain muscle mass and definition? Want to lose weight while having fun?"

Helix said, "Do you want to look like a superhero?"

The fat-ass on the couch cast off the bowl of chips and sprang to his feet, enthusiastically nodding his head. "You bet!"

"Then we've got the solution for you," Supernova said as she and Helix walked confidently across the studio toward a contraption that looked like a cross between a dentist's chair and a catapult. "The Meta-Gym 3000!"

"That's right, Supernova," Helix took over. "The Meta-Gym 3000. I use the Meta-Gym 3000 in my own personal training to get results like this." He struck the classic muscle-man pose, arms hooked and flexed to make his huge biceps bulge.

Deidre wrapped both hands around a bulge and squeezed. "Impressive."

"So is the Meta-Gym 3000."

I sat and watched the full half-hour of it. Helix did most of the talking while Deidre balanced things with timely interjections, frequent nods and a constant smile. It didn't take Helix long to mount up on the thing and begin to demonstrate firsthand just how much fun using the Meta-Gym 3000 was. As a disclaimer appeared on the bottom of the screen telling me that the Meta-Gym 3000 would not give me super-strength, Helix went through a quick series of redundant exercises while the camera lingered on the straining muscles under his clinging bodysuit. Then it was Deidre's turn, and she spent a few minutes repeating various moves that involved her swiveling her hips and ass or scissoring her legs open and closed, all with the cameraman seemingly kneeling between her knees. I wanted to choke Morris.

I spent a few minutes with buff members of the Century City Fire Department who told me their results were so dramatic they had a Meta-Gym 3000 installed in the fire station. Then it was back to Helix.

"But wait, there's more!" he barked. He went on to tell me that if I didn't love the Meta-Gym 3000 as much as he and Supernova did, I could return it within sixty days for a full refund through this special TV offer.

After the Meta-Gym 3000 show ended it was followed by the Captain Fantastic Grill—"You'd need heat vision to cook this fast!". And this time I turned off the television.

But instead of going to bed, I reached for my phone.

It was almost like I was dreaming it. I hit Thana's number as quickly as possible, hoping she would answer before I had time to reconsider what I was about to do. Or why.

Thana acted happy to hear from me, and maybe she really was. I told her that Deidre and I needed her help.

"Now you're scaring me," she said.

"It's nothing bad," I explained and then asked her if there was somewhere we could meet. I suggested Jerry's. I wasn't surprised when she told me she had never heard of it.

"What about Spandex?"

"Pardon?"

"Spandex Ballet. It's a club. It's in the basement of the old Justice Guild Hall. Cheesy superhero theme. You'll love it." We agreed to meet at the bar in an hour.

Chapter Seven
When Strikes Helix

Captain Fantastic, Mach 1, Super Bee and the original Nova Girl weren't the first metahumans to band together in the war against crime (that was the Mystery Men of America), but they were, at the time, by far the most successful. All had been active for quite some time before Mob Macabre mounted an attack on Century City so devastating that it took the combined forces of all four of those heroes to repel it. They all saw the benefits of teaming up right away, and so did the public, and thus was born the Justice Guild. Or at least that's the way Deidre's mom tells the story at every family reunion.

In 1977, considered by most to be their best year ever, the Justice Guild was everywhere. Mach 1 was the first metahuman to appear in a television commercial. At the time, it seemed harmless. In the commercial, Mach 1 was walking up the steps of Guild Hall, exhausted after just defeating an unnamed villain, when a young boy, starstruck, offers him a ice cold Coke. Mach takes the Coke and just as he reaches the top of the steps, turns and tosses the boy his winged helmet. There was a television show based on the exploits of Super Bee. The actress who played her was, amazingly, even prettier than the real Super Bee, and her black and yellow costume, naturally, was far more revealing. I still feel something a little more than nostalgia when I think of her stinger. Even Deidre's mom was in a couple of

115

print ads for Revlon's Charlie perfume.

The Justice Guild had transformed the old abandoned City Hall into their headquarters and every man, woman and child in Century City had taken the tour. We got to see the banks of supercomputers with their blinking lights, the underground garage where Cap parked the Fantasti-Coupe, and the big table where the heroes discussed how to save the world. I'm sure Trey and I had Guild Hall in the backs of our minds when we conceived of the Citadel. Now the Hall was empty again with the exception, apparently, of that basement garage, current home of Spandex Ballet.

It was after ten o'clock when I arrived and it was just warm enough for the rain not to freeze. The reflection of red neon on the wet pavement was like a beacon and I parked and joined the steady stream of people disappearing through the sunken alley entrance. I paid the cover and stepped into a maelstrom of pulsing beats, kaleidoscopic lights, and swirling shadows. The murals showed a stylized art deco Century City skyline assailed by bat-winged demons and defended by caped and square-jawed heroes painted in heavy black outlines shaded with vividly colored dot matrices, all surrounded by plenty of *Biff!*s, *Pow!*s and *Bam!*s. A DJ was playing loud, hypnotic music to a dark, cavernous dance floor packed with young men and women. I immediately regretted not trying harder to convince Thana to meet me at Jerry's. Above me on a suspended walkway mocked up to look like the Bostwick Bay Bridge, a couple of overly energetic girls danced perilously close the platform's edge. Occasionally a shower of sparks would issue forth, for effect, from various points on the ceiling. In a corridor, a trio of glassy-eyed revelers—two men and a woman—absentmindedly slid their hands down each others' pants, just out of reach of the flashing lights. The air smelled of sweat, perfume and weed. I was easily the oldest person I could see.

When I was halfway to the bar I saw her leaning against a rail, sipping on a martini.

"Hey, Jinx," I said. She smiled and kissed me on the cheek,

leaving behind the scent of alcohol. "Sorry I'm late."

Thana glanced at the jeweled watch dangling from her slender wrist. "You're not," she lied.

A green-haired girl in an Electric Lass tank top stopped to take my drink order.

"Where's Deidre?" Thana asked.

"She's with Helix. They're still dealing with the Department of Extra-Human Affairs on the Syzygy thing. She told me not to wait up."

"I'll bet." The waitress returned with my beer. Thana finished her drink and showed the girl her emptied glass before setting it down on the bar top.

I really looked at Thana for the first time since I arrived. She had on a pair of spike heels, a tiny slip of a dress that looked like chain mail and, as far as I could tell, nothing else. She clearly had plans after she got rid of me. I wondered what those plans were.

"So," Thana suddenly said. "Why are we here?"

"Well," I began weakly and Thana held up a finger to me. The green-haired girl walked by again, close enough for Thana to grab her by her bare forearm.

"Go get my drink, right now." And without hesitation, the girl spun on her heels and I watched her make her way to the bar in a hurry.

"I'm just going to come out and say it," I told Thana.

"Good idea," Thana replied. The waitress immediately reappeared with Thana's drink, apologizing for the wait.

"We watched the Livewire video. Deidre and I," I said.

"Good for you. I think that officially makes it everyone in America now." She took a big swig.

"Why didn't you just say it was Helix? When he withdrew your invitation to be a Centurion, why didn't you call him out and tell everyone it was him on the video?"

Thana sighed as she ran a hand through her shiny black hair. It was raked into a fin on the top of her head. "Deidre doesn't know you're here, does she?"

"Don't change the subject."

Thana smiled.

"Why didn't you tell someone who was on that video?" I asked. "Had Eyewitness 8 found out that it was Helix on there, no one would've cared that it was you behind the camera."

"Because I couldn't."

"Why not?"

"Well, one," Thana started counting on her fingers. "It's none of your goddamn business and two, no one would've believed me."

"But he's right there, on the video," I explained.

"I know that. You know that. But you put on a pair of glasses and these stupid bastards that you dedicated your life to protecting, no offense, don't know you from Adam's housecat." She was right. "Seriously. I mean, shit, the guy lives on fucking Westlawn for Christ's sake. He puts on his glasses and some sweatpants and he goes to the fucking grocery store and nobody gives him a second glance. Same with Trace. Unless these fuckers are wearing long underwear and capes, it just doesn't register with people."

"Deidre didn't even recognize him," I agreed.

"That's why he did it. Stayed in disguise, I mean. He knew if the shit ever hit the fan, which, obviously, it fucking did, he could deny it if he had to. And fucking Livewire, that dumb bitch, all she wanted to do was fuck Helix. I had to explain to her five fucking times, 'You *did* fuck Helix.' Jesus." Thana drew on her martini.

"So you didn't use your powers..."

"No. Fuck, no. How many women need their arm twisted to fuck Helix?"

"You could've proven it somehow," I went on.

"Proven what?"

"That it was Trey."

"How? Fucking *how*?" She finished her drink and banged the glass down. "Tell me. I'd love to know. I really would."

"They're in the Citadel in the video."

"Can't prove it. Only other skintights have seen the inside, and no one's going to rat out Helix. Not to help me out."

"He was wearing his Signet Ring."

"You can buy an exact replica at Centurions Café."

"But..." I stuttered, "But... it's him."

"Don't think I haven't lain awake every single night since that cunt leaked the video, trying to figure out how to prove it, because I assure you I have. If I came out and said, 'Hey, you know what? This guy here? He's Helix!' do you know what would happen to me?" She watched me to see if I could answer. "Look, I get paid. I get jobs. Shitty jobs, granted. Private eye shit, mainly. Cheating spouses, that sort of thing. But they're jobs. They pay the fucking bills. And if I came out now and said that shit, no one would fucking believe it and not even the sneaky fucks that hire me now would trust me after that." She finally took a breath. "Trust me on this."

I was quiet.

"Now," she demanded, "Why don't you tell me why you called me?"

"I want you to do that for us," I said suddenly. "Like the Livewire video."

"Excuse me?"

"I want you to video Deidre and me." It sounded like the complete bullshit it was.

"Listen to me, I made that video because Helix asked me to. It had nothing to do with my powers. He came to me and said he could use my help and that if I did this thing for him, he'd make sure I got the invitation. That fucking video put me in court. The video cost me the Centurions."

The only thing I could think of to say was, "I'm sorry."

"Don't be. You did what you had to do. I know that."

I was quiet as long as I thought I had to be before saying, "We wouldn't show it to anyone."

"That's what Livewire said."

"No one will ever see it except us, I promise."

"That's what Trey said," Thana said. "Let me ask you

something. If you're not going to show it to anyone, what's the point?"

"I want..." I started and then paused to make sure I was going to say what I meant. "I want to see Deidre."

"Then video her yourself. Ever heard of a tripod? I thought you were a photographer."

"We have. It's not the same. I want..." I got stuck again.

"I know what you want."

"Really?"

"Really. But I can't help you." Thana almost laughed. "It's funny. Invisibility wasn't even one of Century Man's powers, but I can see right through you."

Thana gave me time to confess to something, but I didn't.

She looked at me for a moment and said, "You know, if you were smart, you'd just forget this. These things never end well. You know that. Fantasies never translate well to the real world. Expectations don't get met. Or worse, expectations get exceeded and someone likes it too much. Then someone gets jealous. Feelings get hurt. Bad things. Believe me."

She was right. But it didn't matter.

"Let's say you go through with it," Thana went on. "Let's say Deidre's okay with it. And let's say that you find someone you both agree on, someone willing to play by your rules. And you go through with it. What if it's the worst experience of her entire life? What if she hates herself for doing it? What if she hates you for making her?"

I had thought of all those possibilities and then some.

"Or think about this: What if she loves it? I mean fucking loves it. What if it's everything both of you had dreamed it would be. What then? Itch scratched? Don't count on it. What if it's the fucking pinnacle, the very apex of sexual experience, and she could never again recapture that thrill?

"What if you knew, going in, that would be the case? Would you still do it? Knowing full well it was all downhill from there? Could you live the rest of your life knowing that every time you made love to your wife she was comparing it to that one time,

120

never again satisfied with just you? Never again content to have plain vanilla sex with her husband? Not happy unless there were super-powers and a camera involved?"

Thana let what she was saying sink in. "Or is it better that it's a fantasy? Could it be that the anticipation is always sweeter than the fulfillment, that the fantasy is always better than the real thing?"

It was a good point. They were all good points. But it didn't matter.

"I just want her to..." I said before I realized I didn't know how I wanted that sentence to end.

"Come?" Thana guessed, a little too easily. She laughed, then stifled it and said, "Sorry. It's not funny. I just..."

"Maybe you should lay your hands on me and make me not want this."

Thana seemed to actually consider it for a minute. She checked her watch and glanced at the club's main entrance. She said, "You do realize you wouldn't need me to convince him, right?"

"What do you mean?"

"Trey."

"Who said anything about Trey?"

"Don't insult me, Will. I'm not stupid, and neither are you."

I didn't say anything.

"He'd love to do it," Thana said. "You know he's got the same problem Deidre does."

"But on the Livewire video..."

"Okay, yeah, he can come. I mean, he can physically ejaculate. That's not the problem. The problem, one of the problems at least, is that he can never fuck a normal human hard enough to bring himself to climax. Anything approaching the force it would take to get him off would tear a normal chick apart like a fucking rag doll." Thana chuckled.

"But, Livewire," I tried to say again.

121

"Livewire's a meta. She's not invulnerable, but she's not normal, either. And anyhow, she was blowing him when he came."

"I was going to say a blowjob."

"Yeah, blowjobs work. No force needed. Not on Helix's part. He can just lie there and let some lucky fan service him. But then what happens when he comes?"

I shrugged my shoulders.

"You saw the video. He goes off like a fucking shotgun. Trace said it. It would've blown Livewire's head off. And then not only is he worried to death about being recognized, he's looking at involuntary manslaughter." Thana laughed cruelly. "Bastard can't even beat off unless he's in the desert or on a mountaintop or some shit."

"Or in the Citadel," I added.

"And I assure you, there's more than one dent up there."

I shook my head in disbelief, more at my own naiveté than anything.

"So, yeah," Thana continued. "If you're offering him the chance to cut loose and not have to hold back? Yeah."

She checked her watch once more and this time I got the hint. I stood to leave and Thana walked out of the club with me, back into the rainy night. The cold and quiet were blessings after the thumping sweatbox of the club.

Thana's hatchback was just a few cars away from where I had parked. She stopped at it.

"Be careful what you wish for, Will. This isn't what you want."

I nodded. "Maybe you're right."

"Always." Thana smiled as she got in her car. "Goodnight, Mighty Century Man."

The next night, Deidre convinced me to meet her for dinner at Centurions Café. She was craving a Skyscraper Burger and obviously could get one nowhere else. And for some reason, Centurions Café also happened to be the only place in town

122

Deidre could go eat and not get pestered for autographs. I used to think that maybe the other diners were simply being respectful of her privacy. Deidre swore it was because no one recognized her in jeans and a sweater, or with brown hair.

Tonight, though, Deidre wasn't wearing a sweater. She was in a very short blue skirt and matching jacket opened to the very edge of something white and lacy underneath. Her magenta lipstick was more in character for Supernova than Deidre. Her heels clicked as she made her way to join me in the bar. She tugged gently, once, at her hemline as she approached, then ran her hands down across her hips, smoothing the tight skirt against her thighs.

"You look..." I started, unable to find a word good enough. "Wow."

Deidre couldn't help but smile.

I said, "You smell really good, too." I had been reduced to a school boy.

Deidre gave me a wink and took me by the hand. "Come on. I'm starving."

A chubby white kid in an ill-fitting Trace costume told us he would be our speedy server tonight. The poor guy couldn't keep his eyes off Deidre's chest, but then again neither could I. She nobly ignored both of us and ordered her usual glass of red and the Helix Cut rib eye, rare.

"What happened to the Skyscraper Burger?" I asked after Trace had ambled away.

"Too much meat."

"I thought that was the point. Skyscraper can get really big, so the burger..."

"I get it. I just didn't want all that meat."

"So you ordered a fourteen ounce rib eye?"

"Shut up," Deidre laughed.

Our drinks came, we talked about the kids' report cards, and then a second glass of wine came for Deidre before our food arrived.

"So, Dr. Delirium is back from the dead," Deidre said to me between bites of her steak.

"Again?"

"Yep. I told Psy-Fi she should've looked for the body, did I not? No body, no death. Superheroics 101."

I had to make a conscious effort to listen to what my wife was saying. As if her mascara and cleavage and lipstick and perfume weren't distracting enough, I couldn't stop feeling guilty about my conversation with Thana. At least three times during dinner I had talked myself into confessing to her where I was last night, but each time I had convinced myself that I had done nothing wrong. Deidre didn't even know I had been gone. I hadn't lied about anything. And besides, I argued in my head, it was about her; she was the reason I went to Thana. She would understand. Not that she would ever find out. Thana was right, I had concluded after having slept on it. Nothing good could come of it.

Deidre pointed at me with her fork. "Are you even listening to me?"

"Of course."

"What'd I just say?"

"'Are you even listening to me?'"

"Smartass," Deidre smiled before turning her attention back to her steak. Trace wandered nearby and Deidre got his attention and ordered a third glass of wine. After he was out of earshot, she said, "Oh, by the way, the boys are spending the night at Mom's so we can be as loud as we want to tonight."

I smiled. "So that's why you're all dolled up tonight. And getting drunk."

Deidre gave me that wink again.

Just as I was polishing off my Mild-Mannered Malt, someone on the other side of the dining room stood from their meal and pointed out the window. "Look!" Someone else added, with equal zeal, "It's the beacon!" Half the restaurant scrambled to the windows, craning their necks to see. Deidre and I watched each other for a few seconds and then stood to see for ourselves.

124

Skintight

There, over the Century City skyline, illuminating the belly of a passing cloud was the unmistakable glowing Century Man symbol.

Deidre looked at me. "I'll fly."

"As long as you're not driving."

The air was frigid. Deidre flew as slowly as she could and still maneuver. There was a time when freezing temperatures and wind chill were only a concept to me, something regular humans had to concern themselves with, like visiting the doctor or using oven mitts. But I was regular human now and I was freezing. Deidre flew toward downtown, toward the beacon, high above the streets and sidewalks lined with twinkling Christmas lights, above the rooftops, but still close enough to hear an occasional taxi horn or corner Santa's bell wafting up. We flew silently into the heart of the city, the buildings growing until we were no longer flying over them but instead between, our fragmented reflections flanking us.

Looming, jutting from the center of city like a lighted spike was the Holloway Building, Century City's tallest building. Deidre began to arc up, climbing in the sky until we were aimed at the ornamental sword-like spire that capped the building, flying straight toward the white shaft of light that originated from it. The streets below receded, the headlights of the cars moving on them like glistening beads of water on a giant spider's web. I hadn't been this high since I could fly myself and for a moment I felt dizzy. The graduated top floors of the building were lit red and green, as they were every Christmas, and we flew through the glow as we approached the source of the beacon, a massive spotlight perched on a precipice near the base of the spire.

Deidre dropped from the sky and lit softly, high heels tapping on the metal platform that surrounded the skyward-facing searchlight. Fifty feet below, the ninety-seventh floor Observation Deck was filled with sightseers, their excited din barely audible over the thrumming of the giant lamp. I could hear them asking, "How long has it been?" and "Do you think he'll show up?"

"I was a little worried this old thing wouldn't fire up," a figure said from the shadows behind the spotlight.

"Thana?" I said.

She walked into the glow, patting the beacon with her hand. "It's been a while."

Thirteen months, to be exact. I had given it to Commissioner Beck almost two decades earlier with the instructions, "Use this to call me." Countless nights that icon had lit the Century City night, calling for help. But it had been dark for over a year.

"What's going on here, Thana?" I said.

Helix, in full costume, his emerald cape fluttering in the constant breeze, strode from behind the beacon and stood next to Thana, arms folded across his chest. Thana said, "Exactly what you wanted."

"I don't understand."

"You don't have to play dumb," Thana said. "Deidre knows where you were last night. She actually called me before you did."

Deidre wouldn't look at me.

"It's okay," said Thana, "We're all on the same page now. Deidre wanted to be sure you were serious about this. And you are, I can tell."

I turned to Deidre and took her hands, waiting for her to look at me. "I didn't mean for this..." I struggled to find something to say that remotely made sense. "We don't have to do this. This isn't..."

"It's okay," Deidre said, squeezing my hands.

"See?" Thana said. "It's okay. She wants it, too."

I turned my back to Thana and Trey. "Say it," I told her. "Tell me. I want to hear it from you." I watched her face, ready to take her away from here if I sensed even the slightest indecision.

"I want this," Deidre said, looking me in the eye. "As long as you do, too."

126

"Believe it or not, only big boy here needed convincing," Thana said, patting Trey on the ass. He was staring at Deidre. "Some bullshit about respecting the two of you too much, I don't know. But he wants to now, don't you?" Thana looked up at Trey. He nodded once, his eyes never leaving Deidre.

"So," Thana said. "Is this going to happen tonight?"

Deidre saw Trey's unabashed gaze but, unlike at the Halloween party, this time she returned it with confidence. I watched her and it was obvious she was prepared to make this happen. My heart hammered against my sternum.

Thana said, "Deidre, you look amazing, girl, but why don't you go ahead and turn into Supernova?"

I shook my head, slowly at first, then faster until I finally spoke up. "This is... Wait. This is wrong." I looked to Deidre for back up. She seemed confused by my reluctance.

"Listen," Thana said, moving close to me, lowering her voice. "I made him want Supernova. He wants the blue costume, the blonde hair, the whole nine yards."

"No, it's not that."

"What, then?" Thana said. "What are you afraid of?" The question felt genuine, not accusatory. I didn't have an answer regardless. Thana was losing her patience. "Do you want this, or not?"

Deidre came to me and held my hands. "Do you love me?"

"Yes."

"Do you trust me?"

"Of course."

"Then trust me," she said.

It started to drizzle. I could hear the drops sizzle as they hit the lens of the beacon. Deidre took a step away from the rest of us and cast her arms out as she began to spin. The burst of light from her transformation lit the underside of the cloud blanket just above, and through the thin air I could hear the tourists on the observation deck below ask each other if it was lightning. Supernova stood now in Deidre's place, skintight bodysuit instead of her skirt and jacket, bobbed blonde hair instead of shoulder-length brunette. She walked by me, brushing my hand with hers as she went to Helix. The light from the beacon bounced off her shining blue costume and illuminated the platform all around her feet with dozens of reflected beams.

I was so nervous I was shaking. Deidre looked at me once more, her eyes flashing with excitement. Helix glanced skyward and, with a knowing nod, the two lifted effortlessly in the rainy night air. I watched them ascend. Thana moved to my side, watching with me. I tried to think of something to say but couldn't. Thana tucked a cigarette between her lips and cupped her hands around the flame of her match. She sighed, a mouthful of smoke disappearing into the dark. She dug in the front pocket of her pants and pulled out her phone. She took another long pull on her cigarette before raising the phone to begin taking video.

"I knew he'd fly," Thana said, pointing her phone at Trey and Deidre. "He's always wanted to do it while flying."

Deidre and Trey were floating two stories above us, just at the edge of the glow of the beacon. Close enough for us to see but too far, I figured, for anyone on the observation deck who might have looked up. I watched Trey, his cape snapping in the wind as he closed in on Deidre.

He said to her, "You are the only thing that has ever made me jealous of him." He glanced down at me. And here I saw it again, that Helix charm. The same magic he so effortlessly worked time and again on his adoring public. The same spell he cast over a nation of hero worshippers. He now held my wife in that same thrall.

She ran her hands over his shaved head, fingernails scratching through the stubble. Her hands slipped down the nape of his neck, around his cabled shoulders and down the expanse of his chest, palms pressed flat. I could see that she was breathing heavily. She let her hands roam over Trey's ridged abdomen, fingers drifting lower until they could toy with the green sash that encircled his waist. Thana kept her phone's camera trained on them and drew again on her cigarette before saying, "Lights, camera... Action."

With slow, confident movements, Deidre untied the sash and then rolled down Trey's trunks, his erection suddenly springing outward as she did so. I could see her staring down at it as she pushed the tights down around his thighs. Trey smiled at her, expecting her to be impressed. Deidre's hands went to it, causing it to rise further still, defying gravity until it was aimed up at her. She seemed to almost flush with pride at having caused it.

She paused and then she looked down at me, as if awaiting my permission to go further. My pulse was like a kettledrum in my ears. I was almost nauseated with a mix of fear and excitement.

Adventurous.

I nodded.

Deidre turned her back to Trey and locked eyes with him over her shoulder. "Fuck me."

Trey cupped Deidre's ass and collected the clinging material of her costume into his fists. He gave a swift yank and the fabric surrendered with a loud rip. He peeled back the torn spandex to expose Deidre's bottom, her pale skin contrasting with the cotton candy blue of her costume. Deidre arched her back, pressing her ass into his Trey's palms, clenching her buttocks into taut bunches of muscle and then letting them relax into soft globes for Trey to knead and spread. He took Deidre's costume in his hands again and split it to her shoulder blades. He wrestled the shredded suit away from her body and cast it down onto the platform at my feet. Deidre stood in the sky, completely naked now. Trey was floating a few feet behind Deidre, staring.

"Fuck me," Deidre said again, bending at the waist and opening her legs to show Trey what was waiting there for him. Trey launched himself forward through the air and, like a hawk sinking its claws into its vulnerable prey, penetrated her. He drove into her almost angrily and Deidre groaned her approval,

129

rising in the air, pushing back against his attack, trying to keep herself from being hurled across the sky. He tangled his fingers in her hair as she clawed at the empty air. For just an instant she seemed to be in pain. I readied myself to stop Trey before he tore my wife apart. How, I had no idea.

"Don't," Thana said in a hushed tone, shooting me a paralyzing glance. I looked at her and then back to my wife. Deidre was panting raggedly, eyes clenched, but taking it. "Don't ruin this."

I returned Thana's stare but said nothing.

"Besides," she said. "She's invulnerable." Thana eyed me cautiously, making sure I wasn't going to interfere, not that I would have known how. "She's kicked the shit out of Man-o'-War," she pointed out. "Something tells me she can handle getting screwed."

I watched them. They were moving through the air now, the force of their thrusts pushing one another, and pushing back again. They rode each other, their bodies rising and falling through the air, swaying and banking with the force of their interaction. Deidre bucked and Trey dropped the full weight of his body on her and they tumbled and dove through the air like angry mating bumblebees.

I could feel Thana staring at me, right next to me, monitoring my reaction to what I was seeing.

"This is..." I started, and then paused. Thana was waiting for what I was going to say. "I can't believe this is actually happening."

Thana inhaled the last of her cigarette, dropped it onto the platform, and crushed it with her shoe. "Are you complaining?"

"No," I said, watching Deidre. My own erection was straining painfully against my pants now and I shifted, trying to relieve the pressure.

Thana was apparently well aware of my condition. "Why don't you just take it out?" I glanced at her as she stepped carefully around the spotlight, searching for a better vantage point to record the action. "Go ahead. That's what you're here for, right?"

I felt suddenly frightened at how easily all this had happened, how easily Deidre had been convinced. And for a brief moment I was overcome with confusion. What if Deidre liked this too much?

"Want to see?" Thana asked. She handed me her phone and I aimed it up at Deidre and Trey. For just an instant, Deidre's eyes met with mine. Her excitement was plain to see. She was excited to be doing this. Excited that I was watching. My uncertainty went away as quickly as it had manifested.

I wondered how many visitors to Century City on the observation deck below could hear Supernova begging Helix to fuck her. They dove and banked, sometimes flipping upside down, spiraling and careening, Thana always chasing them with her phone's viewfinder. They slammed themselves together, pushing themselves to the upper limits of physical endurance, their indestructible, super-human bodies colliding headlong like battering rams, with a sound like bombs bursting.

Deidre was going to come. Around her naked body a translucent veil of purple light began to dance. Her jaw was clenched and a low, guttural growl crept from her throat. Suddenly her entire body buckled as her orgasm surged up through her. At that moment, a brilliant light, like a violet sun, emerged from between her legs, engulfing both her and Trey. Trey didn't stop. He kept fucking her. The light coalesced into beams that shot into the night in all directions, too bright to look at. Thana and I shielded our eyes and Deidre's body glowed white, the night sky around became day and, with a sound like the air itself was on fire, she ignited.

Chapter Eight

Biff. Bam. Pow.

When I awoke the next day it was past two o'clock in the afternoon and I was alone in my bed.

For a moment when I first awakened I thought maybe it hadn't really happened. I thought that maybe it had all been some amazingly vivid dream that seemed real, like dreams sometimes do. But the bedroom was just as we had left it, clothes strewn across the carpet, empty wine bottles on the dresser. And I could smell him; I could smell him on the sheets, on Deidre's pillow. On Deidre's nightstand was our laptop, email open, the most recent one from Thana received five hours earlier with an attachment named *The Adventures of Supernova and Helix.mov.*

"I want everything tonight," Deidre had whispered to me last night as she flew us home from the Holloway Building, Trey following not far behind, Thana in his arms. "Everything we've never been in the right place or the right time or the right frame of mind to do. I want it to happen tonight," Deidre had said. And she got it.

Trey and I fucked Deidre until sunrise. Thana spent the entire time recording us, choreographing and directing us through seemingly endless variations, different positions, locations, and arrangements. Throughout it all was Thana's voice, coaching us, challenging us to fuck Deidre deeper and harder and faster.

Images of the night before flashed through my brain like the four-color panels of a comic book. *Biff!* Deidre's cyan eyes, outlined in black mascara, gazing up at Trey and me. *Bam!* Her magenta lipstick, smeared across her cheek. *Pow!* Her yellow bangs matted to her forehead.

But now Trey was gone, and Thana with him. Deidre had fallen asleep first this morning, wedged between Trey and me. She's a light sleeper and would've awakened when Trey got up. She would've fixed him a cup of coffee before he left. Or at least offered to.

Maybe it was a coincidence, maybe it wasn't, that Deidre floated into the bedroom at the same time I awoke. We looked at each other with what I thought was a sense of disbelief, curiosity, and fear. Deidre crawled into bed and wrapped herself in the warm sheets next to me. We didn't say anything at first. Instead we just lay there in our bed, as we did most mornings, acting as if everything was perfectly normal, as if our marriage hadn't been fundamentally and irrevocably altered.

She was still naked. We were silent for a long time until I finally asked, "When did they leave?"

"I'm not sure." I couldn't tell if she meant she didn't know because she wasn't awake or if she simply didn't remember what time it was when they departed.

"I could feel you watching me," Deidre said suddenly. "Did you like it?"

I opened my mouth to say something and then realized I didn't know the answer.

She said, "I liked you watching."

When I finally thought of something to say, it was, "Was it what you wanted?"

"I think so."

Then I said, "What was it like?"

"What do you mean?"

"Fucking him."

"I don't know. I guess..." Deidre began, but then, "I don't know."

"Tell me," I said. "Tell me what it was like."

"It was like fucking. I don't know. It was... different."

"How?" I asked.

"Thana says I should do three now," Deidre said, changing the subject almost without me noticing.

"Would you?"

"I don't know. Maybe. Trey says I shouldn't change my hair when I'm Supernova. He didn't know I wasn't really blonde."

"Did you like sucking his cock?"

"Wasn't I supposed to?"

"Yes."

"Okay, then."

Neither one of us spoke for a few minutes after that until Deidre said, "I remember when I was a teenager, when Mom finally started letting me hang out at Guild Hall, there used to be a couple of hotlines. Goofy red telephones. Under glass, I swear to god."

"I remember those," I said.

"One was for the Mayor's Office, the other for the Police Commissioner."

"Cool."

"Yep. Each phone had a big red light right where the dial would've been on a normal phone. Whenever either one of them would ring, the red lights would blink on and off. And those phones rang off the hook back then."

"The '70s were rough."

"Oh yeah. Most days I would just stay out of the way, do my homework, and watch those red lights blink on the hotlines. On busy days, when both phones would be ringing at the same time, I used to just sit and stare at them. The Mayor's hotline blinked just a little bit slower than the Police Commissioner's. If they both ran long enough, the fast one got closer and closer to the slow one until finally they would blink at the exact same time. Then they'd get further and further apart until they were as far apart as they could get. And then they'd start getting closer again.

"I remember thinking last night," Deidre said. "When you were both fucking me at the same time, how that was exactly like those hotlines. I could feel both of you inside of me. Pushing against that wall." Her breath was getting heavy. "Your rhythms were always just a little different, sometimes going in just as the other was pulling out. But sometimes you both went in at the exact same time. And when that would happen I'd feel like I was about to burst open."

I watched her, not sure if I was supposed to say anything or just listen. Then she almost giggled. "God, we were loud, weren't we?"

"Do you like being called a whore?" I asked.

"I don't... no," She shook her head. "No."

"You liked it last night."

"Last night, I didn't..."

"You didn't what?"

"Last night I wanted... I wanted to be something different."

Dr. Gunnarsson led me to the same room where I had received the nanobot injection a few days ago. The same table was there, as was the same metal tray. However this time, in place of the needle-pistol was what looked like a colostomy bag and something akin to a thumbtack. At Agnetha's command I repeated the ritual from my last visit, complete with the pulling down of the shorts. With an absolute disregard for gentleness, Agnetha jabbed the thumbtack into my butt. There was a tiny light on the head of the tack that began to flash red.

"What's that for?" I asked.

"That is an ultrasonic beacon that informs the nanobots it is now time to evacuate your body. You will need to urinate now." Agnetha gestured toward a narrow door in the corner of the room and I tugged my shorts up and climbed off the table. "Urinate into this." Agnetha handed me the clear plastic pouch from the table-side tray and off I went.

135

The opening to the bag was circular and resembled an industrial-strength condom. I stuck my dick in it and tried to relax enough to pee. Then, the ignited napalm that had been forced into my body through my butt cheek a few days earlier suddenly came streaming out through my penis. It felt as if my penis had been sliced lengthwise with a razor blade and gasoline poured over it. Then set on fire. My eyes welled with tears and I let a slight grunt slip. I watched as the bag quickly filled with the familiar silvery liquid, this time mingled with amber swirls of urine.

I brought the warm bag out to Agnetha, who was in the process of stretching a pair of latex gloves over her slender fingers. She took the bag and attached what looked like a handheld calculator to it by inserting a jack into a small receptacle in the condom-neck. She inserted the jack of a headset into the calculator-thing and took a seat. After a few minutes she said, "Oh yes, you may remove the evacuation signal from your buttock now."

I plucked the tack from my backside and sat down.

Long stretches of silence from Agnetha followed with her sometimes sitting and simply listening to the headset, sometimes tapping the small keyboard of her device, sometimes nodding and issuing the occasional doctorly, "Hmm." Then there would come a burst of speech from Agnetha, saying things like, "pulsed field gel electrophoresis" and, "asynchronous chromosomal replicons." Certain phrases seemed to make the fluid in the bag gurgle and churn.

"Hmm. This is interesting," she said.

"What?"

"Have you been exposed to any sort of radiation in the past seventy-two hours?"

I thought back over the last three days and tried to remember if I had witnessed Supernova or the Centurions fight a radioactive supervillain. If so, maybe I had been in close enough proximity to register something with Agnetha's nanobots. But the last time I had been near a fight was when

136

Deidre and Trey had taken care of the Priests of Syzygy, and they were simply machines.

Agnetha said, "The nanobots have detected a slight spike in cell activity that occurred during their residence in your body. There's no way to pinpoint exactly when, but that's not important. The spike seems to be similar to when latent meta-genes become active." She was staring at me wide-eyed. "Come with me."

Agnetha stalked the corridors of SMART with me in tow. I knew where she was going and I wanted to tell her to not waste her time or mine but I knew it would do no good. We passed through a series of double-doors, each time Agnetha swiping her security card to gain access until we finally came to a giant steel hatch with a plate that read "Proving Room". Agnetha swiped her card once more and the hatch ponderously opened with a whoosh of air.

It had been a long time since I had been inside the Proving Room. Over a year, in fact. Nothing had changed. The room had always given me the impression of an aircraft carrier hangar implanted deep inside SMART Labs. It was a yawning, open space of grey steel and exposed structure amid the pristine white of the rest of the facility. There was enough room inside of it to dock a cruise ship. Or, more accurately, room enough for metahumans to swoop and dive through the air, teleport from one end to the other, sprint in supersonic bursts, and defy the laws of physics in general. It was a romper room for skintights.

At various stations throughout the room were a treadmill coupled to a turbine, a massive cylindrical glass tank filled with some type of reddish fluid, and a pair of chains with links as big as automobiles. There was a dodecahedron made of concrete, floating weightlessly overhead, tumbling slowly. A hologram of a Tyrannosaurus Rex stood poised for simulated combat.

"Do you remember Attack Formation Delta?" Dr. Gunnarsson asked me.

"Of course."

I smiled to myself and jogged across the floor and took cover behind a bulkhead. I could hear the bay doors on the far end of the hangar slide apart and I didn't have to look to know what was coming through them. On the other side of the bulkhead, fifty yards away, metal footsteps moved toward me.

There were three of them. Seeker/Destroyers, they were called. Machines, vaguely humanoid in shape, roughly twice the size of a man and equipped with a SMART Labs-developed arsenal of high-tech defensive and offensive measures. Enhanced thermal vision, active light-refraction camouflage, motion and vibration sensors. Both upper limbs were outfitted with a variety of weaponry including reciprocating photon-bolt rifles, plasma net guns and neurotransmitter-grenade launchers. All non-lethal of course, but painful as hell.

I had outwitted and outlasted the Seekers countless times as Century Man. At one point I even held the unofficial SMART Labs record for most Seekers taken out in a sixty-second span (a record Helix still hadn't broken). But the Seekers weren't used so much for combat training as they were for establishing the power levels and skill sets of metahumans. And I knew that's what Dr. Gunnarsson had in mind for this exercise. Whatever it was the nanobots told her had given her reason to believe the ability to outperform the Seeker/Destroyers had been rekindled in me.

But even as I crouched behind the bulkhead and waited, I felt nothing. Nothing about my body told me I could again defy gravity or bend steel. I wasn't even sure I could run to the other end of the hangar without having to stop to catch my breath. Physically, I felt positively mundane. And I was sure the Seekers were about to confirm my suspicions.

The footsteps were getting closer, almost on top of me now. They hadn't detected me yet. But it didn't take a metagene to sit still. I let the Seekers take one more step before I leapt from my hiding spot with all the strength and agility of a absolutely normal man.

Even still, my instincts kicked in. I remembered how to do this and I went right, then left, then rolled as the first photon-bolt zapped the floor where I had been a half-second earlier. Looming over me were all three Seekers, their lenses and antennae tracking my every movement now. There would be no more hiding.

The two flanking Seekers moved to cut off any potential escape routes while the center Seeker closed in on me. With metal arms extended, the Seeker loosed another photon blast. I had to throw myself to the floor to dodge it. I rolled out to one side to avoid a descending plasma net released from another Seeker. Adrenaline flowing now, my senses felt heightened somehow. Maybe. I scrambled to my feet, sure now I had the speed to maneuver behind the closest Seeker.

A bolt from a photon rifle impacted against my chest and sent me sprawling headlong across the floor. I'm not sure what hurt worse, the blunt force of the blow or the electricity surging through my body. For a second or two I was completely paralyzed, muscles refusing to respond. I was done.

"Halt," Dr. Gunnarsson said loudly and the Seekers turned in unison and marched away through the same bay doors they had emerged from. Agnetha approached me. I could see the disappointment on her face. I wondered if my own disappointment showed through my pain.

"I'm sorry," I wheezed, the words barely forming.

"No, Will. I am sorry. I thought possibly—"

"It's okay. Really."

Agnetha helped me to my feet and offered to escort me to the nurse's station. But my pride was hurt a lot worse than my body.

Back in Agnetha's office we sat in silence for a few minutes while she poured over her notes once more. She regarded me for a moment before finally speaking.

"I can find no scientific explanation for what happened to your powers, Will." She said the words reticently, as if trying to soften their blow, but I was anything but surprised by them.

139

"Maybe it was a magic of some sort."

"There is no such thing as magic, Will. Only science we do not yet understand. I did not say there was no scientific explanation, only that I have yet to find it."

"Has Century Man returned?" demanded Eyewitness 8's Lola Oh as she pointed her microphone at Police Commissioner Beck's face. Beck kept climbing the steps of police headquarters, doing his best to ignore the cameras and microphones. "Can you confirm the discovery of Supernova's shredded costume at the base of the beacon?"

"Shit," Deidre said. "I knew we should've gone back for it."

"Police are still baffled by the sudden appearance last night of the Century Man beacon in the Century City sky," Lola went on, now addressing the camera. "Although there have been no confirmed sightings of Century Man himself, a spokesman for the Metahuman Crime Division refused to deny his possible return."

The Return of Century Man. That's what they've decided to call the night my wife fucked Helix.

"Other downtown denizens report seeing a brilliant light show over the Century skyline last night not long after the beacon was extinguished." Lola stabbed her mic in the face an elderly lady who had been patiently waiting nearby. "How would you describe the lights you saw?"

"Oh, it was definitely Nova Girl," the old woman started. "The new one. It was that tacky purple and blue light. Not that pretty pink, like her mother used."

Deidre and I both laughed. My chest was still aching from the photon bolt I took to it earlier. But it felt good to laugh. It was the first time we had really laughed since before *it* happened. It. Every other major event in my life had a name; the Hyper-Time Crisis, Operation Mindcrime, the Knave Incident. I didn't know what to call last night but I knew it wasn't the Return of Century Man. If anything, it was the last nail in his coffin.

140

"Have I cheated on you?" Deidre said suddenly and quietly, staring at the television.

"No," I said as quickly as I could, hoping to sound as sure of the answer as I truly was. It was the one thing I did know. My feelings were locked in a battle as epic as any the Centurions had ever waged. I would be almost overwhelmed with jealousy, yet at the same time consumed with a burning desire to watch Deidre do it again. There were so many questions. Questions I wasn't sure I wanted the answers to. But I knew my wife hadn't cheated on me. "No. No, of course not."

"Do you regret it?"she said next.

"No," I told her, not nearly as sure of that response. I didn't regret it. Not yet, anyhow. I had almost expected to, but I didn't. I wasn't sure what I felt, despite the fact that it was all I had thought about, but it wasn't regret.

"Do you remember the first time you ever flew?" Deidre said.

"Yeah, I do, actually."

"Me too. I remember how excited I was. And how scared. I was sure nothing bad would happen; Mom was right there. But I wasn't *that* sure. I couldn't wait to see how different everything looked from up there, but I couldn't wait to be back on the ground again. You know?"

I did know.

"This just in," Lola said on our television. "We're receiving word that security at Casey Asylum has been compromised. We have unconfirmed reports that the patients..."

Before Lola could finish her sentence, there was a blinding flash of light and I turned to see Supernova standing in my kitchen.

"Are you okay?" she asked me.

I nodded.

"Are you sure?

"Everything's fine, baby," I said.

She wouldn't ask me again.

"I have to go," she said. I nodded. I wondered if she was as relieved as I was to have something to take our minds off of It. Before I could tell her to be careful, she was gone. The air in her wake glowed and sizzled for a few seconds before going back to normal. I gathered up my camera and left the house.

The sprawling Nineteenth Century manor of Dr. Augustus Casey clung to the edge of a cliff overlooking Bostwick Bay. Every child who had grown up in Century City knew that the old place was haunted. From the city, looking at the house across the water, it looked like a grand, gray old lady perched on the precipice, ready to jump. Some evenings, just as the sun began to set, a fog seeped out of the woods behind the asylum and rolled off the cliff to covered the bay like a winter's blanket. This was one of those evenings.

Upon his death by suicide in 1954, and in accordance with his last will and testament, Dr. Casey's former home was converted into a hospital for the mentally ill. Under the administration of his son, Adam, the hospital became in the 1970s the home for those members of the metahuman community deemed mentally or emotionally incompetent to stand trial for their crimes. It was a sort of halfway house for supervillains. Dr. Adam Casey felt he could rehabilitate these people, turn them into productive members of society, teach them to use their powers for good. He was killed during a patient uprising in 1981.

In the decades since Dr. Casey's murder, the Casey Asylum for the Criminally Insane had housed at one time or another almost every major metahuman criminal that called Century City home. Phantom Lord, Dr. Delirium, the Somnambulist. They had all spent time there, only to be declared fit to rejoin society where they promptly perpetrated their next fabulous crime against it, no doubt planned while relaxing in Casey Asylum. Since coming under the stewardship of Dr. Ashley Smith five years ago, a dozen patients had attempted to escape the asylum; about half had managed to do so. None, however, had ever broken back into the asylum after publicly declaring his intention to free all of his friends inside. But that was precisely what the lunatic who called himself the Single Bullet Theory had done that afternoon.

For Century City's Metahuman Crime Division, working in concert with Casey Asylum's private security force, there had been more than enough time to re-secure all known exits from the hospital. All doors, windows, fire escapes and utility accesses were either locked and barred or under armed guard. The South Wing, where the most unstable patients were housed, swarmed with MCD officers in full riot gear. Alerts had been issued to asylum staff to avoid at all costs the madman loose among them. He could be disguised, the authorities warned, as a doctor or an orderly or a security guard. Firefighters ringed the entire estate, braced for anything. The police peered through binoculars, scanning Casey Manor for anything that might indicate the Single Bullet Theory's next move.

The sun was hidden now behind Century's skyline. The shadows of the skyscrapers crept like skinny fingers across the waters of the bay and up the cliff. When I arrived there was no sign of the Centurions. This was typical, though; they almost always grouped off-site so as to better coordinate their initial response. I knew they were somewhere, together. I wondered, as I photographed the small army surrounding Casey Asylum, how Deidre had felt upon seeing Helix for the first time after last night. After It. Did they simply say, "Hi", and begin planning how to handle the situation at hand? Did they exchange quick, knowing smiles? Embarrassed glances? Or was there the slightest hint of a smirk on Trey's face? A glint in his eye, when he caught Deidre's, that said, "We've got a secret." Or was it even a secret? What if Trey had told Andre? Bragged to him about finally fucking Supernova?

The crash of wood and glass and metal filled the air before I could wonder any more, and the main entrance to Casey Asylum was ripped from the house and flung into the air. I turned my camera, and my face, just in time to avoid the fragments of the

143

house that flew my way. Where the entrance to the old house had been was now only a gaping hole.

Standing in the hole was a lone, skinny, hawk-nosed, naked man. The Single Bullet Theory had no powers, no extraordinary physical skills, no cache of high-tech weaponry. His only weapon was chaos, and his absolutely unpredictable use of it. He was utterly and completely insane. Legend had it that his entire family, his entire life, was taken from him when a single bullet, fired by a drive-by shooter a block away, ignited a gas main in his downtown apartment, leaving him with nothing. The 'theory,' as he once explained it while torturing a kidnapped Commissioner Beck, was that a single bullet could make even the sanest person embrace the inevitability of chaos. His crimes were among Century City's most infamous: killing the entire animal population of the Century City Zoo with water balloons filled with nitroglycerin, crop-dusting a Comets playoff game with anthrax, decapitating the Mayor's Shih Tzu and sewing a Cabbage Patch Doll's head in its place.

Now he stood in the wreckage, wearing only his trademark grin and the patchwork of disorganized, grotesque tattoos that covered his entire skin from head to toe. Behind him stood G-Force, the metahuman who could manipulate gravity. He was doubtless responsible for the dramatic removal of the asylum's front door. Behind G-Force stood the collected inhabitants of the hospital, ready to unleash themselves on whatever stood between them and freedom, however temporary it might be.

"Vamoose!" howled the Theory, throwing his hands in the air. With that, the patients began to spill out, on foot and through the air, like angry bees from a hive. They were mostly wearing robes and pajamas. Freed from the power-sapping MetaDampers (developed, of course, by Wertham Biotech) that lined the walls of the asylum, the inmates unleashed themselves. I saw Phantasmo take to the sky, effortlessly phasing intangible as the MCD shot energized containment nets at him. Moonchild ran directly into the waiting arms of CCPD, her powers useless in the absence of a full moon. G-Force used his powers to pin an entire flank of officers to the ground as he floated overhead. Coma shot overhead, swatting away rubber bullets like flies.

A fairly new player in the supervillain game, Killshot, cleaved an opening in the defenses with an sweeping pass of the cybernetically-augmented Gatling gun woven with cables and tubing into his shoulder socket where his left arm should have been. He backed away from the overwhelmed police, moving my way, covering his escape with bursts of suppressing fire. His targeting goggles rotated and dilated independently of one another, like a chameleon's eyes. And then he found me in his sights.

Killshot swung his big weapon around to bear on me. I glanced over my shoulder to make sure Killshot wasn't targeting a Centurion or police officer instead of a civilian photographer. He stalked me slowly, ignoring the gunfire that was now ricocheting off the armored panels that encased most of his body. His machine gun-arm was trained on my chest, the red dot of his laser sight tracing a little squiggle on my sternum. Instinctively I readied myself, as if the bullets would've bounced off my bowed chest, and for the slightest moment I almost believed it again, almost felt it again. A beam of intense purple light struck his shoulder, sending pieces of armor and weaponry flying in all directions, and he slumped to the ground.

I looked to the sky and saw the Centurions fast descending. I was vaguely aware of the others; Helix dropping from the air, the others deploying from an invisible hatch in Bettie, her hovering presence betrayed only by the low whistle of her engines. I paid them no attention. I was focused on Supernova and her alone.

I could see her, a sapphire fleck taking on Deidre's familiar shape as she swooped down and skimmed past the Gothic spires and lightning rods of Casey Asylum. If her form was familiar, her costume was not. The last light of sunset glinted off what little there was of it. It was still her famous cyan but now metallic, almost foil-like. The top was small and sleeveless, baring her midriff. Her seven-pointed star was scaled down to half its former size to fit. The bottoms were incredibly short. She was naked otherwise, save for a pair of cuffed magenta gloves and matching boots that resembled her original ones, only these had spike heels. She would've looked more at home on the runway at Secret Identity. The only thing that bothered me more than the costume itself was the fact that Trey had seen her in it before I had.

She flew right past me, arms out to her sides like a hawk scanning for prey. She soared overhead, surveying the chaos, ready to intercept the nearest threat. I watched her fly up and into a tight grouping of airborne escapees, knocking each to the ground with staccato energy bursts from her eyes.

Within minutes, the Centurions had turned the tide. Skyscraper dashed to a clearing on the asylum grounds and began to grow, dwarfing the manor almost instantly. He knelt, leaving a sunken footprint large enough to park a car in, and cupped his giant hands over the opening in the asylum, keeping any more patients from spilling out.

Synapse, free from the dampening cell that held him, had taken over the brain of a policeman and had turned him on his fellow officers, firing at them at point-blank range. As each bullet cleared the muzzle, Trace plucked them from midair and dropped them harmlessly to the ground before depositing Synapse into the custody of the law keepers he had just tried to kill.

Cusp, the girl who could see ten seconds into the future, strolled across the yard in her Casey-issued pajamas, effortlessly dodging bullets and tackles with the aloof knowledge of what the officers and agent were going to do before they themselves did. The air seemed to ripple slightly and Psy-Fi suddenly materialized in front of Cusp, having time-traveled exactly twelve seconds into the future, where she administered a clumsy headlock, enough to subdue Cusp until the police could get their hands on her.

The remaining flightless escapees scrambled toward the cliff in the gathering dark, fanning out across the manor's lawn towards the tantalizing promise of freedom that waited across the bay. As they approached the cliff's edge, a massive, fiery winged serpent came over the crest, belching flame and blocking their path, spreading its wings and filling the sky. Those patients that hadn't fainted reversed course, running for their lives now into the arms of the Century City Police Department's Metahuman Crime Division. I took a photograph of Presto, on the peripheral edge of the scene. His palms were held outward, calmly commanding the dragon illusion he had created now to dissolve, its work done.

Either out of pure genius or complete stupidity, the Single Bullet Theory had managed to remain undetected throughout the melee by choosing to stay put. He hadn't budged since giving the initial command to evacuate the hospital. He stood patiently near what used to be the main entrance, only yards away from the Skyscraper's tree-trunk pinky finger, sometimes masturbating, sometimes not. There was a slight smile on his face as he watched the violent proceedings as if they were some sort of sporting event. Helix, with seemingly nothing better to do, finally noticed the naked lunatic and casually descended to apprehend him, emerald cape swirling behind him. He smirked at the Theory as he drew near. It was the same look he gave me last night above the Holloway Building.

I watched the Theory through my telephoto lens as he checked an imaginary wristwatch just as Helix touched down in front of him. He looked up at Trey, his eyes wide with mock surprise, and mouthed the word, "Ka-Boom." And then suddenly, the two of them were lying face down, thrown to the ground by a tremendous blast, a fiery explosion that roared from the manor behind them. Chunks of stone and pieces of burning wood flew through the sky like a fireworks display, spraying out from the explosion. An entire wall of the South Wing had been destroyed. It was a wall that kept in the worst of them, a wall that separated mad from sane. And it was now reduced to a smoldering pile of rubble. Scattered around it were the limp bodies of Century City's Finest who had been guarding that part of the hospital, mixed in with those they were guarding against. The deep blue sky had been turned gray by the smoke and ash.

Standing in the empty blackened place where the wall had been was Bombshell, the self-proclaimed Human Explosion. Her body was charred and smoking from the blast she had just released from it. From behind her on either side trickled a slow but steady procession of Casey Asylum's deadliest criminals. I saw the Veil and Medicine Man; Subhuman, Skinner and 2x4.

Trace was the first skintight there, followed by Helix and Supernova, urgently corralling the inmates, sometimes forcefully, sometimes brutally. Psy-Fi appeared on the scene, using medical technology gleaned from the 22nd Century to try and save what lives she could. I saw her kneeling over a prone police officer, reviving him even as a second Psy-Fi approached and knelt next to her, mimicking her actions. Psy-Fi jumped to her feet and stared at her doppelganger, the look of confusion mirrored on the other's face.

"Marta!" I heard Deidre call to her over the din of the fray. "You've doubled up. Jump home!" Psy-Fi seemed even more confused than before. "When you jumped forward to stop Cusp, you must have forgotten to jump back! Now you're in the same time twice!" I could tell by the panicked look on Marta's face she understood now. "You've got to get out of here!"

Marta had once futilely tried to explain to us the implications of a "time coil" if she was to ever accidentally co-occupy the same time-space. Deidre yelled at her, "You've got to go the future! Now!"

Psy-Fi frantically tapped a sequence into her wristwatch and simply vanished, the air where she had been almost shimmering.

No sooner had one Psy-Fi disappeared did the other one begin to laugh, her visage morphing to that of the Veil, the shape-shifting metahuman with the ability to replicate the appearance and mannerism of anyone she sees. She scanned the grounds until she saw the Single Bullet Theory running for the cliff's edge.

"One down!" she called to him. Despite ignoring the Veil and her locating gaze, his position had been given away. Before the Veil could even realize what she had done, Trace was on a path to intercept the fleeing freak.

"Theory! Now!" I heard a female voice cry out. I spun to see Cusp, still struggling to free herself from the grasp of the police. I turned back in time to see the Theory stop dead in his tracks and take a half-step sideways. He extended his foot and tripped the zooming Trace, who tumbled uselessly, arms and legs flailing, as he disappeared over the edge of the cliff at what had to be over a hundred miles per hour.

Instantly Trey took to the air, shooting like a missile over the edge after his fallen comrade.

"Three down," I said to myself, counting Trey and Andre along with Marta as Centurions who had been effectively removed from the battlefield.

I saw Presto dashing toward the Theory, black cloak fluttering behind him, and Skyscraper rising and stepping over Casey Asylum. The pair converged to capture the skinny, naked man with no powers. The ground shook with each step the Skyscraper took, closing in on his quarry. As the giant neared the cliff, a sound like the Earth cracking open filled the air. As I fell, I saw the ground beneath Skyscraper begin to surrender. His unfathomable weight was too much for the cliff to support. A part of it as big as a football field sliced away, taking with it Skyscraper, Presto, and the Theory.

Deidre shot after them, scorching the air in her wake. She knew, as I did, that Presto couldn't survive that fall, and the only way the Skyscraper would be able to was by growing large enough to make the drop small by comparison, but his fear of heights had no doubt paralyzed him. It was up to her to save them both. I sprinted to the new edge of the cliff and peered over, seeing only the huge dust cloud that was billowing up from the shore of the bay below.

For what felt like minutes there was silence. The inmates had stopped rampaging, their field general now missing in action. The police stood dumbfounded, slowly lowering their weapons as they realized that, whether by sheer luck or ingenious design, a madman had neutralized every last Centurion. Still the seconds ticked by with no sign of any of them. Almost remorsefully, the inmates began to surrender themselves to the authorities, allowing themselves to be handcuffed or fitted with straightjackets.

"Look!" someone called out.

"Up there!" another added, pointing skyward. All eyes turned and saw Helix and Supernova descending from the smoky sky. Supernova had Presto tucked under one arm and Skyscraper, now back to normal size, under the other. Slung unceremoniously over her shoulder was the Single Bullet Theory. Helix was carrying Trace. They were all visibly shaken. In all fairness, the Theory always looked shaken, though.

Helix and Supernova touched down and let their passengers stand gingerly under their own power. The CCPD swarmed the Theory and escorted him from sight, keeping the press at bay as long as they could. The reporters and photographers rushed in and the Centurions began recounting for them the details of yet another day saved, even as the broken asylum burned and the wounded were treated.

"I wear Calvin Klein," Supernova told me from the television. Her toned naked back was to the viewer, watching over her shoulder. She was wearing only a tight pair of jeans and a mischievous smile. "Or nothing at all."

The image changed to a different commercial but it was still Supernova. She threw her head back, ran her hands through her trademark blonde curls and it changed to a deep brunette. She did it again and this time her hair was a fiery red. "I can be whoever I want to be." She held up a bottle of Clairol Nice 'n Easy. "And so can you." Yet a different commercial appeared, this time Supernova was softly lit from behind as she peeled herself out of her costume, slipped into a steamy shower and

150

began washing her hair. "Underneath it all," she cooed. "I'm still me."

Supernova's image and voice were suddenly replaced with that of Eyewitness 8's Lola Oh. "Supernova insists she is still a role model for young girls and women everywhere, despite recent sexually-suggestive televisions ads like these, and her new costume, which leaves very little to the imagination. Has the once squeaky clean heroine traded in her wholesome image for sex appeal? Is Supernova still a role model? We go straight to the source, her own publicist and manger, Morris J. Kidder. It's all next on *Alter Ego*."

Either Deidre genuinely wasn't paying attention to what was on television or she was ignoring it remarkably well. "Marta finally came back about an hour after she left," she told me as she floated into the kitchen. "When she got to 2174, the future-her told the now-her what had happened. I don't know how she keeps it straight."

A commercial came on for the *Century City Journal* Awards. I deflated at being reminded of the awards. Deidre perked up, giving away that she was, in fact, paying attention. A stern-sounding man with a very deep, very dramatic voice told us that this weekend the historic Hawthorne Hotel ballroom would host the 52nd Annual version of the overwrought, dreadful affair, complete with presentations by Century City's alleged best and brightest. He promised us we would see all of our favorite heroes and that we'd also get to find out who was going to win the coveted Hero and Heroine of the Year Awards, as if there was actually some uncertainty.

Deidre's gown for the show had arrived from Milan today, I knew, but she didn't mention it.

"Welcome back to *Alter Ego*," Lola said. "I want to thank you for being with us. Tonight we ask the question: Is Supernova still a role model? In a recent interview in *Meta People* magazine, Supernova said parents shouldn't be worried if their teenage daughters want to copy her."

Deidre's face came back onscreen. "I feel comfortable in my skin. It's okay to express yourself and have that kind of self-confidence. I don't think that's a bad thing to teach girls."

"But there are many who are not sold on the newfound image of Supernova," Lola said.

"Fuck off, Lola," Deidre said as she flopped onto the couch with a bowl of ice cream. "Want some?" she said, holding a spoonful in my face.

I examined it. "I don't like pistachio."

"Yeah, me either."

"Then why are you eating it?"

"Good question. If I don't stop I'm going to look like a busted can of biscuits in my new costume. Maybe Morris could get me a deal with Pillsbury."

I couldn't help but laugh. She unbuttoned her jeans, which were clearly cutting into her belly.

Lola Oh said, "Much of the new criticism aimed at Supernova stems from just how much we're seeing of her suddenly." The TV showed video clips on random people on the street.

"What happened to her costume?" a middle-aged man asked. "It's wintertime, for Christ's sake."

"Honey, put some clothes on and be our Nova Girl again," a grandmotherly type said.

A young couple, arm in arm, strolled up to Alter Ego's camera. The girlfriend said, "I just don't think her new costume is very practical for fighting crime."

The boyfriend shot her a look. "The woman is bulletproof. What's 'practical' got to do with it? She could fight crime in a G-string and still get the job done."

"Just because she can dress like a stripper doesn't mean she should," the girlfriend said.

"Oh, come on!" Deidre snorted.

"I mean, seriously, what's the point?" the girlfriend asked her partner.

"Extra attention?" The reply was tentative.

Deidre said, "Oh, don't be a pussy now." Between bites of ice cream she made a whip-cracking sound. "Wh-pssh!"

The girlfriend said, "Exactly. And you know why she needs the extra attention? Because no matter how many times Supernova saves the day, Helix is always going to get more press simply because he's a guy."

"Thank you!" Deidre raised her spoon.

"It's the same reason children don't learn about Harriet Quimby or Lise Meitner or Black Eagle in elementary school," the girlfriend said.

"Who?" the boyfriend and I said at the same time.

The girlfriend said, "You wouldn't know them. They didn't wear hot pants."

"By the way," I said to Deidre. "Your mom called."

"Shit."

"Yeah. She said you looked like a tramp. Or was it 'jezebel?'"

"Mom would've said 'jezebel.'"

"You know they're right," I said, unable to keep silent anymore.

"Not again, Will."

"Don't you think it's a little silly to be running around in hot pants this time of year?"

"I'm impervious to temperature extremes. You know that. Everybody knows that."

"So you're going to fight crime half-naked, just because you can?"

"What's the big deal, Will? You wanted me half-naked at the Halloween party."

"That was you. We're talking about Supernova."

"In case you haven't noticed, Supernova and I are the same person."

I wanted to disagree with that last statement but I figured I'd help my cause more by changing my tack. "Maybe you should change your name," I offered. "Maybe you should be Wonderbra Woman. Or how about The Nippler?"

Deidre couldn't help but laugh. "Shut up."

"Or maybe Ass Lass?"

"Shut up." She was laughing harder.

"Get Marta into a thong and you guys could form the Just Ass League."

"You'd like that, wouldn't you?"

Lola Oh said, "The five-time Heroine of the Year, whose secret identity as Deidre Donner was revealed last year, has also been criticized recently for drinking in public. Add to this the near-constant tabloid gossiping about her marriage, her money, her health, and you've got to wonder why Supernova would intentionally court controversy with such a calculated image change. With us now is Supernova's publicist, Morris Kidder."

Deidre's Signet Ring began to chirp. "What now?" she asked herself as she tapped the ring's face. "Supernova."

"I need you in the Citadel," Helix replied.

"Be right there," Deidre told him, and then to me she said, "I'll be right back." She handed me her bowl of ice cream and stood from the couch. She sucked in her belly and buttoned her jeans. And then she vanished.

Lola said, "Morris, thanks for being with us."

"Thanks for having me."

"Is there a strategy, a plan, if you will, to Supernova's new image?" Lola asked.

"Well, it's not a new image, Lola. It's simply an updated costume. She's changed costumes before. She used to wear a skirt when she first debuted as Nova Girl. Deidre hasn't set out to become controversial. The goal is to be inspiring and creative, always thinking about young people, because she is such a role model."

"But the parents are concerned that their fourteen-year-old daughter is going to want to dress like this," Lola countered.

Morris came to Deidre's defense. "The youth of this city, of this country, need people like Supernova. And Supernova isn't young. She's married, got kids. But she thinks young. She has a young attitude. There's a message being conveyed here."

I heard Deidre's ring chirping again, this time from upstairs in our bedroom. Wondering what she had forgotten, I trotted up the stairs to see if she needed any help. The bedroom was dark and empty; Deidre wasn't there. But still the ring beeped away noisily. The sound was coming from inside my nightstand. I opened the top drawer and scattered away the crossword puzzle books and cough drops and saw my own Signet Ring, in the back corner of the drawer, where it had lain forgotten for over a year. It wasn't as loud or clear, or as shiny, as it used to be, but it still worked.

I watched the ring for a moment to make sure it was indeed the culprit. But there was no mistaking it. There was an incoming signal for Century Man. I picked the ring up, started to slip it on my finger, and then decided to just hold it. I gave the symbol a tap and Deidre's voice came out.

"Will, it's me," she said. "Are you there?"

"Yeah."

"I was afraid one of the kids would get to your ring before you did. Are they asleep?"

"Yeah. Where are you?" I stepped to the door of our bedroom and pulled it to.

"I'm at the Citadel."

"Is everything okay?"

"Yes," she said, then, "Trey's up here. We're going to—"

Then the ring fell silent. I held it to my ear, but could hear nothing.

"Deidre?" I said into the ring. "Dee?"

There was static and then silence again. Then more static. And then Deidre's garbled voice. "—is that okay? You don't—"

Silence again. I tapped on my ring, wondering if the months of disuse had shorted it out. "Deidre? Can you hear me?"

I listened intently to my Signet Ring for any type of sound that might let me know what Trey and my wife were doing up there. But I couldn't hear anything. Suddenly the ring came back to life and I heard what sounded like the metal-on-metal scraping of the big table in the War Room being pushed across the floor. Deidre said, "Right there, yeah, that's—" before the ring went dead again.

"Deidre? What's going on?" I asked, even though I knew exactly what the answer was. I think a part of me—a foolish part—had been hoping for it. Then the smarter part of me took over and banished those thoughts. They could be doing anything up there, I told myself. Trey might have called an emergency meeting. Maybe some space junk was on a collision course with the Citadel. They could be rearranging the furniture for all I knew. It was none of my business.

The minutes began to accumulate. My ring remained quiet. My mind raced. *What if they're doing it again? What if she's fucking him?* And then the absurdity of that thought hit me. Deidre was my wife. I trusted her. She would never do anything like that. *But she did.* Not without talking to me about it first. Not without asking permission. *But what if she* was *asking permission and I couldn't hear her through my ring?*

I paced around my bedroom. I tried not to listen for their sounds. Then, just as purposefully, I would press the ring to my ear and try to hear something, anything. But I heard nothing.

Five minutes passed. Then ten. With a struggle that bordered on panic I tried not to imagine what was happening on that goddamned satellite. And then I would try to picture exactly that. Did he have her bent over the War Room table? Was she whispering to him about how big it was and how good it felt? Was he going down on her, the oxygen sizzling as Deidre's orgasm burst from her body, her thighs clamped around his head tight enough to crush a normal man's skull? Or was she on her knees for him, eyes glittering up at him, working for his praise and encouragement, following his every command?

No. Of course not. Stop it, you idiot.

It was exactly seventeen minutes and thirty-seven seconds before my Signet Ring came back to life.

"Be right there," Deidre said. She was out of breath. "Clear out a spot in the basement."

Seconds later I heard the zap of a teleportation. I walked down the basement stairs, unsure of what I should even be bracing myself for. Deidre was standing on the hardened steel floor, her arm draped across the back of Century Man's War Room chair.

"Surprise!" she beamed.

I looked around the basement. For what, I'm not sure. Trey, maybe. I said, "I don't understand."

"It's your chair from the Citadel, silly."

"Yeah, I see that. But what were you..."

"I knew you missed this stupid thing, and Trey's been pestering the rest of us for months to dump it in orbit. So I told him if he wanted to get rid of it he'd have to help me haul it onto a transporter." She was still breathing heavily. "Damn thing's heavy. Anyhow, tonight was the first chance we both had to meet up there."

"So, you and Trey..."

"Yeah, it took both of us to move it."

I went to the chair and ran my hand across the stylized shield etched into it. My hands were trembling.

"Say, 'thank you, honey.'" Deidre said.

"Thank you, honey."

"You're welcome." She gave me a kiss on the forehead. "You're sweating. Everything okay?"

"Yeah, yeah. Thanks. Everything's fine."

Chapter Nine
Altered Egos

Space is cold. Even if you're invulnerable. I had withstood direct hits from Frostbite's ice cannons and gone toe-to-toe with Captain Cryo, but I could never get used to the cold I felt whenever I left Earth's atmosphere.

But the silence always made up for it. Pure, absolute silence. No car horns, television sets, mindless conversations, ringing phones, barking dogs, crying babies. Nothing. No need to constantly filter and sift through all that noise to listen for that one alarm, that one cry for help. Not even my super-hearing could overcome the simple fact that sound can't travel in a vacuum.

But there was no time to enjoy the quiet. Not now. I had a job to do.

I was stationed just above the exosphere, waiting, watching. I knew after the threat was averted, Trey would question why I let it get so close to the planet. But I also knew that my best bet for stopping this thing was with the help of atmospheric drag. And I had seventy-five miles of air beneath me. This was my best chance. *Our* best chance. I knew it.

I knew exactly where to be watching for it. And right on cue it appeared, looming out of the blackness of outer space. An asteroid the size of a city. A planet-killer. The White House had known for a week. The media found out only days ago.

Extinction-level event, they kept saying. Global cataclysm. End of civilization.

Not on my watch.

The asteroid hurtled toward me, tumbling end over end, taking up my field of vision completely and still miles away. In mere seconds it closed that gap, and at the moment of impact I stiffened my body against the leviathan and pushed back with all my might. I could see nothing but rocky asteroid around me, my entire peripheral field filled with it in all directions. I had no idea if I had even slowed it yet, but instantly I could feel the heat of reentry. The shock layer gases ignited. We were burning through the atmosphere, the ionization trail visible to the entire Northern Hemisphere. Then the asteroid shuddered with what felt like an earthquake, and the entire thing split in two. I could see the smaller half tumbling away, slowing, splintering further still, breaking into pieces and succumbing to the fiery forces of reentry in a glittering fireworks shower.

But the largest chunk of it was still coming, still barreling down from the sky, pushing me underneath it. The sky was filled with flame and smoke and steam, the sound like the heavens themselves were being ripped asunder. I gathered my strength, gathered my resolve, and renewed my push upwards against it. And again the mammoth cleaved apart, cracking into gigantic halves and drifting apart. I stayed with the biggest of the pair, praying the atmosphere would destroy the other.

We had broken through the scattered cloud cover now, a plummeting fireball, only deep, blue ocean below. Not deep enough, I knew.

Then, as clear as a bell, a voice was in my ear.

"I'll take it from here."

It was Helix, white and emerald and golden in the bright sky. Time had seemingly stopped. Helix was hoisting the asteroid aloft with one hand, the other hand on his hip. We were floating in the sky, motionless. The trail of smoke and fire had frozen behind the giant rock as if in a photograph.

Trey smiled at me. And I woke up.

Deidre was gone again. The sheets on her side of the bed were still warm. My first thought was that she was with him again, but I reminded myself I was married to Supernova, Defender of Peace and Justice, and that I probably woke more mornings without her than with her. I turned on Eyewitness 8 and watched a few minutes of live coverage of the Centurions wrangling what appeared to be, essentially, an overgrown, mutated diplodocus. It stood on the abandoned Century County Fairgrounds, fifty feet tall, and traded ground-shaking blows with the equally gargantuan Skyscraper as Supernova and Helix buzzed the giant green lizard like colorful gnats. Eyewitness 8's Lola Oh, the fight carefully framed behind her, theorized that the creature had been awakened from some centuries-long slumber, or perhaps had come from outer space, or possibly was the rogue creation of SMART Labs.

I got dressed, dutifully grabbed my camera, and drove to the fairgrounds.

I parked a block away and joined the crowd trotting to the police barricades to watch. Through a gap in the spectators I could see the Centurions and the monster. Eyewitness 8's Eye in the Sky hovered just out of harm's way. The onlookers *ooh*ed and *ahh*ed as the heroes set about subduing the rampaging creature. Skyscraper was five stories tall and riding the thing like a cowboy trying to break a bucking bronco. Trey and Deidre were tiny specks of color against the blue sky, orbiting the beast's head and delivering thunderous blows with each pass. Presto lured the creature toward the dilapidated Ferris wheel with the illusion of a giant T-bone steak. As the giant lizard reached through the wheel for the mirage meal, Psy-Fi used that wristwatch of hers to jack into the old ride's controls and set the wheel in motion. The forgotten motors were still strong enough to wrestle the monster to the ground with a calamitous crash of metal and a shower of electrical sparks. Helix swooped down and effortlessly knotted the Ferris wheel's spokes into makeshift handcuffs around the creature's limbs.

The crowd burst into their customary cheering and applause. As I made my way back to my car I heard a familiar phrase.

"Faster than a streak of lightning!"

I turned to see Thana walking quickly to catch up to me. "Stronger than a hundred men! It's the Mighty Century Man!"

"Where?" I snorted, scanning the sky with mock anticipation.

"Figured I'd find you here," Thana said, falling in next to me. "'Stronger than a hundred men.' I always thought that was cool as hell."

"It's just something the guys at the agency came up with," I said, shaking my head. "A long time ago."

"Good show, huh?" she said, glancing back over shoulder. Just then the giant diplodocus bellowed as it tried in vain to free itself from its amusement park prison. Yet more gawkers flocked to the barricades to get a look.

"If you like that sort of thing," I said.

"Where you headed now?"

I had considered simply going back home, and then thought of Jerry's. "Anywhere but here," I told her.

"Mind giving me a lift back to my place?" Thana nodded toward the fairgrounds' parking lot, where half a dozen cars were pressed into the earth inside a giant diplodocus footprint. Among the casualties was her hatchback.

"That sucks," I said.

Thana shrugged. "Good thing I sprang for the rampaging prehistoric beast rider on my auto insurance." I think she was being serious.

We got in my car and left, talking about nothing in particular for a while, both of us stubbornly refusing to mention anything involving capes or tights or giant prehistoric monsters. Thana caved first and brought up the *Journal* Awards, but only because they were happening later tonight, and only in regards to my chances of winning Photographer of the Year. Thana made sure I understood just how *not* pissed she was to not have been invited. I told her about the stuffy after-show party the *Journal* always threw, and she told me about the wild after-party Spandex Ballet always threw. We talked about everything except Supernova and Helix. But I knew it was only a matter of time. We finally seemed to run out of things to say.

Thana said, "What are you doing?"

"What do you mean?"

"Why did you let her do it?"

I was quiet as I thought about the answers to that question. I finally told the truth, "I don't know."

"Don't get me wrong, I don't care. I really don't. I'm the last person to judge. I'm just curious." Thana stopped and thought. "Is it some kind of possession thing? Like, maybe, you want to be the one who takes her home at the end of the night? You want to be the one she chooses. But she has to have a choice, right? If you love something, set it free?"

It almost sounded right.

Thana said, "It must be a hell of a boost to the ego, huh? To be married to the woman everyone wants to fuck. You must feel like Joe DiMaggio when he was married to Marilyn. Only Joltin' Joe hated it."

Thana studied me as I drove, giving me time to think about how to respond. When I was ready I said, "When I first asked her out, I did it as me, as Will. I didn't want to rely on Century Man to get me a date. I didn't even know there was a Deidre yet. All I knew was Nova Girl. It took some convincing, but she finally said yes. Will Donner, freelance photographer, had gotten a date with Nova Girl. When the big day came, as I was waiting on my patio for Nova Girl to fly in, my doorbell rang. When I opened the door, I saw the most beautiful thing I had ever seen in my entire life. She introduced herself as Deidre and explained that she was Nova Girl's cousin. She was so nervous. Or at least she acted like it. Deidre told me that Nova Girl had been called away but had asked Deidre to go on the date with me in her place.

"We had a blast. She was everything Nova Girl wasn't, the opposite of what I thought I wanted. Nova Girl was bold and

162

Skintight

confident, but Deidre was shy and awkward. She wore clothes that hid her figure, wore her hair in a ponytail. She was so sweet and funny. And I fell in love with her.

"It took us a couple of months to figure out who each other really was. But when we did, when we finally realized, well, we... We did it like..."

"Superheroes?" Thana said.

"Exactly. It was amazing. It was as if we had discovered sex for the first time. Imagine: suddenly realizing your girlfriend can fuck like an atomic bomb. We did everything. Anywhere and everywhere. We did it at the poles. We did it in the stratosphere. In the middle of the Sahara. In the middle of hurricanes. On the summit of the Matterhorn; that was our favorite place. That earthquake in Morocco? That was us."

"Nice," Thana said, genuinely impressed, but still missing the point.

I parked my car across the street from Thana's apartment and shut off the engine.

"I want to feel that again," I said. "That discovery. That mystery. Not knowing where the limits were. But determined to find out. I want that again. The other night at the beacon, seeing Deidre with Trey, I felt it then."

Thana nodded, like she understood, even though I knew she couldn't. "So what now? What happens next?" she asked.

"I don't know."

"I'll tell you what happens. You're like the dope fiends you cape-types leave to the police. Each time they have to do a little more to get that same high. Are you going to keep coming back to me, your connection, begging me to hook you up again? Promising yourself there won't be a next time even though you know there will be? When will it be enough?"

"I may have already found out."

Thana looked at me with either admiration or contempt, I couldn't tell which. She got out of the car and came around to my window. A city bus was rumbling to a halt behind us, its brakes squealing and engine hissing. Thana raised her voice to be heard. "Answer one more thing for me before I go: If you still had your powers would you be doing this?" She knew she had asked me a question I had no answer for. "Think about it."

And with that, she turned to cross the street to her apartment. In that moment, the bus driver hit the gas. With no one waiting, he had decided not to stop after all. The bus was going to hit Thana. Without thinking, without a moment's hesitation, I flung open my car door and dashed in front of the bus, scooping Thana into my arms and setting her on her feet on the opposite sidewalk, all before the bus even passed by. It had all taken a second. Maybe half a second.

Thana and I looked at each other, waiting for the other to confirm what had just happened.

She said, "You... did you just...?"

I watched the bus roar past, the driver staring back at me slack-jawed. I said, "That *was* kind of fast, huh?"

"No shit."

For some reason I looked back across the street, as if there would be a clue there.

"Try to fly," Thana said, her voice low, her eyes wide.

"I can't fly, Jinx."

"You're not supposed to be able to run faster than a speeding bus, but you just did."

"No. No, I don't think I did. I didn't. I couldn't have. The bus... it was slowing down, it..."

"Bullshit, Will! We both saw what you just did. Your powers are back."

"No, Thana," I said as calmly as I could. My legs were trembling. "I don't have any powers."

Thana looked at me in disbelief. I shook my head once, as if trying to physically shed my confusion.

I said, "Listen, what just happened scared the shit out me. You, too. It happened really fast. It doesn't mean my powers are back."

She didn't believe it, I knew, but I could tell she wasn't going to argue any more. She simply smiled and said, "Whatever

164

you say." She turned and walked up the steps to her building, then stopped. "So that's what it feels like to have your life saved by Century Man, huh?"

"The bus wasn't even going that fast."

"Oh, stop." Thana smiled at me. "Thank you."

"Any time," I conceded with a nod. Thana disappear into her apartment.

My entire body was tingling. I looked again at the distance I had just covered and tried to make sense of what had happened. I would have never admitted it to Thana, but I did feel something. Something I hadn't felt in a long time. That speed. That strength. What if Thana was right? What if my powers were coming back? Or maybe they were never really gone. Maybe they were just lying dormant, recharging. Maybe. But they couldn't be, could they?

I knew there was only one way to be sure. Instead of getting back into my car, I ducked down the nearest alley, checking to make sure I was alone. I was. I paced for a few minutes, debating whether or not I was actually foolish enough to try this. Then, before I could change my mind, I began to jog down the alley. I broke into a sprint. Faster. I could feel it. I was going to fly. I reached top speed and planted my feet, the springboard that would launch me into the air and into flight.

But nothing happened. I simply jumped a couple of feet in the air and landed again. No higher than any man of my age could jump. I couldn't fly. My forward momentum kept me staggering and I finally slowed to a stop at the end of the alley. I rested my hands on my knees and tried to catch my breath. And all I felt was old. And stupid.

I tried to tell myself I wasn't going to Jerry's simply to drown my sorrows with a couple of other washed-up, past-their-prime skintights. When I walked in the door, though, and saw Curt and Mort right where I knew they'd be, I couldn't help but feel a sort of kinship, even if they had no idea I had ever been a superhero.

We all greeted each other and I pulled up a stool just as Jerry set a beer in front of me.

"Get any pics of the big lizard?" he asked.

I shook my head and took a draw off my beer. "Didn't even bother."

"I don't blame you," Mort said. "That's the third dinosaur attack we've had this year. This one didn't even look that tough."

"It was fifty feet tall, Mort," Jerry barked. "Do you think you could have taken it?"

Curt eyed Mort with a smirk, waiting for his response.

"In my day, sure. See we didn't have all these fancy super-powers and magic rings and whatnot. All we had was these." Mort put up his dukes. "And this." He pointed to his temple. "And a whole lotta this," he said, patting his chest where his heart was.

Curt was convinced and nodded accordingly.

"We would have figured out a way to take care of that overgrown salamander without wrecking an entire amusement park."

Even Jerry couldn't argue with that.

"These kids nowadays, I swear," Mort went on. "They ain't tough. They don't know what tough is. Nowadays it's all about laser beams and alien technology. Back in my day, it was about how good you were with your mitts. And how quick you could think on your feet. These punks today never had to duke it out with Haymaker or Iron-Head. They never scrapped with Steamhammer."

Curt was punctuating each name with an emphatic nod.

Mort said, "And there wasn't a single one of them me and the Night Watchman here didn't take down."

"What about Knuckleduster?" Jerry said, picking up a glass to polish. Mort deflated in a way that only Jerry could make him.

"You would have to bring him up, you bastard."

Jerry was beaming with pride. "Ask him what happened, Willie."

Curt had his face buried in his hands. I looked to Mort for an explanation.

"Knuckleduster got in a lucky shot."

"Knuckleduster knocked his ass out, is what happened," Jerry clarified. "With one punch."

"One punch?" I asked, incredulous. Curt put his forehead to the bar. "Prizefighter got knocked out in one punch?"

"It was a lucky shot!" Mort pleaded. "And besides, he was a big son of a bitch."

"He was big," Jerry conceded. "I fought him in the ring once. Took a beating, too, I did." Jerry picked up another glass to shine. "But at least he didn't knock me out."

"Yeah?" Mort was off his stool, dukes at the ready, fighting back the laughter himself. "You want I should knock you out right now?" Curt, too, seemed ready for action suddenly.

"Then who would serve you beer, you old fart?"

Mort seemed to consider that a very good point and sat back down, laughing in earnest now with his friend.

"He was a mean bastard, wasn't he?" Jerry offered.

"Toughest bastard I ever fought."

"So, who would win in a fight?" I posed to whoever wanted to answer. "Knuckleduster or Helix?"

"Well, that's apples and oranges, Willie. See, Helix's got them fancy powers. Duster was just a man. A big, bad man. But a man, all the same. Helix, he's... well, he's something more."

"Or less," I said under my breath.

"What about Century Man?" Mort asked suddenly. I froze.

"Century Man," Jerry said, almost ruefully. "He was one of the good guys. Maybe the last of the good guys."

Curt nodded.

"Think he could take Helix?" Mort asked.

Jerry didn't answer right away. Curt seemed unsure himself. I did my best to act uninterested.

Mort said, "I mean, assuming he was to come back. From wherever he is. Century Man, that is. And Helix didn't want to give up control of the Centurions. And it came down to the two of them. *Mano y mano.* Who'd win?"

"Helix is stronger," Jerry thought aloud. "But Century Man is smarter."

"Helix is meaner, too," Mort added. "Remember that time Willie's old lady had to pull Helix off of the Underdweller?" We all nodded. "Helix was going to kill him. Hell, he almost did anyhow."

"Yeah, but Century Man ain't no pushover," Jerry countered. "He didn't take any shit off anybody, least of all Helix. Besides, if it ever came down to it, Century Man would have the rest of the Centurions to back him up. And he's got what matters most: Heart."

"Well, it's not like he's coming back, so I guess it doesn't really matter," I said. "He's gone."

Jerry set down one glass and picked up another. "He may be gone, but he ain't forgotten. He'll be back. Wait and see."

Prizefighter and the Night Watchman nodded in agreement. And I could see the hope in their eyes. But I didn't have to heart to tell them just how wrong they were.

It was after dark when I got home. I found Deidre in front of the bedroom mirror, trying on her gown for the *Journal* Awards. From the doorway, I watched as she studied her reflection, standing in profile, smoothing the shimmering gown to her body. It was long and sleek; sleeveless, the same blue as her costume. Arranged on the bed were the candidates for accompaniment to the gown; various shoes and random pieces of jewelry. On the carpet were the scattered rejects; the pumps she had worn to the Halloween party and a diamond bracelet, among others that didn't make the cut.

Deidre slipped on pair of strappy magenta heels and selected a necklace with a pink topaz pendant in the shape of a seven-pointed star. She checked the mirror again, turning this way and that, making sure she liked what she saw. She smiled and nodded to herself, just barely. Approving, Deidre peeled the gown down her body and carefully stepped out of it. Like a

Peeping Tom, I watched my wife undressed until she was wearing only the high heels and a satin thong in Supernova blue.

"Where did you get those?" I said.

Deidre visibly flinched, startled. She looked at me for a second and then slid her hands onto her hips and adjusted the waistband of her panties. She held her head just a little higher and said, "They were a gift, thank you very much." And then she added with a sweet smile, "From someone very special."

"Did he beat off while you modeled them for him?"

Deidre looked like she had been shot. "You gave them to me, asshole."

And, just like that, I remembered: Christmas, two years ago. I had told Deidre that Supernova needed color-coordinated underwear.

"I'm sorry, baby." She wouldn't look at me. "I just... I guess I'm just a little..."

"Don't you fucking dare say 'jealous.'"

"Jealous."

Deidre turned to me. The look on her face had changed from hurt and anger to something else, something a little bit harder to read. Not quite concern, but something akin to it.

"You wanted it."

"I know."

Deidre watched me for a moment before saying, "Do you still want it?"

"Do you love him?"

"What? God, no." She almost laughed at the idea. "No. No."

"Do you think about him?"

"What do you want me to say? Of course, Will. I think about a lot of people. Do you think about..." She paused for a beat to think of someone. "Thana?"

"We're not talking about me. We're talking about you and Trey."

"There is no 'me and Trey.' Don't forget, this was your idea."

"It was *our* idea."

Silence.

Deidre sat on the bed and I sat next to her. I knew my next question was a mistake before I even asked it, but I had to ask it. It was too much not to know.

"Was he better?"

"Don't, Will."

Okay, I told myself. *Stop.*

"How was it different?"

"How was what different?"

"Fucking him," I said bluntly. "You said last time it was different."

"I don't know, baby."

"Tell me. Please."

"He was..." Deidre started and then stopped, maybe to think about what to say. Or what not to say. "Everything was different. The way he smelled. The way he... He was just more... I don't know, Will."

"More what? Just say it. You won't hurt my feelings."

"More... I don't know... Aggressive, maybe?"

"Do you like that?"

"Sometimes, yeah. I guess," Deidre said. "But I like the way we do it, too. We don't always just fuck. We do that too, you know? But Trey just fucks." She seemed to think that was a compliment to me.

"Do you like the way Trey fucks?"

"Come on, baby. Don't do this."

"Just tell me. Did you like the way Trey fucked you?"

"Yes, okay? Yes. I liked the way he fucked me." Whatever had replaced her anger was gone. "I fucking *loved* the way he fucked me, okay? Wasn't that the whole point? This was your idea, don't fucking forget that. You were the one who—"

"Was he better?"

"It's not like that."

"Tell me."

"I'm not going to compare the two of you. I'm just not."

"That's not what I want."

Skintight

"What, then?"

"Just say it."

"What, that he was better? Is that what you want me to say? Does that turn you on?"

I didn't answer.

"Fuck you," Deidre said. "Fuck you."

I grabbed her. I threw her to the floor and tore her panties from her. I shoved myself into her and fucked with all of my strength and all of my shame and all of my guilt.

And afterwards, I lay on the floor, spent. Deidre got to her feet, teetering precariously on her high heels until she found her balance. Her lipstick was smeared across her face.

"Get up," she said. "We're going to be late."

As we cleared the spires of the Marinelli Building, I could see the line of limousines stretching down Wickline Avenue all the way to the intersection of Adademy and Tabor. The *Journal* Awards (or more properly, the *Century City Journal* Awards for Excellence in Metahuman Heroism) had traditionally been held in the ballroom of the old Hawthorne Hotel on Wheeler Boulevard, but that room had been rendered unusable just yesterday by Killshot. He was still at large after the incident at Casey Asylum. By all accounts, Killshot had practically demolished the hotel and then, in true rookie fashion, waited around for the television cameras to show up before announcing his arrival among Century City's villainous elite. Eyewitness 8 had some shaky footage of Killshot spouting the usual blather about getting revenge on the one truly responsible, etc. No one was sure if the hotel's destruction was motivated by anything other than a desire to inconvenience the metahuman community, but either way it did get the guy some pretty good publicity.

So instead, the awards ceremony had been hastily relocated to the Bowman Theater. It was a smaller venue, to be sure, but apparently the only thing available on such short notice. The *Journal* had a man on the ground serving as a makeshift air traffic controller, armed with a prioritized guest list and a com-

171

link with the Centurions, the Peacemakers, the Unnaturals, as well as any other flight-capable metahumans deemed important enough to merit an announced arrival. Morris had promised the *Journal* an exclusive interview with Supernova and consequently had ensured that his client would be the last to land.

I had declined Deidre's offer to fly me in with her for a couple of reasons. It was cold as hell out here tonight, for one thing. It wasn't nearly as cold, however, as the shoulder Deidre was giving me after my regretful line of questioning in our bedroom. I figured we could each use a little time to decompress and suggested I just call a cab. Deidre didn't disagree.

I was making my way into the theater anonymously when I heard a wave of cheers rise from the gathered crowd being kept at bay by the velvet rope. I looked skyward, along with a sea of paparazzi and fans, and saw Deidre descending from the frigid night sky. The searchlights found her and followed her as she floated down to the elevated runway reserved for the arrival of the metahuman nominees. The long blue gown she was wearing made me realize just how strange it is to see a human being in flight. It was something I never noticed when she was in costume.

Deidre touched down on the red carpeted landing platform. "And finally, Supernova!" the announcer's deep voice boomed over the speakers as the flashbulbs and applause erupted. Deidre made her way down the raised walkway, and I followed on the ground level, unseen. As per Morris's pep talk, Deidre ran the gauntlet with aplomb, politely smiled for every photographer and just as politely ignored requests for autographs. *Don't slow down*, he had told her about ten times. *But don't look like you're in a hurry.*

I joined Deidre and we walked into the theater together. Morris was waiting for us just inside the main entrance, safely out of sight and reach of the crowd outside.

"Deidre, my dear," he said, his voice as nasally as ever. If possible, he looked even shorter and wider in a tux. "You look good enough to eat."

He took her hand and kissed it. Deidre smiled and I realized it was the first compliment she had been given this evening, an honor that should have been her husband's, but had been neglected. All I could do was nod and agree.

"Willie, you're a lucky man." Morris took my hand and shook it, his fat, gold watch jangling.

"I know it," I said.

"Do you?" Deidre said to me.

I looked at her. "I really do."

"You better." I thought I could see the slightest smile.

The three of us were escorted to our seats in the front row by a young man in a dinner jacket who took the opportunity to say to Deidre, "You look lovely tonight, Mrs. Donner." And then as we were sitting, he looked past us and said, "Is there anything I can get you, Ms. Thompkins?"

Thana was sitting in the seat next to Deidre's.

"Another one of these," she said, showing the usher her emptied martini glass. She was already drunk. She reached under her butt and pulled out a crumpled card that read *Reserved for Captain Fantastic.*

Before any of us could ask how she got in, let alone was sitting in the front row, Thana said, "Cap decided he'd rather sit in the balcony." And she tossed the card in the floor.

The show was the predicable blend of bad jokes, overlong acceptance speeches, and questionable fashion choices. There was the requisite somber silence during the *In Memoriam* montage. I was almost afraid they'd include Century Man. The awards themselves were just as predictable; the Centurions versus Damage, Inc. was Fight of the Year. They gave Comeback of the Year to Translucent Lad, Rookie of the Year to G-Net-X. Sidekick of the Year went to Alter Boy. The evening's only unscripted moment came when Space Ace was wheeled out to announce Captain Fantastic as this year's recipient of the

Lifetime Achievement Award. By the time Captain Fantastic had made his way down from the balcony, Space Ace had assumed the Captain was unable to attend tonight's ceremony and accepted the honor on his behalf. The only real highlight, other than Deidre winning her fifth consecutive Heroine of the Year award, was a Broadway-style song and dance number spoofing the Hero of the Year nominees. I laughed when they played Helix as a spray-tanned lunk more concerned with ruining his manicure than saving the day, and stopped laughing when their version of Supernova was mistaken for a streetwalker by a chorus line of billy club-twirling Century City police.

I couldn't wait for the whole thing to be over but I was equally dreading the *Journal*'s after-show party and a concentrated dose of Morris Kidder. I tried to keep my mind off it by people-watching. No matter how many times I saw it, it was always humorous to see people dressed in tuxedos and evening gowns while also wearing masks and cowls.

After Helix was given his first Hero of the Year award and had thanked God, his mom, and the Centurions, especially Supernova, for making it all possible, the house lights came up, the crowd rose in unison and everyone began to file out. Thana grabbed Deidre and me by the hand, holding us back as Morris disappeared into foot traffic.

Thana looked Deidre up and down. She licked her fingertip and touched it to Deidre's hip. "*Tsss*," Thana hissed. "Hot as hell."

Deidre blushed and smiled. "Thanks. You look amazing."

I got my first good look at Thana. She was in red, as she always was when she wanted to make an impression. Her dress was clingy, short, and had a neckline that plunged like a kamikaze. Standing next to Deidre in her shimmering sheath of cyan satin, they made quite a pair. Thana and Deidre were both right, they each looked amazing.

"Wait until we hit the dance floor," Thana said.

"Dance floor?" Deidre asked.

Thana nodded. "We're going dancing."

"We've got the *Journal*'s after-party to attend," Deidre explained. "I would love to, but..."

Thana draped her arm around Deidre's neck. "You're not going to the party," Thana said. "We're going dancing."

"We're going dancing," Deidre repeated, as if it were self-evident. And then to me, she said it again. "We're going dancing."

I didn't argue. As bad as I hated dancing, it was a welcome reprieve from Morris. We were joined suddenly by a tuxedoed Trey, Andre, and Rudy, who seemed to already know the plan. The obligatory congratulations were passed all around. Everyone, even Thana, was quick to pat Andre and Rudy on the back for their Best Partners award. In somewhat of an upset, they beat out the Solar Sisters, due mainly, I was sure, to their tandem rescue last year of President Needham and Marine One. It was an award Deidre and I had won just two years ago.

"Nice job, guys," I told them.

Andre flashed a smile and held up his golden statuette, buffing its head with his tuxedo sleeve." Thanks, man. Fastest I've ever run. I still have nightmares about those helicopter blades." He shuddered. "Hell, Rudy here still has the scars."

Rudy held up his hands to show me the crisscrossing lines the rotors gave him when he cradled Marine One in his palms. "It was the hurt," the big German said, and everybody laughed, including Rudy, even though he no idea what we were laughing at.

"Gang's all here," Thana spoke up. "Let's go."

Chapter Ten
Turbines To Speed

The six of us left the theater through a service door in the rear. A security guard had politely tried to shepherd us back toward the front, but Thana stroked his cheek with the back of her hand and told him he never saw us. We walked past him and out the back door, the guard seemingly staring right through us.

"Look," Deidre said, nudging me as we stepped out into the cold night. She was looking down a side alley. There, parked between a pair of dumpsters and bathed in a halo of light from the streetlight above, sat Captain Fantastic's personal crime-fighting vehicle, the Fantasti-Coupe.

"What the hell?" Andre said.

Thana snickered. "I bet that old bastard got lost looking for the valet."

"Poor guy," I said.

We all walked to the car to have a closer look. Despite being designed in the Seventies, it still looked futuristic and fast. It sat, crouched and poised, its wedge-like shape punctuated with fiberglass fins and louvers and spoilers meant to slice through the air like a knife. The engine looked ready to spill forth from its bay behind the bubble-shaped cockpit, bristling with chrome implements of speed.

Thana peered inside. "He left the fucking keys in it." She opened the driver's side door and turned to the group. "Who wants to go for a ride?"

Andre sneered at the Fantasti-Coupe. "I'll be at the club by the time y'all get that antique cranked. Come on, Rudy. Race ya." And with that, Andre disappeared in a whoosh of swirling debris.

"Verdammt noch mal," Rudy sighed and then quickly began to enlarge his body. His rented tuxedo popped at the seams and fell away in tatters until he was wearing only his malleable black and yellow bodysuit. He grew until he was able to simply stride over the neighboring buildings. The ground beneath our feet shuddered with each step until he was a couple of miles away, trying uselessly to keep up with the Fastest Man on Earth .

"You're driving," Thana said to me, rounding the car and opening the passenger entry.

"We're just going to steal the man's car?" I asked.

"We'll bring it back," she said. "That's called borrowing."

Deidre had joined Thana on the other side of the car. "Come on," she said. "Let's be adventurous."

I looked at my wife and then down at the most famous car in Century City. "I have always wanted to drive this thing," I said, a stupid smile creeping across my face. "We'll bring it back, right?"

"Not a scratch," Thana said. She dragged her ruby fingernails across Deidre's bare shoulder. "Get in the back." Without a word, Deidre climbed into the backseat of the Fantasti-Coupe. Thana gave me a wink and joined Deidre in the backseat of the cockpit. Trey rounded the car and sat in the front passenger's seat.

I slid behind the wheel and surveyed the bank of controls before me. My eyes roamed over the array of switches, knobs and levers, all with embossed label tape affixed beneath. *Smoke Screen, Fantasti-Ray, Oil Slick, Fantasti-Jump, Ejector Seat, Fantasti-Scope, Fantasti-Zooka.* I glanced through the forked spokes of the steering wheel and there, right where Thana had said they were, were the Fantasti-Keys, dangling in the *Ignition Control.*

I hit the starter, which was followed by the unmistakable sound of a vintage American V8 engine growling to life.

"Wait," Thana said from the back, obviously expecting something more akin to a rocket launch. "What about all that 'atomic turbines to speed' stuff Cap used to say before starting the car?"

"It was all bullshit," I said. "I take my car to guy who used to know the guy who worked on the Fantasti-Coupe. It's a Ford 302."

"What about all those things?" she said, pointing to the gadgets on the dash.

"Those are legit."

"Good," Thana said. "I was beginning to think everything I held dear was a lie."

"Shit," Deidre suddenly said. She was looking through the back on the cockpit's canopy.

I looked in the rearview mirror and saw an elderly man in spandex and a cape directing a pair of security guards our way. "It's Captain Fantastic."

"Go, go, go!" Deidre chanted.

I revved the engine and it snarled with power, filling the alley with a window-rattling roar. I shifted into first gear and popped the clutch just as a security guard lunged for the car's door handle. The roar of the engine, low in the throat, was bass to the screeching treble of the tires spinning on the pavement. The Fantasti-Coupe shot forward. In the mirror I could see the guard belly-flopping to the ground.

I found the *Forward Illumination* switch and flipped it.

"Dead end!" Deidre called out. In our headlights was a solid brick wall. I cranked the wheel hard and jammed my foot into the brake pedal, power-sliding the car to a halt with its nose aimed back the way we'd come. In the back, Deidre and Thana were bracing themselves, looking for something to grab hold of. Trey never budged.

I gunned the motor, the whole car twitching and twisting like a caged beast. The security guards were crouched and cowering, awaiting our next move. Behind them, Captain Fantastic was pointing and shaking his fist. I tightened my grip on the wheel and kicked the gas pedal to the floor. The car pounced forward, the bellowing engine drowning out the barked orders of the guards and angry threats of the Captain. They all dove aside as we charged through, tumbling and rolling to the edges of the alley.

"Sorry, Cap!" Deidre called out, knowing the man couldn't hear her. She laughed.

We bounded out of the alley onto Wickline Boulevard. The street was still teeming with Century City police keeping the paparazzi at bay as the awards show attendees made their exits. I floored the gas pedal, fishtailing and weaving, wrestling the wheel and shifter simultaneously. Adrenaline surged through my veins. I split a pair of parked black and white cruisers and wound through the gears, ignoring the speedometer. The Fantasti-Coupe gathered speed, building momentum, our bodies pressed deep into the seats.

In the rear view mirror, a *V*-shaped phalanx of police cars immediately formed, blue lights dancing on each roof.

"Shit," Deidre and Thana said in unison, craning their necks to see.

I threaded the needle of traffic waiting at the intersection of Academy and Tabor Avenue, straddling the two lanes down the middle. I glanced at the passenger's side mirror just as it clipped a stopped car and was amputated, sent flying in a rain of glass and plastic. In the rearview I watched the police cars replicate my maneuver, minus the mirror smashing.

"Do something!" Deidre called from the backseat. I watched the cops in the mirror. I counted five of them. I glanced at Trey; he was watching me, saying nothing, smiling ever so slightly. I scanned the dashboard and stabbed a finger at the first button I thought might help us: *Oil Slick.* In the mirror I could see a steady flow of thick black liquid issuing onto the pavement in our wake, creating a gleaming ribbon of slipperiness. Our closest pursuer realized too late what it was and tried to swerve to avoid the oil, only to send his cruiser into a flat spin. He collided with a fire hydrant and catapulted into a barrel roll before landing roof down on the sidewalk. Thana clapped her hands.

"You think he's okay?" Deidre wondered aloud, echoing my own thoughts.

Trey said, "He's fine." And he was probably right. CCPD cruisers were some of the safest in the country, thanks in no small part to their propensity for getting tossed around and stomped on like Matchbox cars on a regular basis.

In the mirror I could see the other police cars taking a lesson from their dispatched partner and weaving around the oil slick. We closed on slower traffic and I sawed the steering wheel left, banking and drifting into the oncoming lane and then darting back into our own lane just before we would've collided head-on with a delivery truck.

I flipped the *Smoke Screen* toggle switch. A roiling cloud of white smoke billowed behind us, engulfing the police cars until their sweeping blue lights were the only evidence they were still back there. Despite their sudden blindness, the cops again tried to copy my move, the first three somehow slipping through, the fourth scraping its rear quarter panel against the delivery truck in a shower of sparks. The police officer lost control, his cruiser ricocheting off the road until he came to rest against a light pole, facing the other direction.

"Two down," Thana confirmed.

"Three to go," I said.

Deidre chimed, "This is fun!"

We sped away from downtown, the cop cars in hot pursuit. The entrance to the Century Centre Mall loomed ahead and at the last moment I pulled hard on the wheel and dove into the shopping center's sprawling parking lot. I downshifted and aimed the Fantasti-Coupe toward the most heavily occupied section.

"What are you doing?" Deidre yelped.

180

"They'd be crazy to follow us, wouldn't they?"

The three police cars converged and fell in behind me, blue lights flashing in the rearview. I wove around parked cars, shifting gears, braking hard and then accelerating harder, speeding through gaps. Our pursuers were more cautious, allowing me to put precious distance between them and us. I scanned the throughways for pedestrians and oncoming cars, swerving at the last second to avoid a shopper making her way through the parking lot. She froze and watched the Fantasti-Coupe streak past, a familiar site in this town. Police cars chasing after it, however, were not.

I pushed the gas pedal down, pointing the car to the far side of the parking lot, toward the Century Centre Cineplex. I steered the car into the more thickly populated part of the parking lot, the openings between cars become scarcer and narrower, where they existed all. I hooked around a line of cars and then shot the gap between a pair of minivans. Two of the cops made it; the third smashed headlong into a van with a spray of shattered windshield and venting steam.

The remaining pair of Century City's Finest still in tow, we hurtled past rows of parked vehicles. I reached toward the dash again and triggered the *Fantasti-Ray*. From the back of the car, a crackling bolt of red energy lanced toward one of the police cars, slicing through its engine compartment effortlessly. There was a brilliant orange flash of light in the rearview and I saw the fragmented remains of the black and white cruiser tumbling across the pavement.

"One to go," Deidre said, grinning, bouncing her fists on her knees.

I raced toward the exit nearest the Cineplex, aiming for the open road beyond.

"Bad move," Trey said, perfectly calm.

I looked to my destination and saw a line of cars, all departing the Cineplex after a screening on the Captain Fantastic movie. They were waiting on a red light and blocking our escape route. I redirected us to the outer reaches of the

181

parking lot, where the twenty foot tall inflatable Captain Fantastic stood lazily swaying, hands on his hips, chest puffed out like a hot air balloon.

Still the lone police car gave chase, siren blaring, mimicking my every move. I pinned the accelerator against the floorboard and looked at Trey.

"Fantasti-Zooka?" he asked.

"Fantasti-Zooka."

Strangling the wheel, knuckles going white, I pointed the Fantasti-Coupe at the giant blow-up Captain. Trey flipped the switch and the entire car shuddered. With a deafening *FWOOSH*, a rocket fired from the front of the car, spewing sparks and smoke behind it. It sunk into the inflatable superhero's hindquarters and exploded, a blinding fireball lighting up the night sky.

"Bullseye!" Deidre cheered.

Immediately the Captain behind to deflate, a plume of flames bursting forth from his shredded tarpaulin buttocks as he collapsed. Unsure which way he was going to fall, I knew we had only one sure escape. I punched the button on the dashboard labeled *Fantasti-Jump*.

With a jarring thud, we were suddenly airborne, bounced off the pavement by a pneumatic jack beneath the car. We cleared the hunched-over Captain by a few feet at most, his deflating face smiling weakly at us as we floated past. And still we climbed. The Fantasti-Coupe soared through the air, listing ever so slighting to the port side, sailing in a long arc over the shrinking hero. We followed a rainbow trajectory, our flight path taking us well above the stoplights and power lines of the intersection. At the apex of our jump I looked out the window in time to see the final police car being smothered by the flaming and limp remains of Captain Fantastic.

We fell to Earth with a bone-rattling crash of buckling metal and twisting sub-frame. We bounced once, the car banking hard before righting and giving itself back over to my control. I shifted gears and floored it once more, pushing the Fantasti-

Coupe faster and faster still until the cityscape smeared into a blur in my peripheral.

We ditched the Fantasti-Coupe, steaming from a busted radiator, a couple of blocks away from Spandex Ballet and walked the rest of the way. Deidre and Thana carried their high heels in their hands, walking down the road barefoot. By the time we got to the club, most of the adrenaline from the chase had worn off but the girls were still giggling.

Thana led us into the club and all the way to the back, weaving through the crowd like a shark. Waiting for us in a deep semi-circular booth were Andre and Rudy, empty glasses scattered on the table in front of them. Andre was still wearing his tuxedo but had lost the jacket and loosened his bowtie. Rudy had apparently purchased a hooded sweatshirt from the club to wear over his Skyscraper bodysuit, *Biff!* and *Pow!* embroidered on the chest. He and Andre slid over and made room for us.

As Deidre excitedly recounted to Andre and Rudy our evasion of the law, a teenage girl in a bondage version of Night Angel's costume came by and took our beverage orders. Andre pointed out that we were many drinks behind he and Rudy and had some catching up to do. The club seemed even louder and more crowded than it did when I met Thana here. All around us, young people with tattoos and multi-colored hair bounced to the incessant beat. Above us, two half-naked men writhed in a cage. One was perpetually pretending to try to disarm the other of a large, plastic ray gun.

Thana nodded up at them and then said to me, "Sincerest form of flattery." I looked at the two men again and realized I was watching a sort of S&M reenactment of Century Man's fight with Gravitron.

And then Thana asked everyone, loudly, "So, who wants to fuck Supernova tonight?"

Deidre flinched. Andre and Rudy were confused, but Trey just laughed and started on his drink.

"Don't mind me," Thana said. "I might already be a little drunk." She was. She slid out of the booth and took Trey by the hand. "You're dancing with me." He offered no resistance and the two of them went out to the dance floor.

As soon as Trey and Thana were out of range, Rudy asked in his broken English, "We are to be tonight fucking *Dye*-dre?"

"In your dreams, Rudy," Deidre laughed, trying to act appropriately befuddled by Thana's remarks. She punched Rudy in the bicep, a little too hard.

"And it's pronounced *Dee*-dre, you fucking Nazi," Andre said. Rudy laughed.

"Do not forget," Rudy said. "I can step on you."

Andre said, "Like your big schnitzel-eating ass could catch me." Rudy laughed harder.

"And the award for Best Partners goes to Trace and Skyscraper," I said.

"I want to dance," Deidre said, not giving her teammates a chance to inquire further about what Thana had said. Deidre was up and ready, pulling me by my wrist. "Come on."

"No way."

"Come on, baby. I want to dance."

"You know I don't dance."

"Please." She was tugging at me like a child.

"Nope."

"Goddamn," Andre finally said. "Watch out, man." He slid out of the booth, took Deidre by the hand and led her onto the floor. Deidre glanced over her shoulder as the crowd absorbed them, checking to see if I was watching.

"Fastest Man on Earth," Rudy said. We were the only two left at the booth.

"Seriously, congrats on the award," I said.

"Yes. It will go to collect the dust with the others." He chuckled a little and then got serious. "But it is not the same without Century Man."

I thought suddenly about how I had kept Thana from getting flattened by a city bus earlier, then tried to forget it.

184

"Trey is doing a good job," I said.

"You are a liar," Rudy laughed. He took a swig of his beer and changed the subject. "It is rare thing you have. Strong and beautiful woman. You are lucky man."

Like earlier with Morris, all I could do was nod.

I looked to the dance floor and watched Andre dancing with my wife, pressing his body into hers as they moved to the pulsing music. Trey appeared, without Thana, and joined them. The three of them danced together, Trey and Andre taking turns dancing with Deidre, and then sometimes all three would dance together. I couldn't help but think of the Livewire video.

The bodies surrounding the three of them parted and Deidre saw me watching. From in between Trey and Andre she motioned for me to join them. For a moment, I actually considered going out there. Deidre eventually lost interest in trying to convince me and instead focused on the two partners she already had. She moved between them, her arms in the air, her head back.

"You must be loving this," Thana said suddenly, materializing at the table with a fresh drink. "Scoot over."

More drinks arrived and, prompted by Thana and the alcohol, Rudy began to give his honest opinion on his teammates.

"You're among friends here," Thana told him.

With each drink, Rudy became increasingly honest. He couldn't stand Andre, Thana and I learned, "And not just because he thinks I am Nazi." I listened to Rudy, nodding occasionally, responding when necessary, but never once taking my eyes off my wife.

Thana asked Rudy what he thought about Trey. Rudy said he wanted to take on more responsibility within the Centurions but Trey wouldn't have it. "He thinks I am man who only can get big," he added, his English worsening with each drink.

"What do you think of Deidre?" Thana asked.

"Deidre is strong," Rudy nodded. "Strong leader."

"No," Thana said, lowering her voice. "What do you really think about her?"

"I like Deidre," Rudy said, still not going where Thana was leading him.

"Would you do her?"

"I do not understand."

"She's messing with you, Rudy," I bluffed.

"Would you fuck her?" Thana slapped a hand on my back. "Because Century Man here will let just about anyone bang his wife. Isn't that right, Century Man?"

"Fuck you, Thana."

"This is true, Will?" Rudy asked, as hopeful as he was confused.

Deidre, Trey, and Andre suddenly appeared at our table, sweating and smiling, grateful for the refills Thana had ordered for them. I braced myself for whatever might come out of Thana's mouth next.

It was, "Let's get out of here. I know a better place." She whispered something to Andre and he used his Signet Ring to call a cab.

We left Spandex Ballet and got in the taxi, a minivan big enough to hold all six of us. Deidre asked where we were going but Thana either didn't hear the question or simply ignored it. Either way, Deidre didn't ask again. The ride was short and when the cab came to a stop we were in the parking lot of Secret Identity.

Deidre said, "Isn't this a strip club?"

"Yes, ma'am. It truly is," Thana replied as we piled out of the van.

"Is this the place where the bitches dress like superheroes?" Andre asked.

"Like you don't have a membership," Trey was quick to reply.

"You do not need membership," Rudy added. There was a silent pause, and everyone except him burst out laughing. "It is true," he said earnestly.

186

Skintight

Deidre hung in the back of the group as we made our way to the club's front door. Thana waited and took Deidre's hand to walk with her.

"Don't be afraid," Thana said. "It's just boobies."

"I'm not afraid," Deidre laughed.

"Good. Let's have some fun."

Deidre nodded. "Let's have some fun."

The club seemed fairly empty to me, considering it was a Saturday night. I had expected it to be as packed as Spandex Ballet, but maybe with the awards show being on TV, guys who got hard-ons from watching superheroes had already gotten their fill tonight.

It had been years, before I was married, in fact, since I was in a strip club but it was obvious that things hadn't changed much. The place was sparsely populated with an odd collection of people representing disparate social strata. Some were alone, others were in small groups. I was quick to dismiss all of them as lonely, frustrated perverts and then I had to remind myself that I was currently one of them. Only Thana's barked announcement that we should sit in the back turned any heads at all.

A smoky, perfumed haze filled the room, making the colored laser beams and neon lights seem to glow that much brighter, tiny specks of light dancing all around, reflected off the mirror ball spinning over the stage. The music was painfully loud, blaring from a pair of amplifiers suspended from the ceiling. After the pulsing electronic soundtrack of Spandex Ballet, the strip club's hair metal sounded somehow antiquated and potent at the same time.

Deidre stuck close to me, trying to make herself as small as possible as she clung to my arm, not quite ready to make good on her parking lot promise to have some fun. Thana steered us toward the rear of the club and picked a table in the corner.

On the runway, a girl who was supposed to be the Tigress was in the middle of her act, fuzzy tail, whiskers and all. A slow but steady flow of patrons made their way to the edge of the stage to slide dollar bills into her tiger-striped thong. Trey and Andre were talking and laughing with Thana, but the music was too loud to hear what about. Tigress wrapped up her performance and disappeared backstage at least fifteen dollars richer.

Deidre hadn't said a word since we arrived. She was sitting quietly, sipping her drink and nervously eyeing the clientele, like she was afraid that at any moment she would be recognized, or that maybe she would have to hit someone with a Nova Blast. A Latina version of Rocket Queen appeared and asked if any of us were interested in a lap dance. No one accepted, but Andre seemed to consider it before sending her away.

"This is so bad," Deidre finally said. She looked around. "Look at these guys. They're in love. They think this is real."

"Wait," I said. "I seem to remember someone's bachelorette party that included a trip to see Apollo's Army?"

Thana nodded.

Deidre said, "Okay, for starters, that's a touring troupe. We were at a nightclub, not some skeevy joint with an adult bookstore next door. And anyhow, it was all a goof. We did it for laughs. Nobody was getting off on seeing dudes dance around in fireman costumes."

Thana took a sip of her martini and said, "Speak for yourself, honey."

We all laughed. The DJ reminded everyone that in less than an hour their Weekly $500 Amateur Contest would begin, eliciting a few errant whoops from the audience. He then told us to welcome to the stage Starface, which about half the club did with a smattering of applause.

Thana leaned to Deidre and said, "One of us is winning that $500 tonight."

Deidre looked at her with disbelief. "Excuse me?"

"Why do you think we came here?" Thana said. "These pervs want to see super-ladies get naked, then dammit, that's what we'll give them."

"You go right ahead," Deidre laughed.

Thana laid a calming hand on Deidre's arm. "Let's do it. Why not?"

Deidre seemed to actually consider the idea suddenly.

"What about it, Century Man?" Thana asked, "Want your wife to take it off?"

I tried to read Deidre's expression, and make sure I gave the answer she wanted me to. But before I could try, Thana said, "Who am I kidding? Of course you do. How about you, Rudy the Skyscraper? Want to see Supernova get naked?"

Rudy's eyes lit up. He said something in German that was obviously in the affirmative.

Thana pointed at Trey and Andre. "And you know these horny bastards here want you to." She squeezed Deidre's hand. "See? Come on. What do you say?"

Deidre nodded, slightly and slowly at first, then emphatically. "Let's have some fun."

Rudy clapped his hands together. Trey and Andre just shook their heads and chuckled. I watched Deidre and tried to figure out if she really wanted to do it or if she was just trying to appear as impulsive as Thana. Either way, my wife quickly seemed to warm up to the idea, helped along no doubt by the alcohol, not to mention the enthusiastic encouragement of Rudy and Thana. I didn't say anything; I didn't try to discourage her. *Adventurous.*

Starface finished dancing and the DJ told us that anyone entering the $500 Weekly Amateur Contest should come backstage now. Without a word, Deidre and Thana stood.

"Knock 'em dead," I said to my wife as she went with Thana backstage, joined by only a handful of other contestants.

The four of us that were left sat and drank in silence for the next few songs, turning down lap dances and watching a continuous stream of girls shake their bodies on stage. There was a fantasy for everyone; a female version of American Eagle, a more-naked version of Ghost Girl, even a take on Laura Lark, Captain Fantastic's old girlfriend from the *Century City Journal.*

Finally the time had arrived, the DJ announced, for the amateur contest, and the sudden pounding in my chest made me realize just how bad of an idea this was. I knew Deidre wouldn't embarrass herself; she could dance. Every man at my table had just borne witness to that at Spandex Ballet. I knew she could strip, too; she had done it for me on more than one special occasion. But this was altogether different. She was going to strip for a room of drunk strangers, some of whom might recognize her and whip out their cell phones and give Lola Oh even more ammunition. Deidre would also be stripping for four men she knew very well indeed.

The first amateur, the DJ informed us, was Dyna-Girl, and she came out wearing a bikini and a pair of black combat boots, which actually was a fairly good approximation of the real Dyna-Girl's costume. She spent her entire song swinging around the chrome pole at the end of the runway. As the song faded, she finally dropped her top, prompting maybe two or three half-hearted cheers from the suddenly low-key crowd.

Dyna grabbed her bikini top and quickly slipped backstage as Devil Doll was introduced next. Devil Doll had actually put some thought into her costume, going so far as to paint her skin red and fashion her trademark pitchfork out of a broom handle, some clothes hangers, and spray paint. She was only slightly more popular than Dyna-Girl but it was easy to feel what little excitement was in the room slowly fade as each new amateur took the stage in homemade costumes and stumbled through every late-night stripper movie cliché imaginable.

And then Thana appeared. The DJ introduced her as Jinx. He had no clue that she was the genuine article. She emerged from the backstage curtain just as a the slinky riff of Ratt's "Slip of the Lip" began to pump through the speakers. She was still wearing the short red dress she'd worn to the awards. She stalked down the runway in high heels, peeling off her tight dress until she was wearing only her panties and stilettos.

The mood in the club instantly became more charged. Whistles and applause filled the room as men were lured to the

190

edge of the stage by Thana's lithe body and exposed breasts. She spiraled acrobatically around the smooth chrome pole, sliding her hands down it as she sank to the stage. She rolled to her back and grabbed her ankles, pulling her long legs far apart, giving everyone an unobstructed view.

Andre and Trey high-fived like a couple of frat boys. Rudy and I watched quietly, but every bit as intently, as Thana got to her feet and stood directly over the man front and center at the end of the stage. She threaded her fingers through the man's hair and held his head as she grinded the lacy crotch of her panties over his face. She freed him and backed away, and the man simply stood and stared up at Thana with a stupid, bewildered smile on his face. She pulled the waistband of her panties away from her hip and he slipped a crisp dollar between. Thana let the elastic snap back against her skin, holding the bill firmly in place.

Andre laughed, shaking Trey by his big shoulders and pointing to the stage. The pair was positively giddy by now. The next man at the stage also surrendered his dollar, as did every other patron who waited patiently to see Jinx up close and personal. She danced until everyone had a chance to pay for a look, staying long after her song was over and halfway into the next. Finally, at the DJ's urging, she left the stage, her underwear garnished with a fringe of dollar bills. The loudest cheer of the night so far followed Thana through the backstage curtain.

The next and final amateur, the DJ said, was Supernova. My heart leapt into my throat. The throbbing beat of "Smooth Up in Ya" by Bulletboys pulsed through the amps. The curtain parted and Deidre stepped through as the song hit full stride. She had transformed backstage and was wearing her new two-piece costume. It looked downright conservative in this setting.

Any fears I had about Deidre having performance anxiety were immediately dispelled. She strutted down the runway proudly, hands on her hips, the heels of her magenta boots hitting the stage in perfect time to the beat. The crowd was electric. No one present, former and current Centurions excluded, realized they were seeing the real Supernova.

Trey and Andre sprang to their feet and pushed to the stage; Rudy and I followed. We worked our way among Deidre's other admirers just as she reached the edge of the runway and began to dance. She glanced down and saw the four of us, and didn't miss a beat. Her hips swirled and wheeled, her shoulders swam, blonde hair trailing about her jawline as she spun.

She coiled around the pole and touched the tip of her tongue to it, licking up and down its length as she sank to a crouch and then rose again. Trey caught my eye and gave me a nod, acknowledging the fact that we both knew exactly what it felt like to have Deidre do that, like we were part of some secret club. Like we had some kind of bond.

Deidre snaked through the neon haze, her body eclipsing the fanning beams of lasers. She wrapped her arms around herself and snatching the top of her costume over her head. She let the top fall away, revealing her naked breasts, hardened nipples betraying her excitement. She danced like a flame, hands over her head, breasts bouncing. Her face was flush, arms coiling above her head like wisps of smoke.

The crowd wanted more, calling loudly for Supernova to take it all off. Deidre's eyes were bright with obvious excitement as she tugged at the cyan trunks that made up the bottom half of her costume. She stepped closer to the edge of the stage, teasing at removing this last article of clothing from her body. Hands were suddenly all over her, squeezing and grabbing, pulling at her costume. In the stage lights I couldn't be sure, but I thought I saw a shimmering veil of blue energy sheathe her body for a split-second before it disappeared just as quickly.

Deidre stepped back, just out of arms reach but still dancing. She hooked her thumbs behind the waist of her shorts, shimmying them over her hips and down her legs before stepping out of them, flipping them into the crowd with a kick. Naked now except for her boots and the blue satin thong I had interrogated her about earlier, she waved to the adoring crowd and trotted back down the runway, the lone spotlight illuminating the crescents of her ass. Then she was gone, disappeared behind the curtain as her song faded, chased by a round of raucous applause.

No sooner had she departed than the DJ declared her the contest's winner and called her back onstage. Supernova stood on the runway, panties still stuffed full with dollar bills, and beamed as she hoisted the big poster-board check for $500 over her head.

It was well after two a.m. when we left Secret Identity. Deidre had gotten back into her gown since most of her Supernova costume was long gone. Trey and Andre were quick to volunteer to ride in the back of the taxi with the women and Rudy sat in the middle row of the van with me.

All the way home Thana and Deidre frolicked and giggled in the backseat, throwing money at each other. When the laughter finally quieted down I glanced over my shoulder, expecting to see the two passed out. Instead I saw that Deidre had slid to her knees in the floor, her head moving between Thana's thighs. Trey and Andre were staring unabashedly, their eyes wide.

"Suffering Sappho," Andre grinned, elbowing Trey in the ribs.

Rudy had turned around now, watching with the rest of us. "Ach, man," he uttered as he looked on.

I peered into the backseat, watching the women. I could see Thana, breathing heavy, sinking into the seat, running her fingers through Deidre's hair. I could hear Thana talking softly to Deidre, telling her how good at this she was, and then I could hear Deidre, moaning into Thana's pussy.

"You are *sooo* beautiful," my drunken wife slurred as she came up for air. Her lipstick smeared across her face, cheeks flush and chin red from the abrasion. Deidre smiled up at Thana and then went back down. She didn't stop until we got to Thana's apartment.

Thana walked to the cabbie's window, tugging down her dress. She gave him a peck on the cheek and told him he would forget he had ever seen us. He nodded, repeating her words back to her, and drove away. We followed Thana into her apartment and she locked the door behind us. Thana spent a few minutes lighting the dozens of candles that were scattered throughout and then told us to make ourselves comfortable while she made everyone something to drink, and then she disappeared into the kitchen. Deidre sunk into the sofa, drunk and exhausted, her face still red.

Thana came back and divvied out various and sundry cocktails, all in martini glasses, then disappeared again, this time down the hallway. She returned moments later with a laptop. She opened it on the coffee table, clicked on a folder called *Super Friends* and then found the file she was looking for: *HyperB.mov*.

"A little something to set the mood," Thana said. As we watched, an image came on the monitor of Thana herself, naked and on all fours. Mounting her from behind, just as naked, was the Hyperborean.

Thana laughed when she saw the confusion on my face.

"What's wrong, Will?"

I didn't know what to say that wouldn't sound completely naive, so I said nothing.

"Oh, I know," Thana went on. "He's a bad guy, right? A *villain*. I should only fuck the good guys, is that it?"

Trey and Andre laughed a little. I tried to ignore their laughter, tried to ignore my confusion. After the drinks I'd had, it was easy. Thana opened more files and I concentrated on the images on the screen. In short time I had seen Thana blow both Toxic Twins, do it doggie-style with the Lycan, and fuck all three of Mister Schizo's personalities. At one point in a video, Thana was alone and appeared to be having a seizure of some sort in a public restroom.

"You can't tell," Thana explained. "But right there I'm getting fucked by C-Thru."

194

I could hardly believe what I was seeing. This wasn't some porno movie. This was Thana. We watched more. There was nothing, or no one, she wouldn't try.

As the rest of us watched the videos, Thana began rearranging her living room, pushing tables to one side, moving away a floor lamp, clearing the floor before going to Deidre and taking her by the hand. Thana led Deidre to the center of the room, then left her there and sat next to me on the sofa. Thana had her phone in her hands.

"Don't be shy, boys," Thana said. "We all know why we're here."

Deidre looked at me. This was my chance, I knew, to stop this if I wanted to. I said nothing, and that was all the permission any of them needed.

Trey, Andre, and Rudy rose and converged on Deidre. The three men began stripping my wife's gown from her, tugging it off her shoulder and working it down her body until it lay around her feet like a puddle of blue satin. Thana aimed her phone's camera at them, leaning a little closer. The men wiggled Deidre out of her panties and began to paw at her. She stood between them, naked, as they ran their hands all over her. Trey slapped Deidre's naked bottom, hard enough to raise a scarlet handprint on her bulletproof flesh.

Deidre sank to her knees. The men joined her on the floor, and it began. The grunts and groans of the men echoed loudly through Thana's apartment, punctuated periodically by Deidre's higher pitched squeals, creating an almost constant cacophony. Then all would fall suddenly quiet for just an instant before resuming, the eye of a noisy storm when only their labored breathing and the slapping together of bodies could be heard. It took Rudy longer than the others to ignore Thana's camera, but he finally did. Throughout it all, though, was Thana's voice, coaching and coaxing, directing her film.

It was like watching the Centurions attack any other challenge; each member with a specified role, playing to their strengths. Andre was a blur, his body phasing in and out of visibility like a living double exposure as he changed positions above, under, and behind Deidre, all in the time it took his image to travel to my optic nerve. Rudy's entire frame enlarged, his powers overwhelming his self-control until he had to stoop to keep his head from thudding against Thana's nine-foot high ceiling, the floor creaking and groaning beneath him. The difference in the size of his body and Deidre's was disconcerting, like seeing some trick of perspective, Deidre's body coiling and contorting like a worm on a hook. Trey, ever the team leader, would watch until he decided he had been patient enough, and then order Rudy and Andre to stand down as he took his turn.

Then, with the help of Thana's choreography, they all arranged themselves, weaving limbs, pushing and fitting until they were fully interlocked, the men entering Deidre in concert. I could sense their aggression and lack of restraint, the urges they normally had to keep under check not a concern here. They were gathering momentum now, all four of them past the point of no return. They couldn't have stopped now if Hard Corps crashed through the wall with an H-bomb.

Then, in a riot of whimpers, Deidre's body buckled and her climax shot through her like a bolt of electricity, paralyzing her. A halo of intense blue light burst from her body and filled Thana's apartment, searing the air in its wake. I could feel the energy of her orgasm pass through me, engulfing me, suffusing me with its warmth.

One by one, the men came. Trey was first, which seemed to set off Andre and then Rudy, like firecrackers with their fuses twisted together. As each man peaked, I could see Deidre watching their faces, trying to look into their eyes and share that moment when their bodies surrendered to hers. But it wasn't like that.

They lay on the carpet for what felt like forever, all of them spent. Thana's apartment was finally quiet, the only sounds were those of their slowly normalizing breathing, until even that couldn't be heard.

Adventurous. It felt like years since we promised that to

each other. It hadn't even been a month. Tomorrow, after we had slept, after we had thought about it, we might look back and be appalled, but right now, at this very moment, that didn't matter. I tried to remember how we got here from there, but couldn't.

Chapter Eleven
Save The Day

The next day passed as if nothing at all out of the ordinary had happened the night before. We had awakened at Thana's, got up, got dressed and went home like we had been at a sleepover. We showered and grabbed a bite to eat. Deidre picked the kids up from school. We watched a report on Eyewitness 8 about the Fantasti-Coupe being stolen and leading police on a destructive high-speed chase. The only tangible reminder of what we had done was a new file on our laptop labeled *Supernova Strikes Again*.

For a while, it seemed like our old life again. Days passed with no mention of anyone present at Thana's that night. Life began to feel normal again for the first time in a long time. The Centurions were relatively absent from the public eye. A repair on the Citadel was their only real headline. With the exception of a commercial she had to film, Supernova was called into action few times, and always for something like a warehouse fire or bridge collapse; and always solo. There were no occasions to team up with Helix or Trace or Skyscraper. Things were quiet. *Were they too quiet?* Why hadn't Deidre spoken of any of her teammates in a couple of days? Surely there was some reason. What if Deidre was seeing Trey and not telling me? Or Andre. Or Rudy, maybe. Or even Thana. No, of course not. *No.*

Supernova stood alone under the glare of a battery of white-hot spotlights. She shone like an idol, reflecting light in all directions off every curved surface of her body. She was wearing the old costume, the good one; the one-piece bodysuit.

With her slightest movement, shafts of blue light orbited around her, flashing like she was a human disco ball. She ran her hands slowly through her blonde hair and dropped her head slightly, and then gave her sultriest gaze, biting her bottom lip.

"Excuse me while I change into something a little more... *comfortable.*"

And then she began to spin, slowly at first and then, with arms outstretched, faster. Then a burst of light emanated from her chest to engulf and obscure her. Just as quickly the light receded and vanished completely, leaving Supernova to finish her spin and come to a stop, now in her new, more revealing costume.

Only her abbreviated halter top and tiny shorts caught the light now and reflected it back in blue beams. Save for her gloves and boots, the rest of her body was naked; arms, stomach and thighs.

"Like my new look?" Deidre cooed. "I thought so. Verizon Wireless has a new look, too. And just like me, they're ready to show you more than ever. More calling plans, more data plans, and more features. And *un*like me, they've got more coverage than ever. So take another look at Verizon. That is, if you can take your eyes off me."

"Cut!" The call came from off-stage. "Okay, great, Deidre." The director of the commercial, a balding, sweating pile of a man, swung around from behind the camera and waddled over to Deidre, who was at the same time being descended upon by a swarm of stylists, all vying for position, patting her forehead with powder, teasing her hair, adjusting and tugging on her costume. I had hoped she would be forced to go back to her old costume after losing her new one to the crowd at Secret Identity, but Morris had a replacement hastily tailored when Deidre told him it had been damaged in a fight with Razor Maid.

The director said to Deidre, "This time, after you say the part about 'take your eyes off me,' maybe give me one of these," he struck a hands-on-hips pose.

The crew got reset and Deidre went through the motions again, this time ending with the director's requested pose. And then they did it all again. And again. Each time working in some new variation or intonation or emphasis. I stopped counting at Take twenty-three.

Finally the director called for a break and Deidre ducked away from the make-up crew and made her way through the lighting and cameras and stage crew and found me. She took my bottle of water from me and downed it.

"Thanks," she said and handed me back the empty bottle. "Listen, you might as well go on home. I have no idea how much longer this is going to take."

And like lightning, a bolt of suspicion shot through me. Why didn't she want me to wait for her? Had Trey contacted her and asked her to change her plans. Was she meeting him? Where?

No, no. Stop it.

"You sure? I don't mind waiting."

"Seriously. Go on home. I know this is boring you to death. No need for both of us to suffer. I'll call you when I'm freed up."

Trust her. Trust her.

Deidre went back in front of the camera, and I left.

Atomix Comics was within walking distance. I loved going there, always had, even before I became the stuff of comic books myself. I loved the smell of the paper and the ink, loved the innocence of the stories. I loved the clear sense of right and wrong; something that had been missing from my life lately.

Bret, the guy that ran the place, knew his stuff. He could tell you the first appearance of Deathstalker, or when Mach 1 got his original costume back, or which issue Silver Knight's secret identity got revealed. And he could sell you all of them.

After all these years it still struck me as ironic that folks would pay money to read about fictionalized adventures of their

200

heroes when all they had to do was spend enough time downtown to see it in the flesh. And it still felt incongruous to see stories about people I knew, my friends, my wife, even myself, sitting on the racks next to the latest from DC Comics and Marvel.

I remembered coming in here back when I had my powers and listening anonymously as the people talked excitedly about my latest real-life exploits as they flipped through the pages of my fabricated ones. I remembered overhearing folks in restaurants, or in line at the bank, as they recounted for one another my most recent adventure. I liked the way it felt to have a secret. I liked knowing that, despite my mild-mannered appearance and demeanor, there was something that set me apart.

At first, the things Deidre and I were doing had made me feel that again. We had a dirty little secret; a dual life. An alter ego. And, at first, it felt good. But now, it just felt dirty.

I browsed the books along with the handful of other customers Bret had that afternoon. I flipped through the latest issues of *Power of Helix* and *Supernova Action.* If they only knew, I thought. I was still receiving royalty checks, so I shouldn't have been surprised when I saw *Adventures of Century Man* still on the rack.

"What's been going on with Century Man?" I asked Bret.

"Don't waste your time, man," he said, looking up from his Styrofoam tray of Korean takeout. "It's not even the real guy anymore. They killed him off last year when the real Century Man disappeared. The new guy's a clone or some shit. Really cheesy."

I picked up the new issue of *Challenge of the Centurions.* Helix and Supernova were popular enough to merit their own monthly titles. So was Trace. But *Challenge* was the book where the entire team got their moment to shine in the 4-color sun. This month's cover was a crazed Helix dismantling the Statue of Justice with his bare hands while the other Centurions tried futilely to stop him. Inside a zigzag explosion were the shocking words: "Friend Turned Foe?!"

"That's a good one, though," Bret told me. "You're not gonna believe what Helix does, dude."

I looked at Bret and said, "I can only imagine."

When I looked back at the book I saw a small dot of red light meandering across the cover. A laser targeting sight.

I looked past the sales counter, through the store's windows, across the parking lot, across the street. Killshot was there. He was dressed head to toe in desert camouflage that, despite its intended purpose, made him stick out like a sore thumb. His shoulders and chest were armored, his face half-hidden behind his constantly dialing and focusing goggles. There were bandoliers slung over each shoulder, and held straight out in front of him was the massive cybernetic Gatling gun where his left arm once was. He stepped off the curb, into four lanes of traffic. Cars and trucks screeched to a halt, horns blaring at this jaywalking human weapon. I watched him march to the sidewalk in front of the shop.

I heard Bret utter, "Holy shit."

And then all hell broke loose. Killshot's gun roared to life, the glass storefront shattering into a million airborne shards. Atomix Comics filled with the confetti of a thousand shredded funny books. And, just as quickly, the gun fell silent, whirring to a stop. The handful of customers and Bret had hit the deck, buried now under comics, action figures, broken glass and debris. But I was standing, still holding in my hands *Challenge of the Centurions.*

Killshot stepped through the opening he had blasted in the shop, Gatling gun trained on me, glass crunching under his heavy combat boots. He moved toward me until he was at point blank range. A smile creased his face

"Do you have any idea how long I've waited for this?" Killshot said, his breath short.

"I... I think you've mistaken me—"

"I know who you are, Century Man. I know *exactly* who you are."

202

"Listen, I—"

"Do you know what you did to me? You ruined me! Look at me! You took away my arm!" He looked at the weapon where his arm should have been. "I'm more machine than man, now. That wasn't part of the deal!"

I needed to buy some time. It had all happened so quickly. "I can help you. I know people who—"

"Oh, you've done enough for me, Century Man. The time for talking is over. Time for you to die," Killshot snarled as his gun discharged at my chest in a fiery rage, the sound deafening.

But still I stood.

The gun stopped firing. I looked at myself. My body was shrouded in smoke, the shirt I had been wearing was blasted away from my chest, the rest in tatters. But I hadn't felt a thing. The bullets had simply bounced off me. I was unharmed. I was invulnerable.

Killshot's eyes were hidden behind the reflection on his goggles, but his sudden fear was written all over his face. I stepped to him, took his gun-arm in my hands and knotted it like it was a clothes hanger. I could feel the strength surging through me. The strength of a hundred men. I wanted to fly. Right then. Just walk right outside and take off and feel it again. Feel the cold air, feel the altitude, the freedom. It had been so long. It took more than a little effort to resist the urge, but I had something to do first. I had to take care of Killshot and make sure the police would be able to handle him once they got here. And then I could fly.

As I drew back my fist, he slumped to the floor and began sobbing, his hands out to shield himself. "No," he begged. "Not again."

"What... Who are you?" I said. Killshot was careful not to move too quickly as he lifted away his goggles to reveal underneath the face of the Knave of Diamonds.

"You," I said. "How?" Again, I drew back.

"Will, wait." I heard Psy-Fi's voice. She must have been a customer in the comic book shop and I hadn't even noticed. Why else would she have been here?

"Marta?" I said.

She was dusting herself off as she walked through the debris. "I'll explain as much as I can," she said.

I heard the sirens of the police cars coming down the street. Marta nodded towards the sound. "They'll take care of this," she said. "Let's scram before we have to answer some uncomfortable questions."

I didn't want to leave without taking care of the Knave, but Marta was tugging at me. "Hurry."

A tap of my knuckles to Killshot's temple knocked him unconscious. I made sure Bret was okay, and Marta and I were a block away before the police arrived.

It took a while for me to calm down. Marta watched me and waited for me to ask my questions.

"What the hell just happened?" I finally said. "Was that really him?"

"The Knave. Yes."

I didn't know what to ask next, I didn't even know what answers I needed. "Why were you there just now?"

"To keep you from doing something you'd regret. To make sure you found out what you really need to."

"How did you know he'd be there?"

"I'm from the future, Will," Marta said. "We've got history books." She let that sink in before saying, "You would have killed him."

"How did he get out of prison? How'd he get that gun?" It was too much to sort out. "What the hell is going on?"

"He got out the day after Trey put him in. Some poor bastard with a few too many traffic tickets is in maximum lockdown on Styers Island doing the Knave's time for him."

"But why?"

"Trey had me alter the records. Presto and Trace swapped prisoners. Trey gave the Knave access to the tech, helped him fashion the new persona, got him back in the game. I guess he felt he owed him that much."

204

"Owed him?" I asked.

"The Knave Incident, Will. It was all Trey's doing."

"I don't understand."

"Come on, Will." Marta was losing her patience. "How do you think the Knave knew who Deidre was? He's the Knave of Diamonds, for Christ's sake. The guy couldn't steal a necklace without getting caught and he's going to figure out Supernova's secret identity? And then defeat Century Man?"

"What are you saying?"

"Trey gave it to him! Open your eyes!"

"Trey gave *what* to him?"

"Deidre's name. Her address, everything. He gave him the Siphon."

"What are you talking about?"

"He sold you out, Will. He wanted you out of the picture. He gave the Knave Supernova's real name knowing he'd auction it to the highest bidder it as fast as he could. And he did. We're not talking about a criminal mastermind here. He was jewel thief."

"I... I don't..."

"And Trey knew that as soon as Deidre had been outed, you'd go after whoever did it. He knew you would. And you did. And Trey gave the Siphon to the Knave so he'd be ready for you."

"The Siphon?"

"That's what he called it; what Trey called it." Marta hung her head. "He made me build it. He said he'd ruin me if I didn't. So I did, I built the thing. Of course, it took a little while for the Siphon to kick in. You broke the Knave's left arm in four places before it started working."

"Okay, what the hell is a Siphon?"

"It's 22nd Century stuff. All you need to know is it took your powers away when you got close to it. And the Knave had it with him when you two fought." She looked me dead in the eye. "And I'll never forgive myself for creating it."

"So, why are you telling me this now?"

"Because I made a mistake. I shouldn't have helped Trey, no

matter what he threatened. Because Century Man is back."

"Why? Why did my powers come back?"

"I designed the Siphon to be temporary. Trey had no idea. I made it so your powers would resurface as soon as you were exposed to... well, as soon as Deidre..."

"As soon as Deidre *what*?"

Marta blushed. "Had an orgasm."

It all made sense now. Well, the part about my powers coming back, anyhow.

Marta said, "I knew Deidre's orgasms were slightly radioactive from reading the autobiography she publishes a year from now. And I figured it would only be a matter of time before you made her... you know. I just didn't think it would take this long."

"Yeah, well, that's kind of a long story." I said. "Your history books don't say anything about that, do they?"

Marta shook her head.

"Good," I said, and then thought about what I needed to do from here. I said to her, "The Centurions."

"Don't."

"Don't what?"

"Don't go back."

"I have to. I'm the leader. I'm back."

"Trust me. You're not going to want to be a Centurion next week at this time."

I didn't ask what she meant by that.

"Go see Deidre," Marta said. "Go see her before you do anything."

I nodded.

She tapped a couple of times on her wristwatch and disappeared.

Deidre was standing in our kitchen, a mug of wine her hand.

"Hey, baby," she smiled. "How was your day?"

"I ran into an old friend."

"Anybody I know?"

"Yeah."

She didn't care who. "I have a surprise for you."

"Me too."

"Mine first," Deidre said. "Thana's having a little party at the Citadel tonight." She drifted through the air to me and kissed me on the cheek. "We've been invited. How does that sound?"

"I saw the Knave," I said. The color left Deidre's face. I kept going. "I know about Trey. I know he set me up. Tell me why."

"Will, I..." She held her face in her hands for a while, and then looked at me. "He had to get you out of the way."

"For what? Why? I had work to do. I was needed."

"No, you weren't needed. None of us were."

"But the criminals, the—"

"Supervillains? There are no supervillains, Will. There are no bad guys. Not anymore."

"What are you talking about?"

She took a deep breath. "They're all on our side now. Hard Corps, Third Eye, all of them. The fights are staged, Will. Haven't you noticed that no one really gets hurt anymore? Sure, there's always property damage. But when was the last time anyone got even hospitalized?"

"No, this is... You're not..."

"We had put ourselves out of business. We had won. All the bad guys were locked up. Or scared shitless. Without the Atomic Centaurs and Frostbites of the world to beat up on, we were out of a job. And we were close enough to being out of a job as it is, thanks to Estes Wertham and that fucking Code."

Deidre took a minute to organize her thoughts. She was pacing.

"So, a couple of years ago Trey met with the Hyperborean and offered a deal; a deal between us and them. We make sure they never spend much time on Styers Island or in Casey Asylum and they promise to make us look good when we send them back. We pass a percentage of our sponsorship earnings on to them, and everybody's happy. Nobody gets killed, and everybody stays employed. We keep a roof over our heads. It works, Will."

"And these guys we beat to within inches of their lives, guys we sent away for years, they just shook hands and went along with Trey's plan?"

"A lot of them did, yes. It was a lot of money. And they were as tired of fighting as we were. And the ones who didn't agree, well, they're rotting on Styers Island. Or worse."

I couldn't believe what I was hearing.

"And, yeah, there are still some real bad guys. Some upstart meta who isn't in on it, doesn't realize there's a fix on. Or someone too insane to make sense of it. The thing at the asylum the other day, for example. That was real. And most of the E.T. threats are real. Natural disasters are real, too, obviously. Most of them, anyhow. Trey did trigger the Peru landslide last summer," She seemed to realize she was getting sidetracked. "We still do good. We're not bad guys, Will. We still help."

"Help who? Yourselves?"

"Will, you've got to understand. The funding was drying up. We were becoming redundant. The endorsements were the only thing that kept some of us from quitting. And you were so dead set against that."

"So Trey took my powers away just because I was against the endorsement money?"

"No, no, Will. Can't you see? Trey knew if you found out about the deal, you wouldn't stand for it. He knew you couldn't live with that sort of deceit, even if it meant your livelihood. And you were so close to finding out."

"When did you find out?"

She looked away.

"When did you know, Dee?"

"From the start." She started to cry.

"You knew Trey was going to do this to me, to us, and you let him?"

"At the time, I... At the time, it made so much sense. We talked to Dr. Gunnarsson at SMART, and she promised to keep an eye on you—"

"Agnetha was in on it, too?"

"We wanted to make sure you didn't get hurt, Will. Dr. Gunnarsson said she would monitor you, make sure you weren't having ill-effects. Trey promised he would try to clear her father's name, and in return she helped keep our secret."

"I thought she was helping me."

"Trey told me it would be so much better this way. He told me everyone would be happier. He said *you* would be happier. And I believed him. You seemed so tired of it all. Trey said we'd be doing you a favor."

I stared at the floor. "Maybe you did."

"No. No, baby, don't say that." She took me by arms. "It was so wrong and I don't know how to even begin to tell you how sorry I am for..."

"Did Thana do anything to you?"

"What do you mean?"

"Maybe Trey had Thana convince you the deal was a good idea. And that it was a good idea to take away my powers."

"No. I don't think she even knows about the deal."

"Maybe she made you forget that part."

"No, she wouldn't do that."

"She said the same thing about the Livewire video. She said the same thing to me when I asked her to make Trey want to fuck you." I took Deidre's hands in mine. "I don't believe you did this because you wanted to. I can't believe you honestly thought this was a good idea. No way. Not you. Not Supernova. Not my wife."

She tried wiping the tears away but they only came harder.

I made her look at me. "Deidre, my powers are back."

"What?"

"My powers. They're back."

"How?"

"It doesn't matter. We're going to the Citadel tonight and I'm setting things right. Who's going to be there?"

"I don't know. Everybody."

"When we get there, wait for me to make my move."

Deidre nodded.

"Help me make this right."

40,000 feet below me, Century City had slipped behind the veil of dusk. The long shadows of the downtown towers had been absorbed into the umbra of the horizon as the sun sank beneath it. Seven miles up, though, I was still lit by the golden glow of sunset. I soared to the angled edge of light that was slicing through the atmosphere, the last moments of daylight above it, nighttime below.

Higher still I flew, rising in a great parabola through a liquid mountain of clouds, my passage leaving only a whisper in my wake. Vapor condensed and streamed across my face. I banked at the apex of my arc and dove toward the Earth. Wilbur and Orville, Amelia; Yeager, Armstrong and Aldrin. None of them could have known freedom like this. This wasn't physics. This was the nullification of it. This was not rudders or ailerons, the curve of airfoils or the thrust of jet engines. This was the pure and utter defiance of gravity.

Even at my speed, the world below barely seemed to move. The lighted streets looked like slender strings of jewels arranged on velvet. The placid surfaces of the bay and rivers were shards of a fractured mirror. The objects on the ground were shrunk to insignificance. Above me, in the inky blue sky, the planet Venus shone like a diamond. And higher yet, at the peak of the ceiling of the sky, blinked the Citadel.

Then I remembered. The Centurions, Helix and Supernova, all the lies. All the bad things I had forgotten in the joy of flight came crashing back. And I remembered why I had come up here: to think, and plan and prepare for what I had to do when Deidre and I got to the Citadel in a few short hours. My anger at Trey had stolen away my exhilaration at flying. I vowed it would be the last time he would ever take anything from me.

I glided through the air, sweeping back toward the city, and focused my thoughts. My plan, if it could be called that, was to simply arrive at the Citadel with my wife and wait until she had everyone's undivided attention. And then, with the strength of a hundred men, beat the living shit out of all of them. I had no way of knowing who would be waiting there for us. Trey, certainly. Andre. They were my only real concern, though. Barring the presence of a meta with the power level of a Hyperborean or the Quantum Mechanics, there was no one else I couldn't handle on my own. And I wouldn't be on my own.

I flew back home and explained my strategy to Deidre. If she had any doubts, she kept them to herself.

We rode the repulsor lift to the uppermost level of the Citadel. Deidre was wearing the little black dress from the Halloween party. "It will keep them distracted," Deidre had figured, and I agreed.

The door whooshed open and Deidre stepped out into the War Room. I hesitated for just a moment, debating the wisdom of what I was planning to do before deciding I had no real choice. I followed Deidre inside.

Gathered were a dozen, maybe more, metahumans from both sides of the law, male and female, some not entirely human. I recognized all of them. Most were well on their way to getting drunk. Trey, Andre, and Rudy were there, of course, as was Phantasmo, Hellkat, the Atomic Centaur, the Jet Set, and more. I sized them up. Besides the members of the Centurions they were all B-listers at best. Most were in street clothes but others had worn their costumes. Trey was in a tailored suit that looked like it cost more than what I drove.

Trey greeted Deidre with a kiss on the back of her hand and Thana brought her a drink and gave her a hug. Thana led Deidre around the room, making the cursory introductions to the attendees who'd never met Supernova. Everyone knew why they were here, though, and what was supposed to happen, which made the polite handshakes and "nice to meet you's all the more awkward.

I made a conscious effort to avoid eye contact with Trey. I knew my intentions were written all over my face. I knew he would be able to see my barely contained urge to beat him to a crippled pulp. And I was unsure I wanted to stop there. Instead I walked to the viewport and stared through 22,240 miles of space at the Earth and I wondered how long Trey could hold his breath.

Deidre joined me, watching me for a moment before touching my shoulder. "You okay?"

I nodded. "Just act normal."

"What's normal for a situation like this?" she said, and went back to the others. Behind my back I could hear the so-called heroes chatting and laughing with thieves, terrorists and sociopaths.

Thana wasted no more time.

"Unless anyone feels the need to get to know each other a little better, let's get started," she announced. "I know some of you have prison cells to get back to before you're missed." There was scattered laughter at that. Thana raised her cell phone and began to video the proceedings. "Deidre, why don't you be a doll and go ahead and change. Supernova is the guest of honor tonight, after all."

A couple of the men applauded, which made everyone laugh. Deidre looked at me. There was an apprehension in her expression that had been absent at the Holloway Building, and at Thana's apartment. I nodded to Deidre, barely, and tried to tell her with my eyes to trust me, that I wouldn't let anything happen to her.

I glanced around the room at the group Thana had assembled. They were all watching Deidre, waiting for her to do what Thana had asked her to. Deidre extended her arms and began to spin. The uninitiated in the room shielded their eyes against the burst of light that emanated from her body. When the wind and light had subsided, Supernova stood in the middle

212

of the room. Her skimpy new costume elicited a couple of wolf-whistles. If all went as planned it would be the last time anyone saw it.

Thana panned her phone around the room, recording the aroused audience. Phantasmo was openly masturbating now, his ghostly erection glowing ethereally. Circuit Breaker had removed his insulated suit, his naked body crisscrossed with strands of multi-colored wiring. Hellkat was gazing hungrily at Deidre as the Anvil unlaced her corset and caged her breasts with living metal fingers. The Atomic Centaur toyed with what I assumed was the Skink's penis, which coiled and weaved in mid-air, prehensile like his tail. Everywhere I looked now I saw the flash of naked skin as villains and heroes knelt to give head, crawled on hands and knees, or struggled to get out of their clinging costumes. Some of them had moved closer to Deidre, seemingly waiting for permission from her, or Thana, which the latter granted by asking them, "Well, what are you waiting for?"

Now, I heard in my head. *Do something. Now.*

"Stop!" I commanded. Everyone in the room turned, all eyes on me. With a hail of popped buttons I ripped open my shirt to reveal my old costume and the shield of Century Man on my bowed chest. I smiled. "Remember me?"

I leapt into motion before any of them could even react. Trace, I knew, would pose the biggest threat if left unchecked, so I went after him first. I charged him, fists clenched, ready to go. The split-second it took for me to throw my punch must have felt like all day to him, and he watched me out of the corner of his eye, smirking, as he simply sidestepped my attack. My momentum carried me flailing past him. There was a burst of light behind me and I turned to see Andre's singed body lying prone on the floor, blindsided by a Nova Burst.

Deidre's eyes glowed blue as errant crackles of energy spilled from them. From her high ground on the table, she loosed a blast of energy and took out the entire Jet Set, sending them flying against the titanium wall and into a smoldering heap. She swooped to my side and together we went into action.

213

I could feel the forgotten strength coursing through my body. I dropped the Anvil and Rudy with well-placed right hooks. Deidre and I slashed through the group, turning in unison as we went. She leveled the Centaur with a boot to the jaw as I dispatched Circuit Breaker with a single uppercut. Deidre and I cut through the room in a frenzy of kicks and hooks, rushes and elbows. Even had they all been prepared, none of them would've proven worthy opponents for either Supernova or Century Man, much less our combined might, and certainly not taken by surprise as they were. Deidre and I handled the others with the same ease until they lay in a naked pile in the middle of the War Room. We had left only Trey and Thana conscious. Thana had backed herself against the wall, clear of the fray. Trey stood defiantly amid the collapsed casualties, waiting and watching.

"It ends now," I told him. "I know what you did."

"I did what I had to." He seemed to ready himself for a fight, but his eyes betrayed his defeat. I had already won. We both knew that.

"You're done, Trey," Thana said. "I've made sure of that."

I said to Thana, "I want you to know that this is over."

"Almost over," she said. "There's still one more thing I have to do." She held up her phone to remind me of its camera. "I knew this would happen eventually."

"What are you going to do?" Deidre asked her.

"You know, I wasn't going to tell you. I was just going to let you see it on the news tomorrow night like everyone else." Thana was smiling. "But I figured, what kind of villain would I be if I didn't reveal my master plan at the end?"

Thana stepped over an unconscious body as she went to the big viewport and looked out at the Earth. "Deidre, Will," she said. "I'm truly sorry you got caught up in this. But Trey made me a promise." She looked at him. "You promised to make me a Centurion. Remember?"

Trey said nothing.

Thana went on, "But when that bitch, Livewire, leaked the

214

video, you forgot all about that promise, didn't you, big boy? And I took the fall. But now it's your turn to take the fall, Helix." She laughed a little. "And before anyone says it, yes, I could've just used my powers on him. Made him want to make me a Centurion. But that's not what *I* wanted. I wanted to earn it. That one thing. And I did earn it. And he took it away."

Thana looked at the cell phone in her hands. "Now the whole world is going to see the real Helix. They're going to see you chumming around up here with this crew of criminals. And I imagine there might be a few a questions asked."

Trey took a step toward Thana. "I can smash that camera to atoms before you can blink," he growled.

"True, true," she said. "But unless you can convert yourself to electrons you won't be able to stop everyone from seeing the video I took at my apartment. Or the video I took that night above the Holloway Building. I've already emailed those to Lola Oh. And it won't be like the Livewire video. This time it will stick. You were in costume when you fucked Deidre the first time. So was she. That video alone is enough to disgrace you and your precious Centurions."

"You used me, Thana?" I said. "You used my wife and my marriage to get back at Trey for keeping you out of the Centurions?"

"I know it's fucked up," Thana conceded. "But you got what you wanted, didn't you?"

"Did you use your powers on my wife?"

"Really? You think she had to be tricked into it?"

I started toward Thana, hands forming fists. Deidre stepped in my path. "Don't. She's not worth it." She held me by my arms. "It's over."

Deidre was right. And she made her own fist and threw it against Thana's face with just a fraction of her strength. I could hear Thana's nasal bone splinter before she slumped heavily to the floor.

"Okay," Deidre said. "Now it's over."

I surveyed the unconscious bodies littering the War Room.

215

Trey was watching me, eyes shifting between me and his only escape route: the repulsor lift. I slowly moved to block his path.

"I can't let you leave here, Trey. I'm taking you in. You've got to know that."

"You want to fight? Fine. I've wanted to kick your ass for a long time."

Trey and I circled one another. He readied himself for the attack, broadening his stance. I did the same. I could sense Deidre inching closer, looking for an opening to help.

"He's mine, Dee," I said. She took a step back.

Trey smiled. "You sure that's a good idea, Will? You don't really think you can take me without your wife's help, do you?"

Deidre said, "Will, don't let him—"

Trey stepped toward me and swung his fist into my jaw like a sledgehammer. I reeled, but if his fist was a hammer, my jaw was an anvil. I stood my ground. Trey tried to mask his surprise, used to seeing his foes fold after just one of his mighty blows. In that moment I struck back, my knuckles connecting with the underside of his chin, the sound like the cracking of timber. It knocked Trey back a full step.

He dragged the back of his hand across his chin and brought it back smeared with red. I wondered how long it had been since he'd seen his own blood. He launched himself through the air, a double-fisted battering ram hitting my chest with the force of a locomotive. He attacked me with a crazed frenzy, the likes of which he'd never shown against even Hard Corps or Damage, Inc., raining blows down on me. I fought back as best I could, parrying many of the wild attacks and sending them harmlessly wide yet absorbing far too many others. Trey's punches crashed against my face, my sternum, my abdomen. I could feel my left eye swelling shut and my insides knotting up. Trey suddenly ceased his attack and surveyed the damage. My own trickle of blood started now from the corner of my mouth.

Deidre gasped. "Will?"

I waved her off.

Trey said, "I don't know how you got your powers back and

216

I don't really care. It won't matter anyhow. Your best was never good enough to—"

With a sudden burst of power I flew forward. Trey recoiled, but not fast enough. My fist caught him in the jaw, dislocating it and spinning his entire body around in a drunken pirouette. The bastard didn't fall, though. He righted himself and lurched at me, swinging crazily. With a growl of rage, he barreled into me and we both spilled onto the floor, grappling and struggling. Trey freed one of his arms and struck at me with his elbow, driving it into my ribs, certainly cracking them. I finally captured that arm and wrenched it almost completely around, leveraging Trey off of me and onto the floor. I could feel his humerus break.

We both rose to stand on wobbly legs, both leaking blood from our faces and knuckles. Trey's twisted arm hung uselessly by his side. His crisp white dress shirt was spattered with blood, both his and mine.

"You're beaten, Trey," I panted. "End this."

"You can't beat me," he spat through jangly teeth.

I watched the realization creeping across Trey's face, maybe for the first time ever, that he might actually lose. Humiliation gave way to fear, which was quickly banished to reveal pure, white-hot anger. With a howl of fury he rushed me, butting my midsection and sending us both careening into the titanium wall. The metal panels buckled and caved, steam bursting forth from the ruptured pipes within, the air filling with the acrid smell of scorched wiring.

With a shove I cast Trey off me and instantly shot toward him through the air, smashing my fist into his face. Then the other fist. Then again. He stumbled backward with every shot. Loud cracks filled the War Room. Trey batted away one blow only to have the next one land with crushing force across the bridge of his nose, shattering it. He shuffled backward and dropped to a knee, and then somehow found the strength to stand again. He slashed with his crumpled hand and missed. I threw a punch into Trey's face that sent him sprawling against the War Room's wide viewport. I was on him instantly, striking

217

him again, harder still, the force causing a webbing of fissures to spread across the aluminosilicate window.

"Will!" Deidre called. "Stop!"

I landed blow after blow on Trey's wilting body. I was going to punch him through the glass; punch him into the airless void of outer space, and watch as he tumbled away into the abyss. Still I whaled at him and he could only shrink under each blow, convulsing with pain, his knees buckling, his body folding under the barrage.

"Will!" I heard Deidre's voice again. It sounded distant at first, then it was right beside me. Her hand was on my shoulder. "Will." I looked at her. "You've won."

I looked down at the mighty Helix. He was curled against the viewport like a wounded animal. In the cracked viewport above him was my reflection, hulking over him, my face a mask of blood and rage. I stood down. The battle was finished.

"I'm Eyewitness 8's Lola Oh and you're watching a very special *Alter Ego*. Before we begin, I need to take a minute to warn our audience that, due to the extremely graphic nature of our program tonight, viewer discretion is sternly advised. If you are easily offended, please tune out now."

Deidre and I watched as Lola began to air, over and over again—with a running commentary of disdain and disgust—severely censored and very brief excerpts of what she had dubbed "the Jinx Tapes." Lola speculated, for the benefit of all her equally disgusted viewers, that the complete, unedited versions of this depravity could be found on the Internet.

Once Lola felt the audience had gotten their fill of blurred copulation, she talked to Hal Larsen about the impact of the videos and what it meant now that the secret identities of Helix and Trace had been exposed. A local official, speaking on condition of anonymity, told Lola that the presence of known and, in most cases, convicted metahuman criminals in the Citadel video alongside Helix, Supernova, et al., had prompted the Metahuman Code Authority to cease all metahuman funding immediately and indefinitely.

Lola showed a clip of Dr. Estes Wertham calling on the government to outlaw metahuman activity once and for all, and then taking the opportunity to introduce a new and improved version of MetaCheck. Finally, Morris Kidder phoned in to deny any prior knowledge of the videos and to reiterate that he had no idea of Supernova's whereabouts and had not spoken to her in the past twenty-four hours.

The next morning, Eyewitness 8's Lola Oh announced that the Centurion's press advisers had been circulating word that Helix would soon be making a statement about the scandal. Lola went on to report that the news for Helix this day had gone from bad to worse. In exchange for amnesty, Tommy Kohn, a.k.a. the Knave of Diamonds, a.k.a. Killshot, had implicated Helix as the mastermind behind the scheme to remove Century Man as the leader of the Centurions. An independent investigator had concluded that Helix was present in the infamous Livewire video as well. A government-commissioned team had begun work to assess what the Centurions would owe the city in property damage repairs in the year since Helix had assumed leadership. The press was herded out to Dewey Plaza, chosen for its view of the Holloway Building in the distance. When Helix emerged, he was wearing street clothes. His right arm was in a sling and he had an assortment of bandages affixed to his face. He introduced himself and, with little fanfare or preamble, conceded his role in all of it and announced his surrender to local authorities.

The system as we knew it had quite utterly collapsed.

Lost in the maelstrom of the media feeding frenzy was the subtle appearance of Century City's newest metahuman duo, Moxie and Nimbus.

Epilogue

My impact with the granite cornerstone of First Century Loan & Trust dazed me. I was wedged deeply in the crater my body had just made, powder and pulverized pebbles showering down on my shoulders. Traffic on Braswell Avenue had screeched to a halt, drivers watching through windshields, passengers leaping out to join stunned pedestrians, pointing in awe and shouting, "It's him! It's Nimbus!"

I dislodged myself from the building and stood, brushing the rubble from the shield symbol on my chest. Like the rest of my costume, Zack and Luke had designed it. It was close enough to my old shield to mean something to me, but just different enough to keep a connection from being made. I gave myself a once-over. Not a scratch. Dr. Gunnarsson was right. I was stronger than ever.

The crowd called my name but I couldn't take the time to acknowledge them. I wouldn't be able to when this was over, either, which was a shame. I crossed Braswell, floating over the jam-packed cars and lighting on the other side, boots crunching in broken glass and gravel. Half a block away was the thing I'd been careless enough to let sling me against the building. An armored twelve foot tall robot was lumbering down Braswell Avenue, two overturned vehicles and a decapitated fire hydrant in its wake, a plume of water arcing into the air like a geyser.

I'd missed this more than I'd realized.

I crouched, finding my footing among the debris, and fired myself toward the machine. My body was arrow-straight, parallel to the ground, mere feet above it. Fists hitting the thing first, I cleaved through its right leg, exploding its knee joint, bolts and scraps of metal spraying out before me. I banked and landed, turning to watch just as the robot began to list to one side.

Again I sprang into the air, lancing toward the lame machine. I slammed into its square chest, knuckles driving into the plating, caving it in. It flew backwards, tumbling head over heels before crashing into the base of a lamp post. The post snapped and folded, dropping onto the robot like a felled tree. Severed wiring hissed and sizzled, fountains of sparks issued forth.

I leapt to the machine's side, raising its limp arm and hoisting the bulk of its body, using my back as a fulcrum. I moved to the middle of the street, into a clearing. I began rotating, dragging the robot around me until its centrifugal motion lifted it into the air. Like an Olympian hammer thrower, I swung the robot around me faster and faster, three, then four revolutions until I hurled it toward the heavens.

Watching and waiting in the sky was Moxie. She was floating, the sun at her back. A breeze toyed with her skirt and ponytail. Her features were half-hidden behind a pair of aviator's goggles, but her smile was plain to see. As the tumbling robot neared her, her body clenched and shafts of violet-blue energy erupted from the lenses of her goggles. The searing bolts engulfed the machine completely, its silhouette visible for a split-second before it seemed to dissolve in the light. When the energy beams dissipated, the robot was gone; vaporized.

"You in the cape!" came the calls from behind me. The voice was amplified by a bullhorn. "Century City Police! Freeze!"

I turned to face them; a dozen members of the Metahuman Crime Division, decked out in full riot gear, all wielding Wertham MetaDampener cannons trained on me.

"My apologies, officers." I saluted them. "I really must be

221

going." In the time it took them to squeeze their triggers, I was airborne, rocketing into the bright afternoon sky. I joined Moxie and we rose through the glass canyons of downtown until we were above the skyline.

Side by side, we flew higher still. From up here, Century City looked almost exactly the same as it always had. It was anything but.

In the wake of the scandal a new law, the Metahuman Vigilantism Act, was passed, effectively legislating costumed heroes out of existence. Any instance of anyone using the metagene to interfere in any way with law enforcement would be violating the law. It was broad and ambiguous, at best. A number of high-profile arrests had been already been made. Solstice and Equinox were slapped with a fine for foiling a bank robbery. Rocket Queen got a suspended sentence for defusing a hostage situation. Captain Fantastic got nabbed doing forty-seven in a thirty-five in the Fantasti-Coupe, but the ticket was dropped when it was determined no use of super-powers was involved.

Wertham Biotech stock skyrocketed. Local, state, and federal government agencies, in addition to employers and educators, were buying MetaCheck kits quicker than the company could make them. You couldn't renew your driver's license, register to vote or apply for a loan without taking Dr Wertham's test. The only real change to Century City's skyline in the last year was the transfer of the title "tallest building" to the new Wertham Building, a chrome ice pick of a structure that rose ten stories higher than the Holloway Building.

Other than Estes Wertham, Thana was the only real winner in what had become known as the Centurions Scandal (shattered nose aside). After months on the interview circuit and a bestselling tell-all about the whole thing entitled *The Adventures of the Centurions*, she launched CapeDate.com, a metahuman dating service whose members numbered in the thousands before being bought by eHarmony for a sum rumored to be seven figures.

Andre's lawyer got him out of any serious charges. Despite multiple eyewitnesses, the prosecution simply couldn't prove that Andre was privy to Trey's plan. Same for Rudy. The only evidence was Thana's videos and, however unadvisable, it's not against the law to have sex with known criminals. I did hear that Janet had divorced Andre, and that Rudy had returned to Germany to resume his career in propulsion physics. Beyond that, I knew little about either's whereabouts these days.

Deidre and I soared out over Bostwick Bay, above Styers Island, and I could see Deidre glance down at the grey prison complex the sprawled across the dot of land. Trey was down there, somewhere. He'd been in the CCPD's Metahuman Detention Center for a full year now. By all accounts he was a model prisoner. He would be up for parole in seven years. There were murderers in that prison who would do less time.

We'll never know how close Deidre came to making the MDC her new home. She had taken, happily, a plea deal with the D.A. that included her testimony against Trey, accepting financial culpability for all property damage she knowingly inflicted, as well as a series of speaking engagements and public service announcements aimed at minors about the responsibilities that accompany the metagene.

We'd paid for the repairs to Dewey Plaza, Century State University's football field and Champions Fountain out of pocket, which, truth be told, didn't even dent the nest egg Deidre had built over the years thanks to her Clairol, Verizon, and Calvin Klein deals. No, what knocked out our bank account was the fact that she'd given her money away as quickly as Morris had let her.

Deidre donated enough money to the Century City public school system that they would've named the newly constructed elementary school after her if not for fear of taxpayer backlash. SMART Labs had no such qualms, and gratefully opened the doors to the Ray Girl Center for Metahuman Studies, named, at Deidre's request, in honor of her grandmother. In the lobby is a twenty foot tall mural of Grandma in her heyday, flying over a

WWII battlefield in her flared skirt and bomber jacket. She looked pretty hot.

The new schools, research facilities and community centers had all gone a long way to mitigating the damage done to Deidre's public image, but there were still the occasional scowls and whispers whenever we went out. I supposed there always would be. Things had changed too much for certain people not to harbor some resentment.

Alter Ego went off the air due to a lack of advertisers. The *Journal* Awards were discontinued. The Centurions Café chain quickly changed its name to Capes Café. They took down the plastic Citadel over the entrance. The last time Deidre and I ate there, though, the scale replica of Bettie, Psy-Fi's jet, was still hanging from the ceiling, as was the mannequin wearing Presto's costume. Even in their federally mandated exile, they were both still as popular as ever thanks to not appearing in any of Thana's videos. The restaurant had, however, deleted any reference to Helix, Supernova, Trace, or Skyscraper from their menus and gift shop. Outlawed or not, people still loved their heroes, just not *those* heroes.

The booming meta-tourism industry that Century City had been known for was running on fumes. No longer could visitors ride in open-roof buses and expect to see a caped crusader waving to them as he glided overhead. Instead, the pilgrims who still came here did so to tour the sites of famous battles, to see where extraordinary men and women in brightly colored costumes once bravely defended peace and justice.

The skintights weren't all gone, though. There were still a few us fast enough or powerful enough or invisible enough to elude capture by the police or the feds; those of us who wanted to help, even if the authorities didn't want us to.

I still took my photos, usually of Moxie, and the *Journal* still snatched them up. People still wanted someone to cheer for. It paid the bills. Deidre's endorsements deals had all been terminated even before the MVA made them illegal. Morris had been approached about a book deal, which Deidre was seriously considering. It was either that or get a real job, and the property damage lawsuits were still rolling in. Morris said he figured the movie rights wouldn't be far behind the book, and I'd be lying if I said the idea of seeing my wife's life story on the big screen didn't excite me. Maybe there'd even be a two-story inflatable of Supernova down at the Century Centre Cineplex.

I was still coming to terms with what Deidre had done. She was, too. It was a challenge unlike any we'd ever faced. We couldn't punch it or zap it or fling it into orbit. But we would face it together.

Deidre banked and looped around me once before pulling up in formation off my starboard side, arms extended before her. The wind rushed through her chestnut hair. She smiled.

"Race you to the Matterhorn?"

"You're on."